THE INFINITE SEA

'REMARKABLE . . . Just read it' *Entertainment Weekly*

'Nothing short of AMAZING' *Kirkus Reviews*

'WILDLY ENTERTAINING . . . I couldn't turn the pages fast enough' Justin Cronin, *The New York Times*

'The pace is RELENTLESS' *Heat*

'Chilling' *Sun*

'A modern sci-fi MASTERPIECE' *USA Today*

'Packs real POWER' *SFX*

'Everyone I trust is telling me to READ THIS BOOK'
The Atlantic Wire

'It will leave you BREATHLESS and SPEECHLESS and wanting, no, needing book two like yesterday'
– Tee, 5-star Goodreads.com review

'ACTION-PACKED' MTV.com

'An EPIC sci-fi adventure about a terrifying alien invasion. You'll read it in one sitting' *Bookseller*

'This is DAMN and WOW territory. Quite simply, one of the best books I've read in years'
Melissa Marr, *New York Times* bestselling author

'My emotions. I cannot. WHAT IS THIS BOOK DOING TO ME?' @readsthings

'HEARTFELT, violent, paranoid, EPIC, filled with big heroics and bigger surprises . . . A SURE THING for reviewers and readers alike' Booklist (starred review)

'BREATHTAKINGLY FAST-PACED AND ORIGINAL, *The 5th Wave* is a reading tsunami that grabs hold and won't let go' Melissa De La Cruz, *New York Times* bestselling author of the Blue Bloods series

'A fantastic read. *The 5th Wave* is an ELECTRIFYING page turner' Kathy Reichs, *New York Times* bestselling author

'A TWISTY survival story that borrows elements from romance, horror and dystopian fiction' *Wall Street Journal*

'This book's SCARY!' *Teen Now*

'A GRIPPING SF trilogy about an Earth decimated by an alien invasion . . . the question of what it means to be human is at the forefront' *Publishers Weekly*

'This book is STUNNING . . . You must read it'
– Krys, 5-star Goodreads.com review

'Borrow this one from your teen's nightstand while they're at school' *People Magazine*

'SPECTACULAR' TheFoundingFields.com

'*The 5th Wave* will THRILL you, CHILL you, and challenge you to keep the pages turning fast enough' Hypable.com

Books by Rick Yancey

THE 5TH WAVE
THE INFINITE SEA

THE SECOND BOOK OF THE 5TH WAVE

THE INFINITE SEA

RICK YANCEY

PENGUIN BOOKS

Published by the Penguin Group
Penguin Books Ltd, 80 Strand, London WC2R 0RL, England
Penguin Group (USA) Inc., 375 Hudson Street, New York, New York 10014, USA
Penguin Group (Canada), 90 Eglinton Avenue East, Suite 700, Toronto, Ontario, Canada M4P 2Y3
(a division of Pearson Penguin Canada Inc.)
Penguin Ireland, 25 St Stephen's Green, Dublin 2, Ireland (a division of Penguin Books Ltd)
Penguin Group (Australia), 707 Collins Street, Melbourne, Victoria 3008, Australia
(a division of Pearson Australia Group Pty Ltd)
Penguin Books India Pvt Ltd, 11 Community Centre, Panchsheel Park, New Delhi – 110 017, India
Penguin Group (NZ), 67 Apollo Drive, Rosedale, Auckland 0632, New Zealand
(a division of Pearson New Zealand Ltd)
Penguin Books (South Africa) (Pty) Ltd, Block D, Rosebank Office Park,
181 Jan Smuts Avenue, Parktown North, Gauteng 2193, South Africa

Penguin Books Ltd, Registered Offices: 80 Strand, London WC2R 0RL, England

penguin.com

First published in the USA by G. P. Putnam's Sons, Penguin Group (USA) LLC 2014
Simultaneously published in Great Britain by Penguin Books 2014
011

Printed in Great Britain by Clays Ltd, St Ives plc

British Library Cataloguing in Publication Data
A CIP catalogue record for this book is available from the British Library

TRADE PAPERBACK ISBN: 978–0–141–34584–0

PAPERBACK ISBN: 978–0–141–34587–1

www.greenpenguin.co.uk

Penguin Books is committed to a sustainable
future for our business, our readers and our planet.
This book is made from Forest Stewardship
Council™ certified paper.

For Sandy, guardian of the infinite

My bounty is as boundless as the sea,
My love as deep; the more I give to thee,
The more I have; for both are infinite.

—William Shakespeare

THE WHEAT

THERE WOULD BE no harvest.

The spring rains woke the dormant tillers, and bright green shoots sprang from the moist earth and rose like sleepers stretching after a long nap. As spring gave way to summer, the bright green stalks darkened, became tan, turned golden brown. The days grew long and hot. Thick towers of swirling black clouds brought rain, and the brown stems glistened in the perpetual twilight that dwelled beneath the canopy. The wheat rose and the ripening heads bent in the prairie wind, a rippling curtain, an endless, undulating sea that stretched to the horizon.

At harvesttime, there was no farmer to pluck a head from the stalk, rub the head between his callused hands, and blow the chaff from the grain. There was no reaper to chew the kernels or feel the delicate skin crack between his teeth. The farmer had died of the plague, and the remnants of his family had fled to the nearest town, where they, too, succumbed, adding their numbers to the billions who perished in the 3rd Wave. The old house built by the farmer's grandfather was now a deserted island surrounded by an infinite sea of brown. The days grew short and the nights turned cool, and the wheat crackled in the dry wind.

The wheat had survived the hail and lightning of the summer storms, but luck could not deliver it from the cold. By the time the refugees took shelter in the old house, the wheat was dead, killed by the hard fist of a deep frost.

Five men and two women, strangers to one another on the eve of that final growing season, now bound by the unspoken promise that the least of them was greater than the sum of all of them.

The men rotated watches on the porch. During the day the cloudless sky was a polished, brilliant blue and the sun riding low on the horizon painted the dull brown of the wheat a shimmering gold. The nights did not come gently but seemed to slam down angrily upon the Earth, and starlight transformed the golden brown of the wheat to the color of polished silver.

The mechanized world had died. Earthquakes and tsunamis had obliterated the coasts. Plague had consumed billions.

And the men on the porch watched the wheat and wondered what might come next.

Early one afternoon, the man on watch saw the dead sea of grain parting and knew someone was coming, crashing through the wheat toward the old farmhouse. He called to the others inside, and one of the women came out and stood with him on the porch, and together they watched the tall stalks disappearing into the sea of brown as if the Earth itself were sucking them under. Whoever—or *whatever*—it was could not be seen above the surface of the wheat. The man stepped off the porch. He leveled his rifle at the wheat. He waited in the yard and the woman waited on the porch and the rest waited inside the house, pressing their faces against the windows, and no one spoke. They waited for the curtain of wheat to part.

When it did, a child emerged, and the stillness of the waiting was broken. The woman ran from the porch and shoved the barrel of the rifle down. *He's just a baby. Would you shoot a child?* And the man's face was twisted with indecision and the rage of everything ever taken for granted betrayed. *How do we know?*

he demanded of the woman. *How can we be sure of anything anymore?* The child stumbled from the wheat and fell. The woman ran to him and scooped him up, pressing the boy's filthy face against her breast, and the man with the gun stepped in front of her. *He's freezing. We have to get him inside.* And the man felt a great pressure inside his chest. He was squeezed between what the world had been and what the world had become, who he was before and who he was now, and the cost of all the unspoken promises weighing on his heart. *He's just a baby. Would you shoot a child?* The woman walked past him, up the steps, onto the porch, into the house, and the man bowed his head as if in prayer, then lifted his head as if in supplication. He waited a few minutes to see if anyone else emerged from the wheat, for it seemed incredible to him that a toddler might survive this long, alone and defenseless, with no one to protect him. How could such a thing be possible?

When he stepped inside the parlor of the old farmhouse, he saw the woman holding the child in her lap. She had wrapped a blanket around him and brought him water, little fingers slapped red by the cold wrapped around the cup, and the others had gathered in the room and no one spoke, but they stared at the child with dumbstruck wonder. *How could such a thing be?* The child whimpered. His eyes skittered from face to face, searching for the familiar, but they were strangers to him as they had been strangers to one another before the world ended. He whined that he was cold and said that his throat hurt. He had a bad owie in his throat.

The woman holding him prodded the child to open his mouth. She saw the inflamed tissue at the back of his mouth, but she did not see the hair-thin wire embedded near the opening of his throat. She could not see the wire or the tiny capsule connected to the wire's end. She could not know, as she bent over the child to peer into his mouth, that the device inside the child was calibrated to detect the carbon dioxide in her breath.

Our breath the trigger.

Our child the weapon.

The explosion vaporized the old farmhouse instantly.

The wheat took longer. Nothing was left of the farmhouse or the outbuildings or the silo that in every other year had held the abundant harvest. But the dry, lithe stalks consumed by fire turned to ash, and at sunset, a stiff northerly wind swept over the prairie and lifted the ash into the sky and carried it hundreds of miles before the ash came down, a gray and black snow, to settle indifferently on barren ground.

— BOOK ONE —

I

THE PROBLEM OF RATS

1

THE WORLD IS a clock winding down.

I hear it in the wind's icy fingers scratching against the window. I smell it in the mildewed carpeting and the rotting wallpaper of the old hotel. And I feel it in Teacup's chest as she sleeps. The hammering of her heart, the rhythm of her breath, warm in the freezing air, the clock winding down.

Across the room, Cassie Sullivan keeps watch by the window. Moonlight seeps through the tiny crack in the curtains behind her, lighting up the plumes of frozen breath exploding from her mouth. Her little brother sleeps in the bed closest to her, a tiny lump beneath the mounded covers. Window, bed, back again, her head turns like a pendulum swinging. The turning of her head, the rhythm of her breath, like Nugget's, like Teacup's, like mine, marking the time of the clock winding down.

I ease out of bed. Teacup moans in her sleep and burrows deeper under the covers. The cold clamps down, squeezing my chest, though I'm fully dressed except for my boots and the parka, which I grab from the foot of the bed. Sullivan watches as I pull on the boots, then when I go to the closet for my rucksack and rifle. I join her by the window. I feel like I should say something before I leave. We might not see each other again.

"So this is it," she says. Her fair skin glows in the milky light. The spray of freckles seems to float above her nose and cheeks.

I adjust the rifle on my shoulder. "This is it."

"You know, Dumbo I get. The big ears. And Nugget, because Sam is so small. Teacup, too. Zombie I don't get so much—Ben won't say—and I'm guessing Poundcake has something to do with his roly-poly-ness. But why Ringer?"

I sense where this is going. Besides Zombie and her brother, she isn't sure of anyone anymore. The name Ringer gives her paranoia a nudge. "I'm human."

"Yeah." She looks through the crack in the curtains to the parking lot two stories below, shimmering with ice. "Someone else told me that, too. And, like a dummy, I believed him."

"Not so dumb, given the circumstances."

"Don't pretend, Ringer," she snaps. "I know you don't believe me about Evan."

"I believe *you*. It's his story that doesn't make sense."

I head for the door before she tears into me. You don't push Cassie Sullivan on the Evan Walker question. I don't hold it against her. Evan is the little branch growing out of the cliff that she clings to, and the fact that he's gone makes her hang on even tighter.

Teacup doesn't make a sound, but I feel her eyes on me; I know she's awake. I go back to the bed.

"Take me with you," she whispers.

I shake my head. We've been through this a hundred times. "I won't be gone long. A couple days."

"Promise?"

No way, Teacup. Promises are the only currency left. They must be spent wisely. Her bottom lip quivers; her eyes mist. "Hey," I say softly. "What did I tell you about that, soldier?" I resist the impulse to touch her. "What's the first priority?"

"No bad thoughts," she answers dutifully.

"Because bad thoughts do what?"

"Make us soft."

"And what happens if we go soft?"

"We die."

"And do we want to die?"

She shakes her head. "Not yet."

I touch her face. Cold cheek, warm tears. *Not yet.* With no time left on the human clock, this little girl has probably reached middle age. Sullivan and me, we're old. And Zombie? The ancient of days.

He's waiting for me in the lobby, wearing a ski jacket over a bright yellow hoodie, both scavenged from the remains inside the hotel: Zombie escaped from Camp Haven wearing only a flimsy pair of scrubs. Beneath his scruffy beard, his face is the telltale scarlet of fever. The bullet wound I gave him, ripped open in his escape from Camp Haven and patched up by our twelve-year-old medic, must be infected. He leans against the counter, pressing his hand against his side and trying to look like everything's cool.

"I was starting to think you changed your mind," Zombie says, dark eyes sparkling as if he's teasing, though that could be the fever.

I shake my head. "Teacup."

"She'll be okay." To reassure me, he releases his killer smile from its cage. Zombie doesn't fully appreciate the pricelessness of promises or he wouldn't toss them out so casually.

"It's not Teacup I'm worried about. You look like shit, Zombie."

"It's this weather. Wreaks havoc on my complexion." A second smile leaps out at the punch line. He leans forward, willing me to answer with my own. "One day, Private Ringer, you're going to smile at something I say and the world will break in half."

"I'm not prepared to take on that responsibility."

He laughs and maybe I hear a rattle deep in his chest. "Here." He offers me another brochure of the caverns.

“I have one,” I tell him.

“Take this one, too, in case you lose it.”

“I won’t lose it, Zombie.”

“I’m sending Poundcake with you,” he says.

“No, you’re not.”

“I’m in charge. So I am.”

“You need Poundcake here more than I need him out there.”

He nods. He knew I would say no, but he couldn’t resist one last try. “Maybe we should abort,” he says. “I mean, it isn’t *that* bad here. About a thousand bedbugs, a few hundred rats, and a couple dozen dead bodies, but the view is fantastic . . .” Still joking, still trying to make me smile. He’s looking at the brochure in his hand. *Seventy-four degrees year ’round!*

“Until we get snowed in or the temperature drops again. The situation is unsustainable, Zombie. We’ve stayed too long already.”

I don’t get it. We’ve talked this to death and now he wants to keep beating the corpse. I wonder about Zombie sometimes.

“We have to chance it, and you know we can’t go in blind,” I go on. “The odds are there’re other survivors hiding in those caves and they may not be ready to throw out the welcome mat, especially if they’ve met any of Sullivan’s Silencers.”

“Or recruits like us,” he adds.

“So I’ll scope it out and be back in a couple of days.”

“I’m holding you to that promise.”

“It wasn’t a promise.”

There’s nothing left to say. There’re a million things left to say. This might be the last time we see each other, and he’s thinking it, too, because he says, “Thank you for saving my life.”

“I put a bullet in your side and now you might die.”

He shakes his head. His eyes sparkle with fever. His lips are gray. Why did they have to name him Zombie? It's like an omen. The first time I saw him, he was doing knuckle push-ups in the exercise yard, face contorted with anger and pain, blood pooling on the asphalt beneath his fists. *Who is that guy?* I asked. *His name is Zombie.* He fought the plague and won, they told me, and I didn't believe them. Nobody beats the plague. The plague is a death sentence. And Reznik the drill sergeant bending over him, screaming at the top of his lungs, and Zombie in the baggy blue jumpsuit, pushing himself past the point where one more push is impossible. I don't know why I was surprised when he ordered me to shoot him so he could keep his unkeepable promise to Nugget. When you look death in the eye and death blinks first, nothing seems impossible.

Even mind reading. "I know what you're thinking," he says.

"No. You don't."

"You're wondering if you should kiss me good-bye."

"Why do you do that?" I ask. "Flirt with me."

He shrugs. His grin is crooked, like his body leaning against the counter.

"It's normal. Don't you miss normal?" he asks. Eyes digging deep into mine, always looking for something, I'm never sure what. "You know, drive-thrus and movies on a Saturday night and ice cream sandwiches and checking your Twitter feed?"

I shake my head. "I didn't Twitter."

"Facebook?"

I'm getting a little pissed. Sometimes it's hard for me to imagine how Zombie made it this far. Pining for things we lost is the same as hoping for things that can never be. Both roads dead-end in despair. "It's not important," I say. "None of that matters."

Zombie's laugh comes from deep in his gut. It bubbles to the surface like the superheated air of a hot spring, and I'm not pissed anymore. I know he's putting on the charm, and somehow knowing what he's doing does nothing to blunt the effect. Another reason Zombie's a little unnerving.

"It's funny," he says. "How much we thought all of it did. You know what really matters?" He waits for my answer. I feel as if I'm being set up for a joke, so I don't say anything. "The tardy bell."

Now he's forced me into a corner. I know there's manipulation going on here, but I feel helpless to stop it. "Tardy bell?"

"Most ordinary sound in the world. And when all of this is done, there'll be tardy bells again." He presses the point. Maybe he's worried I don't get it. "Think about it! When a tardy bell rings again, normal is back. Kids rushing to class, sitting around bored, waiting for the final bell, and thinking about what they'll do that night, that weekend, that next fifty years. They'll be learning like we did about natural disasters and disease and world wars. You know: 'When the aliens came, seven billion people died,' and then the bell will ring and everybody will go to lunch and complain about the soggy Tater Tots. Like, 'Whoa, seven billion people, that's a lot. That's sad. Are you going to eat all those Tots?' *That's* normal. *That's* what matters."

So it wasn't a joke. "Soggy Tater Tots?"

"Okay, fine. None of that makes sense. I'm a moron."

He smiles. His teeth seem very white surrounded by the scruffy beard, and now, because he suggested it, I think about kissing him and if the stubble on his upper lip would tickle.

I push the thought away. Promises are priceless, and a kiss is a kind of promise, too.

2

UNDIMMED, THE STARLIGHT sears through the black, coating the highway in pearly white. The dry grass shines; the bare trees shimmer. Except for the wind cutting across the dead land, the world is winter quiet.

I hunker beside a stalled SUV for one last look back at the hotel. A nondescript two-story white rectangle among a cluster of other nondescript white rectangles. Only four miles from the huge hole that used to be Camp Haven, we nicknamed it the Walker Hotel, in honor of the architect of that huge hole. Sullivan told us the hotel was her and Evan's prearranged rendezvous point. I thought it was too close to the scene of the crime, too difficult to defend, and anyway, Evan Walker was dead: It takes two to rendezvous, I reminded Zombie. I was overruled. If Walker really was one of them, he may have found a way to survive.

"How?" I asked.

"There were escape pods," Sullivan said.

"So?"

Her eyebrows came together. She took a deep breath. "*So* . . . he could have escaped in one."

I looked at her. She looked back. Neither of us said anything. Then Zombie said, "Well, we have to take shelter *somewhere,* Ringer." He hadn't found the brochure for the caverns yet. "And we should give him the benefit of the doubt."

"The benefit of what doubt?" I asked.

"That he is who he says he is." Zombie looked at Sullivan, who was still glaring at me. "That he'll keep his promise."

"He promised he'd find me," she explained.

"I saw the cargo plane," I said. "I didn't see an escape pod."

Beneath the freckles, Sullivan was blushing. "Just because you didn't see one . . ."

I turned to Zombie. "This doesn't make sense. A being thousands of years more advanced than us turns on its own kind—for what?"

"I wasn't filled in on the why part," Zombie said, half smiling.

"His whole story is strange," I said. "Pure consciousness occupying a human body—if they don't need bodies, they don't need a planet."

"Maybe they need the planet for something else." Zombie was trying hard.

"Like what? Raising livestock? A vacation getaway?" Something else was bothering me, a nagging little voice that said, *Something doesn't add up*. But I couldn't pin down what that something was. Every time I chased after it, it skittered away.

"There wasn't time to go into all the details," Sullivan snapped. "I was sort of focused on rescuing my baby brother from a death camp."

I let it go. Her head looked like it was about to explode.

I can make out that same head now on my last look back, silhouetted in the second-story window of the hotel, and that's bad, really bad: She's an easy target for a sniper. The next Silencer Sullivan encounters might not be as love struck as the first one.

I duck into the thin line of trees that borders the road. Stiff with ice, the autumn ruins crunch beneath my boots. Leaves curled up like fists, trash and human bones scattered by scavengers. The cold wind carries the faint odor of smoke. The world will burn for a hundred years. Fire will consume the things we made from wood and plastic and rubber and cloth, then water and wind and time will chew the stone and steel into dust. How baffling it is that we imagined cities incinerated by alien bombs and death rays when all they needed was Mother Nature and time.

And human bodies, according to Sullivan, despite the fact that, also according to Sullivan, they don't need bodies.

A virtual existence doesn't require a physical planet.

When I'd first said that, Sullivan wouldn't listen and Zombie acted like it didn't matter. For whatever reason, he said, the bottom line is they want all of us dead. Everything else is just noise.

Maybe. But I don't think so.

Because of the rats.

I forgot to tell Zombie about the rats.

3

BY SUNRISE, I reach the southern outskirts of Urbana. Halfway there, right on schedule.

Clouds have rolled in from the north; the sun rises beneath the canopy and paints its underbelly a glistening maroon. I'll hole up in the trees until nightfall, then hit the open fields to the west of the city and pray the cloud cover hangs around for a while, at least until I pick up the highway again on the other side. Going around Urbana adds a few miles, but the only thing riskier than navigating a town during the day is trying it at night.

And it's all about risk.

Mist rises from the frozen ground. The cold is intense. It squeezes my cheeks, makes my chest ache with each breath. I feel the ancient yearning for fire embedded deep in my genes. The taming of fire was our first great leap: Fire protected us, kept us warm, transformed our brains by changing our diets from nuts and berries to protein-rich meat. Now fire is another weapon in our enemy's arsenal. As deep winter sets in, we're crushed between two unacceptable risks: freezing to death or alerting the enemy to our location.

Sitting with my back against a tree, I pull out the brochure. *Ohio's Most Colorful Caverns!* Zombie's right. We won't survive till spring without shelter, and the caves are our best—maybe only—bet. Maybe they've been taken or destroyed by the enemy. Maybe they're occupied by survivors who will shoot strangers on sight. But every day we stay at that hotel, the risk grows tenfold.

We don't have an alternative if the caves don't pan out. Nowhere to run, nowhere to hide, and the idea of fighting is ludicrous. The clock winds down.

When I pointed this out to him, Zombie told me I think too much. He was smiling. Then he stopped smiling and said, "Don't let 'em get inside your head." As if this were a football game and I needed a halftime pep talk. *Ignore the fifty-six to nothing score. Play for pride!* It's moments like those that make me want to slap him, not that slapping him would do any good, but it would make me feel better.

The breeze dies. There's an expectant hush in the air, the stillness before a storm. If it snows, we'll be trapped. Me in these woods. Zombie in the hotel. I'm still twenty or so miles from the caverns—should I risk the open fields by day or risk the snow holding off at least till nightfall?

Back to the *R* word. It's all about risk. Not just ours. Theirs, too: embedding themselves in human bodies, establishing death camps, training kids to finish the genocide, all of it crazy risky, stupid risky. Like Evan Walker, discordant, illogical, and just damn *strange.* The opening attacks were brutal in their efficiency, wiping out 98 percent of us, and even the 4th Wave made some sense: It's hard to muster a meaningful resistance if you can't trust one another. But after that, their brilliant strategy starts to unravel. Ten thousand years to plan the eradication of humans from Earth and *this* is the best they can come up with? That's the question I can't stop turning over and over in my head, and haven't been able to, since Teacup and the night of the rats.

Deeper in the woods, behind me and to my left, a soft moan slices through the silence. I recognize the sound immediately; I've heard it a thousand times since they came. In the early days, it was nearly omnipresent, a constant background noise, like the hum of traffic on a busy highway: the sound of a human being in pain.

I pull the eyepiece from my rucksack and adjust the lens carefully over my left eye. Deliberately. Without panic. Panic shuts down neurons. I stand up, check the bolt catch on the rifle, and ease through the trees toward the sound, scanning the terrain for the telltale green glow of an "infested." Mist shrouds the trees; the world is draped in white. My footsteps thunder on the frozen ground. My breaths are sonic booms.

The delicate white curtain parts, and twenty yards away I see a figure slumped against a tree, head back, hands pressed into its lap. The head doesn't glow in my eyepiece, which means he's no civilian; he's part of the 5th Wave.

I aim the rifle at his head. "Hands! Let me see your hands!"

His mouth hangs open. His vacant eyes regard the gray sky through bare branches glistening with ice. I step closer. A rifle identical to mine lies on the ground beside him. He doesn't reach for it.

"Where's the rest of your squad?" I ask. He doesn't answer.

I lower my weapon. I'm an idiot. In this weather, I would see his breath and there is none. The moan I heard must have been his last. I do a slow 360, holding my breath, but see nothing but trees and mist, hear nothing but my own blood roaring in my ears. Then I step over to the body, forcing myself not to rush, to notice everything. No panic. Panic kills.

Same gun as mine. Same fatigues. And there's his eyepiece on the ground beside him. He's a 5th Waver all right.

I study his face. He looks vaguely familiar. I'm guessing he's twelve or thirteen, around Dumbo's age. I kneel beside him and press my fingertips against his neck. No pulse. I open the jacket and pull up his blood-soaked shirt to look for the wound. He was hit in the gut by a single, high-caliber round.

A round I didn't hear. Either he's been lying here for a while or the shooter is using a silencer.

Silencer.

According to Sullivan, Evan Walker took out an entire squad by himself, at night, injured and outnumbered, sort of a warm-up to his single-handed blowing up of an entire military installation. At the time, I found Cassie's story hard to believe. Now there's a dead soldier at my feet. His squad MIA. And me alone with the silence of the woods and the milky white screen of fog.

Doesn't seem that far-fetched now.

Think fast. Don't panic. Like chess. Weigh the odds. Measure the risk.

I have two options. Stay put until something develops or night falls. Or get out of these woods, fast. Whoever killed him could be miles away or hunkered down behind a tree, waiting for a clear shot.

The possibilities multiply. Where's his squad? Dead? Hunting down the person who shot him? What if the person who shot him was a fellow recruit who went Dorothy? Forget his squad. What happens when reinforcements arrive?

I pull out my knife. It's been five minutes since I found him. I'd be dead by now if someone knew I was here. I'll wait till dark, but I have to prepare for the probability that another breaker of the 5th Wave is rolling toward me.

I press against the back of his neck until I find the tiny bulge beneath the scar. *Stay calm. It's like chess. Move and countermove.*

I slice slowly along the scar and dig out the pellet with the tip of the knife, where it sits suspended on a droplet of blood.

So we'll always know where you are. So we can keep you safe.

Risk. The risk of lighting up in an eyepiece. The opposing risk of the enemy frying my brain with the touch of a button.

The pellet in its bed of blood. The awful stillness of the trees and the clinching cold and the fog that curls between branches like fingers interlacing. And Zombie's voice in my head: *You think too much.*

I tuck the pellet between my cheek and gums. Stupid. I should have wiped it off first. I can taste the kid's blood.

4

I AM NOT ALONE.

I can't see him or hear him, but I feel him. Every inch of my body tingles with the sensation of being watched. An uncomfortably familiar feeling now, present since the very beginning. Just the mothership silently hovering in orbit for the first ten days caused cracks in the human edifice. A different kind of viral plague: uncertainty, fear, panic. Clogged highways, deserted airports, overrun emergency rooms, governments in lockdown, food and gas shortages, martial law in some places, lawlessness in others. The lion crouches in the tall grass. The gazelle sniffs the air. The awful stillness before the strike. For the first time in ten millennia, we knew what it felt like to be prey again.

The trees are crowded with crows. Shiny black heads, blank black eyes, their hunched-shouldered silhouettes reminding me of little old men on park benches. There are hundreds of them perched in the trees and hopping about the ground. I glance at the body beside me, its eyes blank and bottomless as the crows'. I know why the birds have come. They're hungry.

I am, too, so I dig out my baggie of beef jerky and only-slightly-expired gummy bears. Eating is a risk, too, because I'll have to remove the tracker from my mouth, but I need to stay alert, and to stay alert, I need fuel. The crows watch me, cocking their heads as if straining to hear the sound of my chewing. *You fat asses. How hungry could you be?* The attacks yielded millions of tons of meat. At the height of the plague, huge flocks blotted out the sky, their shadows racing across the smoldering landscape. The crows and other carrion birds closed the loop of the 3rd Wave. They fed on infected bodies, then spread the virus to new feeding grounds.

I could be wrong. Maybe we're alone, me and this dead kid. The more seconds that slip by, the safer I feel. If someone is watching, I can think of only one reason why he'd hold the shot: He's waiting to see if any more idiotic kids playing soldier show up.

I finish my breakfast and slip the pellet back into my mouth. The minutes crawl. One of the most disorienting things about the invasion—after watching everyone you know and love die in horrible ways—was how time slowed down as events sped up. Ten thousand years to build civilization, ten months to tear it down, and each day lasted ten times longer than the one before, and the nights lasted ten times as long as the days. The only thing more excruciating than the boredom of those hours was the terror of knowing that any minute they could end.

Midmorning: The mist lifts and the snow begins to fall in flakes smaller than crows' eyes. There's not a breath of wind. The woods are draped in a dreamlike, glossy white glow. As long as the snow stays this light, I'm good till dark.

If I don't fall asleep. I haven't slept in over twenty hours, and I feel warm and comfortable and slightly spacy.

In the gossamer stillness, my paranoia ratchets up. My head is perfectly centered in his crosshairs. He's high in the trees; he's lying motionless like a lion in the brush. I'm a puzzle to him. I should be panicking. So he holds his fire, allowing the situation to develop. There must be some reason I'm hanging out here with a corpse.

But I don't panic. I don't bolt like a frightened gazelle. I am more than the sum of my fear.

It isn't fear that will defeat them. Not fear or faith or hope or even love, but rage.

Fuck you, Sullivan said to Vosch. It's the only part of her story that impressed me. She didn't cry. She didn't pray. She didn't beg.

She thought it was over, and when it's over, when the clock has wound to the final second, the time for crying, praying, and begging is over.

"Fuck you," I whisper. Saying the words makes me feel better. I say them again, louder. My voice carries far in the winter air.

A flutter of black wings deep in the trees to my right, the petulant squawking of the crows, and through my eyepiece, a tiny green dot sparkling among the brown and white.

Found you.

The shot will be tough. Tough, not impossible. I'd never handled a firearm in my life until the enemy found me hiding in the rest stop outside Cincinnati, brought me to their camp, and placed a rifle in my hand, at which point the drill sergeant wondered aloud if command had slipped a ringer into the unit. Six months later, I put a bullet into that man's heart.

I have a gift.

The fiery green light is coming closer. Maybe he knows I've spotted him. It doesn't matter. I caress the smooth metal of the trigger and watch the blob of light expand through the eyepiece. Maybe he thinks he's out of range or is positioning himself for a better shot.

Doesn't matter.

It might not be one of Sullivan's silent assassins. It might be just some poor lost survivor hoping for rescue.

Doesn't matter. Only one thing matters anymore.

The risk.

5

AT THE HOTEL, Sullivan told me a story about shooting a soldier behind some beer coolers and how bad she felt afterward.

"It wasn't a gun," she tried to explain. "It was a crucifix."

"Why is that important?" I asked. "It could have been a Raggedy Ann doll or a bag of M&Ms. What choice did you have?"

"I didn't. That's my *point.*"

I shook my head. "Sometimes you're in the wrong place at the wrong time and what happens is nobody's fault. You just want to feel bad so you'll feel better."

"Bad so I feel better?" With a deep blush of anger spreading beneath her freckles. "That makes absolutely no friggin' sense."

"'I killed an innocent guy, but look how guilty I feel about it,'" I explained. "Guy's still dead."

She stared at me for a long time. "Well. I see why Vosch wanted you for the team."

The green blob of his head advances toward me, weaving through the trees, and now I can see the glint of a rifle through the languid snow. I'm pretty sure it isn't a crucifix.

Cradling my rifle, leaning my head against the tree as if I'm dozing or looking at the flakes float between the glistening bare branches, lioness in the tall grass.

Fifty yards away. The muzzle velocity of a M16 is 3,100 feet per second. Three feet in a yard, which means he has two-thirds of a second left on Earth.

Hope he spends it wisely.

I swing the rifle around, square my shoulders, and let loose the bullet that completes the circle.

The murder of crows rockets from the trees, a riot of black wings and hoarse, scolding cries. The green ball of light drops and doesn't rise.

I wait. Better to wait and see what happens next. Five minutes. Ten. No motion. No sound. Nothing but the thunderous silence of snow. The woods feel very empty without the company of the birds. With my back pressed against the tree, I slide up and hold still another couple of minutes. Now I can see the green glow again, on the ground, not moving. I step over the body of the dead recruit. Frozen leaves crackle beneath my boots.

Each footstep measures out the time winding down. Halfway to the body, I realize what I've done.

Teacup lies curled into a tight ball beside a fallen tree, her face covered in the crumbs of last year's leaves.

Behind a row of empty beer coolers, a dying man hugged a bloody crucifix to his chest. His killer didn't have a choice. They gave her no choice. Because of the risk. To her. To them.

I kneel beside her. Her eyes are wide with pain. She reaches for me with hands dark crimson in the gray light.

"Teacup," I whisper. "Teacup, what are you doing here? Where's Zombie?"

I scan the woods but don't hear or see him or anyone else. Her chest heaves and frothy blood boils over her lips. She's choking. I gently push her face toward the ground to clear her mouth.

She must have heard me cursing. That's how she found me, by my own voice.

Teacup screams. The sound knifes through the stillness, bounces and ricochets off the trees. *Unacceptable.* I press my hand down hard over her bloody lips and tell her to hush. I don't know who shot the kid I found, but whoever did it can't be far. If the sound of my rifle doesn't bring him back to investigate, her screaming will.

Damn it, shut up. Shut up. What the hell are you doing out here, sneaking up on me like that, you little shit? Stupid. Stupid, stupid, stupid.

Teeth scrape frantically against my palm. Tiny fingers seek my face. My cheeks painted with her blood. With my free hand, I tug open her jacket. I've got to compress the wound or she'll bleed out.

I grab the collar of her shirt and rip downward, exposing her torso. I wad up the remnant and press it just below her rib cage, against the bullet hole weeping blood. She jerks at my touch with a strangled sob.

"What did I tell you about that, soldier?" I whisper. "What's the first priority?"

Slick lips slide over my palm. No words come out.

"No bad thoughts," I tell her. "No bad thoughts. No bad thoughts. Because bad thoughts make us go soft. They make us soft. Soft. Soft. And we can't go soft. We can't. What happens when we go soft?"

The woods brim with menacing shadows. Deep in the trees, there's a snapping sound. A boot crunching on the frozen ground? Or an ice-encrusted branch, splintering? We could be surrounded by a hundred enemies. Or zero.

I race through our options. There aren't many. And they all suck.

First option: We stay. The problem is stay for what. The dead recruit's unit is unaccounted for. Whoever killed the kid is also unaccounted for. And Teacup has no chance of surviving without medical attention. She has minutes, not hours.

Second option: We run. The problem is *where*. The hotel? Teacup would bleed to death before we make it back, plus she may have taken off for a good reason. The caverns? Can't risk going through Urbana, which means adding miles of open fields and many hours to a journey that ends at a place that probably isn't safe, either.

There's a third option. The unthinkable one. And the only one that makes sense.

The snow falls heavier, the gray deepens. I cup her face with one hand and press the other into the wound, but I know it's hopeless. My bullet tore through her gut; the injury is catastrophic.

Teacup is going to die.

I should leave her. Now.

But I don't. I can't. Like I told Zombie on the night Camp Haven blew, the minute we decide one person doesn't matter, they've won, and now my words are the chain that binds me to her.

I hold her in my arms in the awful dead stillness of the woods in snow.

6

I EASE HER DOWN onto the forest floor. Drained of all color, her face is only slighter darker than the snow. Her mouth hangs open, her eyelids flutter. She's slipped into unconsciousness. I don't think she'll wake again.

My hands are shaking. I'm struggling to keep it together. I'm pissed as hell at her, at myself, at the seven billion impossible dilemmas their arrival brought, at the lies and the maddening inconsistencies and all the ridiculous, hopeless, stupid unspoken promises that have been broken since they came.

Don't go soft. Think about what matters, right here, right now; you're good at that.

I decide to wait. It can't be much longer. Maybe after she's dead, the softness inside me will pass and I'll be able to think clearly. Every uneventful minute means I still have time.

But the world is a clock winding down, and there are no such things as uneventful minutes anymore.

A heartbeat after I decide to stay with her, the percussive thrum of rotors shatters the silence. The sound of the choppers snaps the spell. Knowing what matters: besides shooting, the thing I'm best at.

I can't let them take Teacup alive.

If they take her, they may be able to save her. And if they save her, they'll run her through Wonderland. There's the tiniest chance that Zombie's still safe at the hotel. A chance that Teacup wasn't running from anything, just snuck off to find me. One trip by either of us down the rabbit hole and everybody's doomed.

I pull my sidearm from the holster.

The minute we decide . . . I wish I had a minute. I wish I had thirty seconds. Thirty seconds would be a lifetime. A minute would be an eternity.

I level the gun at her head and lift up my face to the gray. Snow settles on my skin, where it quivers for a moment before melting.

Sullivan had her Crucifix Soldier and now I have mine.

No. I am the soldier. Teacup is the cross.

7

I FEEL HIM THEN, the one standing deep in the trees, motionless, watching me. I look, and then I see him, a lighter human-shaped shadow between the dark trunks. For a moment, neither of us moves. I know, without understanding how, that he is the one who shot the kid and the other members of his squad. And I know the shooter can't be a recruit. His head does not glow in my eyepiece.

The snow spins, the cold squeezes. I blink, and the shadow is gone. If the shadow was ever there.

I'm losing my grip. Too many variables. Too much risk. Shaking uncontrollably, I wonder if they've finally broken me; after surviving the tsunami that took my home, the plague that took my family, the death camp that took my hope, the innocent little girl who took my bullet, I am terminal, done, finished, and was it ever in question, never *if* but always *when*?

The choppers bear down. I have to finish what I started with Teacup or I'll join her where she lies.

I sight along the barrel of my pistol into the pale, angelic face at my feet, my victim, my cross.

And the roar of the Black Hawks' approach makes my thoughts seem like the tiny squeaking whimpers of a dying rodent.

It's like the rats, isn't it, Cup? Just like the rats.

8

THE OLD HOTEL swarmed with vermin. The cold had killed off the cockroaches, but other pests survived, especially bedbugs and carpet beetles. And they were hungry. Within a day, all of us were covered with bites. The basement belonged to the flies, where corpses had been brought during the plague. By the time we checked in, most of the flies had died off. So many dead flies that their black husks crunched beneath our feet when we went down there the first day. That was also the last day we went into the basement.

The entire building reeked of rot, and I told Zombie that opening the windows would help dissipate the smell and kill off some of the bugs. He said he'd rather get bit and gag than freeze to death. As he smiled to drench you in his irresistible charm. *Relax, Ringer. It's just another day in the alien wild.*

The bugs and the smell didn't bother Teacup. It was the rats that drove her crazy. They had chewed their way into the walls, and at night their gnawing and scratching kept her (and therefore me) awake. She tossed and turned, whined and bitched and generally obsessed, because practically any other thoughts about our situation ended up in a bad place. In a vain attempt to distract her, I began teaching her chess, using a towel for a board and coins for the pieces.

"Chess is a stupid game for stupid people," she informed me.

"No, it's very democratic," I said. "Smart people play, too."

Teacup rolled her eyes. "You want to play just so you can beat me."

"No, I want to because I miss playing it."

Her mouth dropped open. "*That's* what you miss?"

I spread the towel on the bed and positioned the coins. "Don't decide how you feel about something before you try it." I was around her age when I began. The beautiful wooden board on a stand in my father's study. The gleaming ivory pieces. The stern king. The haughty queen. The noble knight. The pious bishop. And the game itself, the way each piece contributed its individual power to the whole. It was simple. It was complex. It was savage; it was elegant. It was a dance; it was a war. It was finite and eternal. It was life.

"Pennies are pawns," I told her. "Nickels are rooks, dimes are knights and bishops, quarters are kings and queens."

She shook her head. Ringer is an idiot. "How can dimes and quarters be both?"

"Heads: knights and kings. Tails: bishops and queens."

The coolness of the ivory. The way the felt-covered bases slid over the polished wood, like whispered thunder crashing. My father's face bent over the board, lean and unshaven, red-eyed and purse-lipped, encrusted with shadows. The sickly sweet smell of alcohol and fingers that thrummed like hummingbirds' wings.

It's called the game of kings, Marika. Would you like to learn how to play?

"It's the game of kings," I said to Teacup.

"Well, I'm not a king." She crossed her arms. So *over* me. "I like checkers."

"Then you'll love chess. Chess is checkers on steroids."

My father tapping his chipped nails on the tabletop. The rats scratching inside the walls.

"Here's how the bishop moves, Teacup."

This is how the knight moves, Marika.

She jammed a stale piece of gum into her mouth and chewed angrily as the dry shards crumbled. Minty breath. Whiskey breath. *Scratch, scratch, tap, tap.*

"Give it a chance," I begged her. "You'll love it. I promise."

She grabbed the corner of the towel. "Here's what I feel." I saw it coming, but still flinched when she flung the towel and the coins exploded into the air. A nickel popped her in the forehead and she didn't even blink.

"Ha!" Teacup shouted. "I guess that's checkmate, bitch!"

Reacting without thinking, I slapped her. "Don't ever call me that. *Ever.*"

The cold made the slap more painful. Her bottom lip poked out, her eyes welled up, but she didn't cry.

"I hate you," she said.

"I don't care."

"No, I hate you, Ringer. I hate your fucking guts."

"Cussing doesn't make you grown-up, you know."

"Then I guess I'm a baby. Shit, shit, shit! Fuck, fuck, fuck!" She started to touch her cheek. She stopped herself. "I don't have to listen to you. You aren't my mother or my sister or *anybody.*"

"Then why have you been latched on to me like a pilot fish since we left camp?"

Now a tear did fall, a single drop that trailed down her scarlet cheek. She was so pale and thin, her skin as luminescent as one of my father's chess pieces. I was surprised the slap hadn't shattered her into a thousand bits. I didn't know what to say or how to unsay what had been said, so I said nothing. Instead, I laid a hand on her knee. She pushed my hand away.

"I want my gun back," she said.

"Why do you want your gun back?"

"So I can shoot you."

"Then you're definitely not getting your gun back."

"Can I have it back to shoot all the rats?"

I sighed. "We don't have enough bullets."

"Then we poison them."

"With what?"

She threw up her hands. "Okay, so we set the hotel on fire and burn them all up!"

"That's a great idea, only we happen to be living here, too."

"Then they're gonna win. Against us. A bunch of *rats.*"

I shook my head. I didn't follow her. "Win—how?"

Her eyes widened in disbelief. Ringer the moron. "Listen to them! They're *eating* it. And pretty soon we won't be living here because there won't be any *here* to live in!"

"That's not winning," I pointed out. "They wouldn't have a home, either."

"They're *rats,* Ringer. They can't think that far ahead."

Not just the rats, I thought that night after she finally fell asleep next to me. I listened to them inside the walls, chewing, scratching, screeching. Eventually, with the help of weather, insects, and time, the old hotel would collapse. In another hundred years, only the foundation would remain. In a thousand, nothing at all. Here or anywhere. It would be as if we had never existed. Who needs the kind of bombs used at Camp Haven when they can turn the elements themselves against us?

Teacup was pressed tight against me. Even under mounds of covers, the cold squeezed hard. Winter: a wave they didn't have to engineer. The cold would kill off thousands more.

Nothing that happens is insignificant, Marika, my father told me during one of my chess lessons. *Every move matters. Mastery is in understanding how much each time, every time.*

It nagged at me. The problem of rats. Not Teacup's problem. Not the problem *with* rats. The problem *of* rats.

9

I SEE THE CHOPPERS closing in through the leafless branches clothed in white, three black dots against the gray. I have seconds.

Options:

Finish Teacup and take my chances against three Black Hawks equipped with Hellfire missiles.

Leave Teacup to be finished by them—or worse, saved.

One last option: Finish both of us. A bullet for her. A bullet for me.

I don't know if Zombie is okay. I don't know what—if anything—drove Teacup from the hotel. What I do know is our deaths may be his only chance to live.

I will myself to squeeze the trigger. If I can fire the first round, the second will be much easier. I tell myself it's too late—too late for her and too late for me. There's no avoiding death, anyway. Isn't that the lesson they've been hammering into our heads for months? No hiding from it, no running from it. Put it off for a day, and death will surely find you tomorrow.

She looks so beautiful, not even real, nestled in a bower of snow, her dark hair shimmering like onyx, her expression in sleep the indescribable serenity of an ancient statue.

I know that killing both of us is the only option with the least risk to the most people. And I think of rats again and how sometimes, to pass the interminable hours, Teacup and I would plot our campaign against the vermin, stratagems and tactics, waves of attack, each more ridiculous than the last, until she dissolved into hysterical laughter, and I gave her the same speech I gave Zombie on the firing range, the same lesson that now comes home to me, the fear that binds killer to prey and the bullet connecting both as if by a silver cord. Now I am the killer *and* the prey, a circle of a completely different kind, and my mouth has gone dry as the sterile air, my heart as cold: The temperature of true rage is absolute zero, and mine is deeper than the ocean, wider than the universe.

So it isn't hope that makes me slip the sidearm back into its holster. It isn't faith and it sure isn't love.

It's rage.

Rage, and the fact that I have a dead recruit's implant still lodged between my cheek and gums.

10

I LIFT HER UP. Her head falls against my shoulder. We take off through the trees. A Black Hawk thunders overhead. The other two choppers have split off, one to the east, one to the west, cutting off any escape. The high, thin branches bend. Snow whips sideways into my face. Teacup weighs nothing; I could be carrying a wad of discarded clothes.

We come out of the trees as a Black Hawk roars in from the

north. The blast of air whips my hair with cyclonic fury. The chopper hovers above us and now we are motionless, standing in the middle of the road. No more running. No more.

I lower Teacup to the blacktop. The helicopter is so close, I can see the black visor of the pilot and the open door to the hold and the cluster of bodies inside, and I know I'm in the middle of a half dozen sights, me and the little girl at my feet. And every second that passes means I've survived that second and, with each second, the increased probability I'll survive the next. It might not be too late, not for me, not for her, not yet.

I do not glow in their eyepieces. I am one of them. I must be, right?

I sling the rifle from my shoulder and slip my finger through the trigger guard.

II

THE RIPPING

11

FROM THE TIME I could barely walk, my father would ask me, *Cassie, do you want to fly?* And my arms would shoot over my head. *Are you kidding me, old man? Damn straight I want to fly!*

And he would grab my waist and toss me into the air. My head would snap back and I would hurtle like a rocket toward the sky. For an instant that lasted a thousand years, it felt as if I'd keep flying until I reached the stars. I would scream with joy, that fierce roller-coaster-ride fear, my fingers clutching at clouds.

Fly, Cassie, fly!

My brother knew that feeling, too. Better than me, because the memory was fresher. Even after the Arrival, Dad was launching him into orbit. I saw him do it at Camp Ashpit a few days before Vosch showed up and murdered him in the dirt.

Sam, m'boy, do you want to fly? Lowering his voice from baritone to bass like an old-time carny hustler, though the ride he was selling was free—and priceless. Dad the launching pad. Dad the landing zone. Dad the tether that kept Sams—and me—from hurtling into the nullity of deep space, a nullity himself now.

I waited for Sam to ask. That's the easiest way to break horrible news. Also the lowest. He didn't ask, though. He told me.

"Daddy's dead."

A tiny lump beneath a mound of covers, brown eyes big and round and blank like the teddy bear's pressed against his cheek.

Teddy bears are for babies, he told me the first night at Hotel Hell. *I'm a soldier now.*

Burrowed in the bed next to his, another solemn, pint-sized soldier staring at me, the seven-year-old they call Teacup. The one with the adorable baby-doll face and haunted eyes who doesn't share a bed with a stuffed animal; she sleeps with a rifle.

Welcome to the post-human age.

"Oh, Sam." I left my post by the window and sat beside the cocoon of covers swaddling him. "Sammy, I didn't know how—"

He slugged me in the cheek with a balled-up, apple-sized fist. I never saw it coming, in both meanings of the phrase. Bright stars exploded in my vision. For a second I was afraid he'd detached my retina.

Okay. Rubbing my cheek. *I deserved that.*

"Why did you let him die?" he demanded. He didn't cry or scream. His voice was low and fierce, simmering with rage. "You were supposed to take care of him."

"I didn't let him die, Sams."

My father bleeding, crawling in the dirt—*Where are you going, Dad?*—and Vosch standing over him, watching my father crawl the way a sadistic kid might a fly that he's dewinged, grimly satisfied.

Teacup from her bed: "Hit her again."

Sam snarled at her, "You shut up."

"It wasn't my fault," I whispered, my arm wrapped around the bear.

"He was soft," Teacup said. "That's what happens when you go—"

Sam was on her in two seconds. Then it was all fists and knees and feet and dust flying from the blankets and *Dear God, there's a rifle in that bed!* and I shoved Teacup away, scooped Sam into my arms, and held him tightly against my chest while he swung his arms and kicked his legs, spitting and gnashing his teeth, and Teacup was shouting obscenities at him and promising she'd put him down like a dog if he ever touched her again. The door flew open and Ben burst into the room wearing that ridiculous yellow hoodie.

"It's cool!" I shouted over the screaming. "I've got this!"

"Cup! Nugget! Stand down!"

Like a switch being flipped, the minute Ben barked the order, both kids fell silent. Sam went limp. Teacup flopped against the headboard and folded her arms over her chest.

"She started it." Sam pouted.

"I was just thinking of painting a big red *X* on the roof," Ben said. He holstered his pistol. "Thanks, guys, for saving me the trouble." He grinned at me. "Maybe Teacup should bunk in my room until Ringer gets back."

"Good!" Teacup said. She jumped out of bed, marched to the door, turned on her heel, went back to the bed, grabbed the rifle, and yanked on Ben's wrist. "Let's go, Zombie."

"In a minute," he said gently. "Dumbo's on the watch. Take his bed."

"My bed now." She couldn't resist a parting shot: "A-holes."

"*You're* the a-hole!" Sammy shouted after her. The door slammed in that quick, violent way of hotel doors. "A-hole."

Ben looked at me, right eyebrow cocked. "What happened to your face?"

"Nothing."

"I hit her," Sammy said.

"You hit her?"

"For letting my daddy die."

Now Sam lost it. As in tears, not fists, and the next thing I knew, Ben was kneeling and my baby brother was crying in his arms, and Ben was saying, "Hey, it's okay, soldier. It's going to be okay." Stroking the crew cut I was still getting used to—Sammy just didn't seem like Sammy without the mop of hair—saying that dumb-ass camp name over and over. *Nugget, Nugget.* I knew it shouldn't, but it bothered me that everyone had a nom de guerre but me. I liked *Defiance.*

Ben picked him up and deposited him in the bed. Then he found Bear lying on the floor and placed him on the pillow. Sam knocked him away. Ben picked him up again.

"You really want to decommission Teddy?" he asked.

"His name isn't Teddy."

"Private Bear," Ben tried.

"Just Bear, and I never want to see him again!" Sam yanked the covers over his head. "Now go away! Everybody. Just. Go. Away!"

I took a step toward him. Ben *tsk*ed at me and jerked his head toward the door. I followed him out of the room. A large shadow hulked by the window down the hall: the big, silent kid named Poundcake, whose silence did not fall into the creepy category, more like the profound stillness of a mountain lake variety. Ben leaned against the wall, hugging Bear to his chest, mouth slightly open, sweating despite the freezing temperature. Exhausted after a tussle with a couple of kids, Ben was in trouble, which meant we all were.

"He didn't know your dad was dead," he said.

I shook my head. "He did and he didn't. One of those things."

"Yeah." Ben sighed. "Those things."

A lead ball of silence the size of Newark dropped between us. Ben was absently stroking Bear's head like an old man strokes a cat while reading the newspaper.

"I should go back to him," I said.

Ben sidestepped to the door, blocking my way. "Maybe you shouldn't."

"Maybe you shouldn't poke your nose into—"

"Not the first person in his life to die. He'll deal."

"Wow. That was harsh." *We're talking about the guy who was my father, too, Zombie boy.*

"You know what I meant."

"Why do people always say that after they say something totally cruel?" Then I said it, because I may have certain issues with self-editing: "I happen to know what it's like to 'deal' with death all by yourself. Just you and nothing else but the big empty of where everything used to be. It would have been nice, really, really nice, to have had someone there with me . . ."

"Hey," Ben said softly. "Hey, Cassie, I didn't—"

"No, you didn't. You really didn't." *Zombie.* Because he didn't have feelings, dead inside like a zombie? There were people at Ashpit like that. *Shufflers,* I called them, human-shaped sackfuls of dust. Something irreplaceable had crumbled inside. Too much loss. Too much pain. Shuffling, blank-eyed, slack-jawed mutterers. Was that Ben? Was he a shuffler? Then why did he risk everything to rescue Sam?

"Wherever you were," Ben said slowly, "we were there, too."

The words stung. Because they were true and because someone else said practically the same thing to me: *You're not the only one who's lost everything*. That someone else suffered the ultimate loss. All for my sake, the cretin who must be reminded, again, that she's not the only one. Life is full of little ironies, but it's also pockmarked with some the size of that big rock in Australia.

Time to change the subject. "Did Ringer leave?"

Ben nodded. *Stroke, stroke.* The bear was bugging me. I tugged it from his arms.

"I tried to send Poundcake with her," he said. He laughed softly. "Ringer." I wondered if he was aware of how he said her name. Quietly, like a prayer.

"You know we have no backup plan if she doesn't come back."

"She'll come back," he said firmly.

"What makes you so sure?"

"Because we have no backup plan." Now an all-out, full smile, and it's disorienting, seeing the old smile that lit up classrooms and hallways and yellow school buses overlaid on his new face, reshaped by disease and bullets and hunger. Like turning a corner in a strange city and running into someone you know.

"That's a circular argument," I pointed out.

"You know, some guys might feel threatened being surrounded by people smarter than they are. But it just makes me more confident."

He squeezed my arm and limped across the hall to his room. Then it's the bear and the big kid down the hall and the closed door and me in front of the closed door. I took a deep breath and stepped inside the room. Sat beside the lump of covers. I didn't see him but knew he was there. He didn't see me but knew I was there.

"How did he die?" Muffled voice buried.

"He was shot."

"Did you see?"

"Yes."

Our father crawling, hands clawing the dirt.

"Who shot him?"

"Vosch." I closed my eyes. Bad idea. The dark snapped the scene into sharp focus.

"Where were you when he shot him?"

"Hiding."

I reached to pull down the covers. Then I couldn't. *Wherever you were.* In the woods somewhere off an empty highway, a girl zipped herself up in a sleeping bag and watched her father die again and again. Hiding then, hiding now, watching him die again and again.

"Did he fight?"

"Yes, Sam. He fought very hard. He saved my life."

"But you hid."

"Yes." Crushing Bear against my stomach.

"Like a big fat chicken."

"Not like that," I whispered. "It wasn't like that."

He slung the blankets aside and bolted upright. I didn't recognize him. I'd never seen this kid before. Face ugly and twisted by rage and hate.

"I'm going to kill him. I'm going to shoot him in the head!"

I smiled. Or tried to, anyway. "Sorry, Sams. I have dibs."

We looked at each other and time folded in on itself, the time we had lost in blood and the time we had purchased in blood, the time when I was just the bossy big sister and he was the annoying little brother, the time when I was the thing worth living for and he was the thing worth dying for, and then he crumpled into my arms, the bear smushed between us the way we were trapped between the before-time and the after-time.

I lay down next to him and together we said his prayer: *If I should die before I wake* . . . And then I told him the story of how Dad died. How he stole a gun from one of the bad guys and single-handedly took out twelve Silencers. How he stood up to Vosch, telling him, *You can crush our bodies but never our spirit.* How he sacrificed himself so I could escape to rescue Sam from the evil galactic horde. So one day Sam could gather the ragtag remnants of humanity and save the world. So his memories of his father's last moments aren't of a broken, bleeding man crawling in the dirt.

After he fell asleep, I slipped out of bed and returned to my post by the window. A strip of parking lot, a decrepit diner ("All You Can Eat Wednesdays!"), and a stretch of gray highway fading into black. The Earth dark and quiet, the way it was before we showed up to fill it with noise and light. Something ends. Something new begins. This was the in-between time. The pause.

On the highway, beside an SUV that had run into the median strip, starlight glinted off the unmistakable shape of a rifle barrel, and for a second my heart stopped. The shadow toting the gun darted into the trees and I saw the shimmer of jet-black hair, glossy and perfectly, annoyingly straight, and I knew the shadow was Ringer.

Ringer and I didn't start off on the right foot, and the relationship just went downhill from there. She treated everything I said with a kind of icy contempt, like I was lying or stupid or just crazy. Especially when Evan Walker came up. *Are you sure? That doesn't make any sense. How could he be both human and alien?* The hotter I got, the colder she got, until we canceled each other out like either side of a chemical equation. Like $E=MC^2$, the kind of chemical equation that makes massive explosions possible.

Our parting words were a perfect example.

"You know, Dumbo I get," I told her. "The big ears. And Nugget, because Sam is so small. Teacup, too. Zombie I don't get so much—Ben won't say—and I'm guessing Poundcake has something to do with his roly-poly-ness. But why Ringer?"

Her answer was an icy stare.

"It makes me feel a little left out. You know, the only gang member without a street name."

"Nom de guerre," she said.

I looked at her for a minute. "Let me guess, National Merit Scholar, chess club, math team, top of your class? And you play an instrument, maybe a violin or cello, something with strings. Your dad worked in Silicon Valley and your mom was a college professor, I'm thinking physics or chemistry."

She didn't say anything for a couple thousand years. Then she said, "Anything else?"

I knew I should stop. But I was in now, and when I go in, I go all the way in. That's the Sullivan way. "You're the oldest—no, an only child. Your dad is a Buddhist, but your mom is an atheist. You were walking at ten months. Your grandmother raised you because your parents worked all the time. She taught you tai chi. You never played with dolls. You speak three languages. One of them is French. You were on the Olympic development team. Gymnastics. You brought home a B once and your parents took away your chemistry set and locked you in your room for a week, during which time you read the complete works of William Shakespeare." She was shaking her head. "Okay, not the comedies. You just couldn't get the humor."

"Perfect," she said. "That's amazing." Her voice was as flat and thin as a piece of aluminum foil fresh from the roller. "Can I try you?"

I stiffened up a little, bracing myself. "You can *try.*"

"You've always been self-conscious about your looks, especially your hair. The freckles are a close second. You're socially awkward, so you read a lot and you've kept a journal since middle school. You had only one close friend and your relationship was codependent, which means every time you fought with her, you slid into a deep depression. You're a daddy's girl, never that close to your mother, who always made you feel like no matter what you did, it wasn't good enough. It didn't help that she was prettier than you. When she died, you felt guilty for secretly hating her and for being secretly relieved that she was gone. You're stubborn and impulsive and a little hyper, so your parents enrolled you in something to help with your coordination and concentration, like ballet or karate, probably karate. You want me to go on?"

Well, what was I going to do? I saw only two options: laugh or punch her in the face. Okay, three: laugh, punch her in the face, or give back one of her own stoic stares. I opted for number three.

Bad idea.

"Okay," Ringer said. "You're not a tomboy and you're not a girly girl. You're in that gray area in between. Being an in-between meant you always secretly envied the ones who weren't, but you saved most of your resentment for the pretty girls. You've had crushes but never a boyfriend. You pretend you hate boys you like and like boys you hate. Whenever you're around someone who's prettier or smarter or better than you in any way, you get angry and sarcastic, because they remind you of how ordinary you feel inside. Go on?"

And tiny-voiced me: "Sure. Whatever."

"Until Evan Walker came along, you had never even held a boy's hand, except on elementary school field trips. Evan was kind and undemanding and, as an added bonus, almost too beautiful to look at. He made himself an empty canvas you could paint with your longing for a perfect relationship with the perfect guy who would ease your fear by never hurting you. He gave you all those things you imagined the pretty girls had that you never did, so being with him—or the *idea* of him—was mostly about revenge."

I was biting my lower lip. My eyes burned. I clenched my fists so hard, my nails were biting into my palms. Why, oh, why didn't I go with option two?

She said, "You want me to stop now." Not a question.

I lifted my chin. *And* Defiance *shall be my nom de guerre!* "What's my favorite color?"

"Green."

"Wrong. It's yellow," I lied.

She shrugged. She knew I was lying. Ringer: the human Wonderland.

"Seriously, though, why 'Ringer'?" That's it. Put her back on the defensive. Well, she never actually was on the defensive. That would be me.

"I'm human," she said.

"Yeah." I peeked through the crack in the curtains to the parking lot two stories below. Why did I do that? Did I really think I'd see him standing there, lurker that he was, smiling up at me? *See? I said I'd find you.* "Someone else told me that, too. And, like a dummy, I believed him."

"Not so dumb, given the circumstances."

Oh, now she was being kind? Now she was cutting me some slack? I didn't know which was worse: ice maiden Ringer or compassionate queen Ringer.

"Don't pretend," I snapped. "I know you don't believe me about Evan."

"I believe *you.* It's his story that doesn't make sense."

Then she walked out of the room. Just like that. Right in the middle, before anything was resolved. Who, besides every male person ever born, *does* that?

A virtual existence doesn't require a physical planet . . .

Who was Evan Walker? Shifting my eyes from the highway to my baby brother and back again. Who were you, Evan Walker?

I was an idiot for trusting him, but I was hurt and alone (*alone* as in thinking I was the last human being in the freaking universe) and majorly mind screwed because I had already killed one innocent person, and *this* person, this Evan Walker, didn't end my life when he could have; he saved it. So when the bells went off, I ignored them. Plus it didn't hurt (help?) that he was impossibly gorgeous and equally impossibly obsessed with making me feel like I mattered more to him than he did to himself, from bathing me to feeding me to teaching me how to kill to telling me I was the one thing he had left worth dying for to proving it all by dying for me.

He began as Evan, woke up thirteen years later to find out he wasn't, then woke again, he told me, when he saw himself through my eyes. He found himself in me, and then I found him in me and I was in him and there was no space between us. He began by telling me everything I wanted to hear and ended telling me the things I needed to: The principal weapon to eradicate the human hangers-on were the humans themselves. And when the last of the "infested" were dead, Vosch and company would pull the plug on the 5th Wave. Purge over. House clean and ready to move in.

When I told Ben and Ringer all this—minus the part about Evan being inside me, a bit too nuanced for Parish—there was a lot of dubious staring and significant looks from which I was painfully excluded.

"One of them was in *love* with you?" Ringer asked when I finished. "Wouldn't that be like us falling in love with a cockroach?"

"Or a mayfly," I shot back. "Maybe they have a thing for insects."

We were meeting in Ben's room. Our first night at the Walker Hotel, as Ringer dubbed it, mostly, I think, to get under my skin.

"What else did he tell you?" Ben asked. He was sprawled on the bed. Four miles from Camp Haven to the hotel, and he looked like he'd just sprinted a marathon. The kid who patched me and Sam up, Dumbo, wouldn't commit when I asked him about Ben. Wouldn't say if he'd get better. Wouldn't say if he'd get worse. Of course, Dumbo was only twelve. "Capabilities? Weaknesses?"

"They have no bodies anymore," I said. "Evan told me that it was the only way they could make the journey. Some were downloaded—him, Vosch, the other Silencers—some are still on the mothership, waiting for us to be gone."

Ben rubbed his mouth with the back of his hand. "The camps were set up to winnow out the best candidates for brainwashing . . ."

"And to dispose of the ones who weren't," I finished. "Once the 5th Wave was rolled out, all they had to do was sit back and let the stupid humans do their dirty work."

Ringer was sitting by the window, silent as a shadow.

"But why use us at all?" Ben wondered. "Why not download enough of their troops into human bodies to finish us off?"

"Not enough of them, maybe," I guessed. "Or setting up the 5th Wave posed the least risk."

"What risk?" Shadow-Ringer said, breaking her silence.

I decided to ignore her. For a lot of reasons, the main one being you engaged with Ringer at your own peril. She could humiliate you with a single word.

"You were there," I reminded Ben. "You heard Vosch. They'd been watching us for centuries. But Evan proved that, even with thousands of years to plan, something can still go wrong. I don't think it ever occurred to them that by becoming us, they might actually *become* us."

"Right," Ben said. "So how can we use that?"

"We can't," Ringer answered. "There's nothing Sullivan's told us that will help, unless this Evan person somehow survived the blast and can fill in the blanks."

Ben was shaking his head. "Nothing could have survived that."

"There were escape pods," I said, grasping at the same straw I'd been reaching for since he said good-bye.

"Really?" Ringer didn't sound like she believed me. "Then why didn't he put you in one?"

I told her, "Look, I probably shouldn't tell someone holding a high-powered semiautomatic rifle this, but you're really starting to get on my nerves."

She acted surprised. "Why?"

"We've got to get a handle on this," Ben said sharply, cutting off my answer, which was a good thing: Ringer *was* holding an M16 and Ben had told me she was the best shot in the camp. "What's the plan? Wait for Evan to show up or run? And if we run, where to?" Cheeks flaming with fever, eyes shining. It's fourth and long with four seconds left. "Is there anything else Evan told you that might help? What are they going to do with the cities?"

"They're not going to blow them up," Ringer said. She didn't wait for me to answer. Then she didn't wait for me to ask how the hell she would know that. "If that was the plan, they would've blown them up first. Over half the world's population lived in urban areas."

"So they plan to use them," Ben said. "Because they're using human bodies?"

"We can't hide in a city, Zombie," Ringer said. "Any city."

"Why?"

"Because it isn't safe. Fires, sewage, disease from all the rotting corpses, other survivors who must know by now they're using human bodies. If we want to stay alive as long as possible, we have to keep moving. Keep moving and stay alone as long as possible."

Oh, boy. Where did I hear *that* rule before? My head felt light. My knee was killing me. The knee shot by a Silencer. *My* Silencer. *I'll find you, Cassie. Don't I always find you?* Not this time, Evan. I don't think so. I sat on the bed next to Ben.

"She's right," I said to him. "Staying anywhere for more than a few days is not a good idea."

"Or staying together."

Ringer's words hung in the icy air. Beside me, Ben stiffened. I closed my eyes. Heard that rule, too: *Trust no one.*

"Not going to happen, Ringer," Ben said.

"I take Teacup and Poundcake. You take the rest. Our chances double."

"Why stop there?" I asked her. "Why don't we all split up? Our chances quadruple."

"Septuple," she corrected me.

"Well, I'm no math whiz," Ben said. "But it seems to me splitting up plays right into their strategy. Isolate, then exterminate." He gave Ringer a hard look. "Personally, I like the idea of someone having my back."

He pushed himself from the bed and swayed for a second. Ringer told him to lie back down. He ignored her.

"We can't stay, but we have nowhere to go. You can't get to nowhere from here, so where do we go?" he asked.

"South," Ringer said. "As far south as possible." She was looking out the window. I understood—a decent snow and you're trapped until it thaws. Ergo, get somewhere where it doesn't snow.

"Texas?" Ben said.

"Mexico," Ringer answered. "Or Central America, once the water recedes. You could hide in the rain forest for years."

"I like it," Ben said. "Back to nature. There's just one little flaw." He spread his hands. "We don't have passports."

He watched her, holding the gesture, like he was waiting for something. Ringer looked back at him, expressionless. Ben dropped his hands with a shrug.

"You're not serious," I said. This was getting ridiculous. "Central America? In the middle of winter, on foot, with Ben hurt and two little kids. We'll be lucky to make it to Kentucky."

"Beats hanging around here waiting for your alien prince to come."

That did it. I didn't care if she was holding an M16. I was grabbing a handful of those silky locks and slinging her out that window. Ben saw it coming and stepped between us.

"We're all on the same team here, Sullivan. Let's keep it together, okay?" He turned to Ringer. "You're right. He probably didn't make it, but we're gonna give Evan a chance to keep his promise. I'm in no shape for a road trip anyway."

"I didn't come back for you and Nugget so we could be the featured guests at a turkey shoot, Zombie," Ringer said. "Do what you think is right, but if things get hot, I'm out of here."

I said to Ben, "Team player."

"Maybe you're forgetting who saved your life," Ringer said.

"Oh, kiss my ass."

"That does it!" Ben boomed in his best quarterback, I'm-the-guy-in-charge-here voice. "I don't know how we're making it through this unholy mess, but I do know that *this is not the way.* Stow the crap, both of you. That's an order."

He fell back onto the bed, gasping for air, a hand pressed against his side. Ringer left to find Dumbo, which left Ben and me alone for the first time since our reunion deep in the bowels of Camp Haven.

"Something weird," Ben said. "You would think, with ninety-nine percent of us gone, the two percent would get along better."

Um, that would be one percent, Parish. I started to point that out and then saw him smiling, waiting for me to correct his math, knowing it would nearly impossible for me to resist. He played with the stereotype of the dumb jock the way someone Sammy's age played with sidewalk chalk: in broad, clumsy strokes.

"She's a psycho," I said. "Seriously, something's off. You look in her eyes and there's no one *there* there."

He shook his head. "I think there's a lot there. It's just . . . real deep."

He winced, hand tucked in the pocket of that hideous hoodie like he was doing a Napoleon impression, pressing on the bullet wound that Ringer had given him. A wound he asked for. A wound so he could risk everything to save my little brother. A wound that now may cost him his life.

"It can't be done," I whispered.

"Of course it can," he said. He laid his hand on top of mine.

I shook my head. He didn't understand. I wasn't talking about us.

The shadow of their coming fell upon us and we lost sight of something fundamental within the absolute dark of that shadow. But simply because we couldn't see it didn't mean it wasn't there: My father mouthing to me, *Run!* when he couldn't. Evan pulling me from the belly of the beast before giving himself up to it. Ben plunging into the jaws of hell to snatch Sam from them. There were some things—well, there was probably only one thing—unblemished by the shadow. Confounding. Indefatigable. Undefeatable.

They can kill us, even down to the last of us, but they can't kill—can *never* kill—what lasts in us.

Cassie, do you want to fly?

Yes, Daddy. I want to fly.

12

THE SILVER HIGHWAY that faded into the black. The black seared by starlight unleashed. The leafless trees with arms upraised like thieves caught in the act. My brother's breath congealing in the frigid air as he slept. The window fogging as I breathed. And, beyond the frosty glass, beside the silver highway in the searing starlight, a tiny figure darting beneath the upraised arms of the trees.

Oh, crap.

I launched across the room and smashed into the hall, where Poundcake whipped around, rifle up, *Relax, big boy,* then busted into Ben's room, where Dumbo leaned against the windowsill and

Ben sprawled on the bed closest to the door. Dumbo stood up. Ben sat up. And I spoke up: "*Where's Teacup?*"

Dumbo pointed at the bed next to Ben's. "Right here." Giving me a look like *This crazy chick's lost it.*

I went to the bed and whipped aside the mound of covers. Ben cursed and Dumbo backed up against the wall, his face turning red.

"I swear to God she was just there!"

"I saw her," I told Ben. "Outside—"

"Outside?" He rolled his legs off the side of the bed, grunting with the effort.

"On the highway."

Then he understood. "Ringer. She's going after Ringer." He slapped his open hand on the mattress. "Damn it!"

"I'll go," Dumbo said.

Ben held up his hand. "Poundcake!" he hollered. You could hear the big kid coming. The floor protested his passage. He stuck his head in the room, and Ben said, "Teacup took off. After Ringer. Go grab her little butt and bring it back here so I can whale on it."

Poundcake lumbered off and the floor went *Thanks a lot!*

Ben was strapping on his holster. "What are you doing?" I asked.

"Taking Poundcake's post until he gets back with that little shit. You stay with Nugget. I mean, Sam. Whoever. We need to pick one name and stick to it."

His fingers were shaking. Fever. Fear. A little of both.

Dumbo's mouth opened and closed, but no sound came out. Ben noticed. "At ease, Bo. Not your bad."

"I'll take the hall," Dumbo said. "You stay here, Sarge. You shouldn't be on your feet."

He rushed from the room before Ben could stop him. Ben, now looking at me with sparkly eyes, fever bright. "I don't think I told you," he said. "After we went rogue in Dayton, Vosch dispatched two squads to hunt us down. If they were still in the field when the camp blew . . ."

He didn't finish the thought. Either he thought he didn't need to or he couldn't. He stood up. Staggered. I went to him and he threw his arm around my shoulders without embarrassment. There's no nice way to say this: Ben Parish smelled sick. The sour odor of infection and old sweat. For the first time since I realized he wasn't a corpse, I thought he might be one soon.

"Get back in bed," I told him. He shook his head, then his hand loosed on my shoulder and he fell back, hitting the edge of the mattress with his butt and sliding down to the floor.

"Dizzy," he murmured. "Go get Nugget and bring him in here with us."

"Sam. Can we go with Sam?" Whenever I heard *Nugget,* I thought of the McDonald's drive-thru and hot French fries and strawberry-banana smoothies and McCafé Frappé Mochas topped with whipped cream and drizzled with chocolate.

Ben smiled. And it broke my heart, that luminous smile on that wasted face. "We'll go with it," he said.

Sam barely sighed when I pulled him from the bed and carried him into Ben's room. I laid him in Teacup's vacated bed, tucked him in, touched his cheek with the back of my hand, an old habit left over from the plague days. Ben was still sitting on the floor, head thrown back, staring at the ceiling. I started toward him, and he waved me back.

"Window," he gasped. "Now we're blind on one side. Thanks a lot, Teacup."

"Why would she take off like—?"

"Ever since Dayton, she's been latched on to Ringer like a pilot fish."

"All I ever saw them do is fight." Thinking of the chess brawl, the coin smacking Teacup in the head, and *I hate your fucking guts!*

Ben chuckled. "It's a thin line."

I glanced down at the parking lot. The asphalt shone like onyx. *Latched on to her like a pilot fish.* I thought of Evan lurking behind doors and around corners. I thought of the unblemished thing, the thing that lasts, and I thought the only thing with the power to save us also had the power to slay us.

"You really shouldn't be on the floor like that," I scolded him. "It's warmer up on the bed."

"A half of a half of a half of a degree, right. This is nothing, Sullivan. A head cold next to the plague."

"You had the plague?"

"Oh, yeah. Refugee camp outside Wright-Patterson. After they took over the base, they hauled me in, pumped me full of antivirals, then put a rifle in my hand and told me to go kill some people. How about you?"

A crucifix clutched in a bloody hand. *You can either finish me or help me.* The soldier behind the beer coolers was the first. No. The first was the guy who shot Crisco in a pit of ashes. That's two, and then there were the Silencers, the one I shot right before I found Sam and the one right before Evan found me. Four, then. Was I missing somebody? The bodies pile up and you lose track. *Oh God, you lose track.*

"I've killed people," I said softly.

"I meant the plague."

"No. My mom . . ."

"How about your dad?"

"Different kind of plague," I said. He glanced over his shoulder at me. "Vosch. Vosch murdered him."

I told him about Camp Ashpit. The Humvees and big flatbed full of troops. The surreal appearance of the school buses. *Just the kids. Room only for the little ones.* The gathering of the rest in the barracks and Dad sending me with my first victim to find Crisco. Then Dad in the dirt, Vosch towering over him, while I hid in the woods, and Dad mouthing *Run.*

"Weird that they didn't put you on a bus," Ben said. "If the point was to build an army of brainwashed kids."

"I saw mostly little kids, Sam's age, some even younger."

"At camp, they separated anyone under five, kept them in the bunker . . ."

I nodded. "I found them." In the safe room, their faces lifted up to mine as I hunted for Sam.

"Which makes you wonder: Why keep them?" Ben said. "Unless Vosch expects a very long war." The way he said it, as if he doubted that that was the reason. He drummed his fingers on the mattress. "What the hell is going on with Teacup? They should be back by now."

"I'll go check," I said.

"Like hell you will. This is turning into every horror movie ever made. You know? Getting picked off one by one. Uh-uh. Five more minutes."

We fell silent, listening. But there was only the wind whispering in the poorly sealed window and the constant undercurrent of rats scratching in the walls. Teacup was obsessed with them. I listened to hours of her and Ringer plotting their demise. That annoying lecturing tone of Ringer's, explaining how the population was out of control: The hotel had more rats than we had bullets.

"Rats," Ben said, as if he read my mind. "Rats, rats, rats. Hundreds of rats. Thousands of rats. More rats than us now. Planet of the rats." He laughed hoarsely. Maybe he was delirious. "You know what's been bugging the hell out of me? Vosch telling us they've been watching us for centuries. Like, how is that possible? Oh, I get how it's *possible,* but I don't get why they didn't attack us *then.* How many people were on Earth when we built the pyramids? Why would you wait until there're seven billion of us spread out over every continent with technology a little more advanced than spears and clubs? You like a challenge? The time to exterminate the vermin in your new house isn't after the vermin outnumber you. What about Evan? He say anything about that?"

I cleared my throat. "He said they were divided over whether to exterminate us."

"Huh. So maybe they debated it for six thousand years. Dicked around because nobody could make up his mind, until someone said, 'Oh, what the hell, let's just off the bastards.'"

"I don't know. I don't have the answers." I was feeling a little defensive. As if *knowing* Evan meant I should *know* everything.

"Vosch could have been lying, I guess," Ben mused. "I don't know, to get in our heads, mess with us. He messed with me from the start." He looked at me, then looked away. "Shouldn't admit this, but I worshipped the guy. I thought he was, like . . ." He twirled his hand in the air, searching for the words. "The best of us."

His shoulders began to shake. At first, I thought it must be the fever, and then I thought it could be something else, so I left my spot by the window and went to him.

For guys, breaking down is a private thing. Never let them see you cry, means you're weak, means you're soft, a baby, a wuss. Not very manly and all that BS. I couldn't imagine the pre-Arrival Ben Parish crying in front of anyone, the guy who had everything, the boy who all the other boys wanted to be, the one who broke others' hearts and never suffered his own to be broken.

I sat beside him. I didn't touch him. I didn't speak. He was where he was and I was where I was.

"Sorry," he said.

I shook my head. "Don't be."

He wiped the back of his hand against one cheek, then the other cheek. "You know what he told me? Well, more like promised. He promised he would empty me. He would empty me and fill me up with hate. But he broke that promise. He didn't fill me with hate. He filled me with hope."

I understood. In the safe room, a billion upraised faces populating the infinite, and the eyes that sought mine, and the question in those eyes too horrible to put into words, *Will I live?* It's all connected. The Others understood that, understood it better than most of us. No hope without faith, no faith without hope, no love without trust, no trust without love. Remove one and the entire human house of cards collapses.

It was like Vosch *wanted* Ben to discover the truth. Wanted to teach him the hopelessness of hope. And what could be the point of *that*? If they wanted to annihilate us, why didn't they just go ahead and annihilate us? There must be a dozen ways to wipe us out quickly, but they drew it out in five waves of escalating horror. *Why?*

Up to now, I always thought that the Others felt nothing toward us except disdain with maybe a little disgust mixed in, the way we feel about rats and cockroaches and bedbugs and other nasty lower forms of life. *Nothing personal, humans, but you gotta go.* It never occurred to me that it could be entirely personal. That simply killing us isn't enough.

"They hate us," I said, as much to myself as to him. Ben looked at me, startled. And I looked back at him, scared. "There's no other explanation."

"They don't hate us, Cassie," he said gently, the way you talk to a frightened little kid. "We just had what they want."

"No." Now my cheeks were wet with tears. The 5th Wave had one explanation and only one. Any other possible reason was absurd.

"This isn't about ripping the planet away from us, Ben. This is about ripping *us*."

13

"THAT'S IT," Ben said. "Time's up."

Then he was up, but he didn't get very far. Halfway to his feet before plopping down hard on his butt. I put a hand on his shoulder.

"I'll go."

He smacked his thigh with his palm. "Can't let it happen," he muttered as I opened the door and poked my head into the hallway. Can't let what happen? Losing Teacup and Poundcake?

Losing all of us one by one? Losing the battle against his injuries? Or losing the war in general?

The hall was empty.

First Teacup. Then Poundcake. Now Dumbo. We *were* disappearing faster than campers in a slasher movie.

"Dumbo!" I called softly. The ridiculous name echoed in the cold, stagnant air. My mind raced through the possibilities. Least likely to most: Somebody quietly neutralized him and stashed his body; he was captured; he saw or heard something and went to investigate; he had to pee.

I lingered in the doorway for a couple of seconds in case the last possibility was true. When the hall stayed empty, I stepped back into the room. Ben was upright, checking the magazine of his M16.

"Don't make me guess," he said. "Never mind. I don't need to guess."

"Stay here with Sam. I'll go."

He shuffled to a stop an inch from my nose. "Sorry, Sullivan. He's your brother."

I stiffened. The room was freezing; my blood was colder. His voice was hard, flat, without any feeling at all. *Zombie. Why do they call you Zombie, Ben?*

Then he smiled, a very real, very Ben Parish–y smile. "Those guys out there—they're *all* my brothers."

He sidestepped me and stumbled toward the door. The situation was escalating quickly from impossibly dangerous to dangerously impossible. I couldn't see any other way: I scrambled over Ben's bed and grabbed Sam by the shoulders. Shook him hard. He woke up with a soft cry. I slammed my hand over his mouth to stopper the noise.

"Sams! Listen! Something's wrong." I pulled the Luger from the holster and pressed it into his little hands. His eyes widened with fear and something that unnervingly resembled joy. "Ben and I have to check it out. Put on the night latch—you know what a night latch is?" Big-eyed nod. "And put a chair under the knob. Look through the little hole. Don't let . . ." Did I need to spell out *everything*? "Look, Sams, this is important, very important. Very, very important. You know how we tell the good guys from the bad guys? The bad guys shoot at us." Best lesson my father ever taught me. I kissed the top of Sam's head and left him there.

The door clicked shut behind me. I heard the night latch slide into the notch. *Good boy.* Ben was halfway down the hall. He motioned for me to join him. He pressed his lips, fever-hot, against my ear.

"We clear the rooms, then we go down."

We worked together. I took the point while Ben covered me. The Walker Hotel had an open door policy: Every lock had been busted at some point as survivors sought refuge during the waves. Also helpful was the fact that the Walker was perfect for the family on a budget. The rooms were roughly the size of Barbie's Dreamhouse. Thirty seconds to check one. Four minutes to clear them all.

Back in the hall, Ben crushed his lips into my ear again.

"*The shaft.*"

He dropped to one knee in front of the elevator doors. Gestured for me to cover the stairway door, then pulled out his ten-inch combat knife and shoved the blade into the crack. *Ah,* I thought. *The old hide-in-the-elevator trick!* So why was I covering the stairs? Ben pushed open the doors and waved me over.

I saw rusty cables and a lot of dust and smelled what I assumed to be dead rat. I hoped it was dead rat. He pointed at the darkness pooling below, and then I understood. We weren't checking the shaft—we were using it.

"I'm clearing the stairs," he breathed in my ear. "You stay in the elevator. Wait for my signal."

He placed his foot against one door and leaned back against the other to hold them open. Patted the tiny space between his hip and the edge. Mouthed, *Let's go.* Carefully I eased over his legs, planted my butt in the space, and dropped my legs over the side. The top of the elevator looked twenty miles down. Ben smiled reassuringly: *Don't worry, Sullivan. I won't let you fall.*

I inched forward until my butt dangled in open space. Nope, that won't work. I swung back to the edge, then maneuvered onto my knees. Ben grabbed my wrist and gave me a thumbs-up with his free hand. I knee-walked down the shaft wall, gripping the edge until my arms were fully extended. *Okay, Cassie. Time to let go now. Ben's got you. Yeah, dumbass, and Ben's hurt and about as strong as a three-year-old. When you let go, your weight is going to pull him off his perch and you'll both drop. He'll land on top of you and break your neck and then he'll slowly bleed to death all over your paralyzed body . . .*

Oh, what the hell.

I let go. I heard Ben grunt softly, but he didn't drop me and he didn't tumble down on top of me. Bending from the waist as he lowered me down, until I saw his head silhouetted in the opening, his face masked in shadow. My toes brushed against the roof of the elevator. I gave him a thumbs-up, though I wasn't sure if he could see it. Three seconds. Four. And then he let go.

I sank to my knees and felt around for the service hatch. Some grease, some dirt, and a lot of greasy dirt.

Before electricity, they measured brightness in candlepower. The light down here was about one half of one half of one candle.

Then the doors above me closed and the candlepower dropped to zero.

Thanks, Parish. You could have waited till I found the hatch.

And, when I did, the latch was stuck, probably rusted shut. I reached for my Luger with the thought of using the butt end as a hammer, then remembered I'd entrusted my semiautomatic pistol to a five-year-old's care. I pulled the combat knife from my ankle holster and gave the latch three hard whacks with the handle. The metal screeched. A very loud screech. *So much for stealth.* But the latch gave. I pulled the hatch open, which resulted in another very loud screech, this time from the rusty hinge. *Well, sure, this sounds really loud to* you, *kneeling right next to it. Outside the shaft, probably only a tiny mouselike squeaky-squeak. Don't get paranoid!* My father had a saying about paranoia. I never thought it was very funny, especially after hearing it two thousand times: *I'm only paranoid because everyone is against me.* Only a joke, I used to think. Not an omen.

I dropped into the utter dark of the elevator car. *Wait for my signal.* What signal? Ben neglected to cover that. I pressed my ear to the crack between the cold metal doors and held my breath. Counted to ten. Breathed. Counted to ten again. Breathed. After six ten counts and four breaths and hearing nothing, I started getting a little antsy. What was happening out there? Where was Ben? Where was Dumbo? Our little band was being ripped apart one person at a time. A big mistake splitting up, but each time we didn't have a choice. We were being outplayed. Someone was making this look foolishly easy.

Or multiple someones: *After we went rogue in Dayton, Vosch dispatched two squads to hunt us down.*

That was it. That had to be it. One or possibly both squads had found our hiding place. We waited here too long.

That's right, and why did you wait, Cassiopeia "Defiance" Sullivan? Oh yeah, because some dead guy promised he'd find you. So you closed your eyes and jumped off the cliff into that emptiness, and now you're shocked there's no big fat mattress at the bottom? Your fault. Whatever happens now. You're responsible.

The elevator was not large, but in the pitch dark it seemed the size of a football stadium. I was standing in a vast underground pit, no light, no sound, a lifeless, lightless void, frozen to the spot, paralyzed by fear and doubt. Knowing—without understanding how I knew—that Ben's signal wasn't coming. Understanding—without knowing how I understood—that Evan wasn't coming, either.

You never know when the truth will come home. You can't choose the time. The time chooses you. I'd had days to face the truth that now faced me in that cold, black space, and I'd refused. I wouldn't go there. So the truth decided to come to me.

When he touched me on our last night together, there was no space between us, no spot where he ended and I began, and now there was no space between me and the darkness of the pit. He promised he would find me. *Don't I always find you?* And I believed him. After distrusting everything he said from the moment I met him, for the first time, in the last words he spoke, I believed.

I pressed my face against the cold metal doors. I had the sensation of falling, miles upon miles of empty air beneath me. I would never stop falling. *You're a mayfly. Here for a day and then gone.* No. I'm still here, Evan. You're the one who's gone.

"You knew from the moment we left the farmhouse what would happen," I whispered into the void. "You knew you were going to die. And you went anyway."

I couldn't stay upright anymore. I had no choice. I slid down to my knees. Falling. Falling. I would never stop falling.

Let go, Cassie. Let go.

"Let go? I'm falling. I'm falling, Evan."

But I knew what he meant.

I'd never let him go. Not really. I told myself a thousand times a day he couldn't have survived. Lectured myself that our holing up in this fleabag motel was useless, dangerous, crazy, suicidal. But I clung to his promise because letting go of the promise meant I was letting go of *him.*

"I hate you, Evan Walker," I whispered to the void.

From inside the void—and from the void inside—silence.

Can't go back. Can't go forward. Can't hold on. Can't let go. Can't, can't, can't, can't. What can *you do? What can you* do?

I lifted my face. *Okay. I can do that.*

I stood up. *That, too.*

I squared my shoulders and slipped my fingertips into the place where the two doors met.

I'm stepping out now, I told the silent deep. *I'm letting go.*

I forced the doors apart. Light flooded into the void, devouring the smallest shadow, down to the last one.

14

I STEPPED INTO the lobby, our brave new world in microcosm. Shattered glass. Mounds of trash piled into corners, like autumn leaves blown there by the wind. Dead bugs on their backs, legs curled up. Bitter cold. So quiet, your breath was the only sound: After the Hum vanished, the Hush.

No sign of Ben. Between the second floor and the stairs, something must have happened to him and not a good something. I eased toward the stairway door, fighting the instinct to haul ass back to Sam before he disappeared like Ben, like Dumbo, like Poundcake and Teacup, like 99.9 percent of everyone on Earth.

Debris crackling beneath my boots. Cold air burning my face and hands. My hands gripping the rifle and my eyes barely blinking in the weak starlight that blared spotlight-bright after the absolute dark of the elevator.

Slow. Slow. No mistakes.

Stairway door. I held the metal handle for a good thirty seconds, ear pressed against the wood, but all I heard was the thumping of my heart. Slowly, I pushed down the handle, pulled the door open to create a crack just wide enough to peek through. Totally dark. Totally soundless. *Damn it, Parish. Where the hell are you?*

Nowhere to go but up. I slid into the stairwell. *Snick*: The door closed behind me. Plunged into darkness again, but this time I was determined to keep it on the outside, where it belonged.

The tart smell of death hung in the musty air. A rat, I told myself. Or a raccoon or some other woodland creature that got trapped in here. My boot came down on something squishy. Tiny bones crunched. I wiped off the gooey remains on the edge of a step; I didn't want to slip, tumble down to the bottom, break my neck, lie helplessly waiting for whoever it was to find me and put a bullet in my brain. That would be bad.

I reached the tiny landing, *one more flight, deep breath, almost there,* and then the shot rang out, followed by another, then a third, then a whole barrage as whoever was shooting emptied the magazine. I rocketed up the remaining steps, slammed through the door, and charged down the hall toward the room that was now missing a door, the room where my baby brother was, and my toe caught on something—a soft something I didn't see in my mad dash for Sam—and I went airborne, landing with a jaw-popping force on the thin carpeting, jumped up, glanced back, and saw Ben Parish lying lifelessly there, arms outstretched, dark wet blotch of blood seeping through that ridiculous yellow hoodie, and then Sam screamed and *I'm not too late, not too late,* and *here I come, you sonofabitch, here I come,* and in the room a tall shadow loomed over the tiny figure whose tiny finger yanked impotently at the trigger of the empty gun.

I fired. The shadow whirled toward me, then pitched forward, reaching for me.

I slammed my foot down on its neck and jammed the muzzle of the rifle against the back of the shadow's head.

"Excuse me," I gasped; I had no breath. "But you have the wrong room."

III

THE LAST STAR

15

AS A CHILD, he dreamed of owls.

He hadn't thought of the dream in years. Now, as his life slipped away, the memory came back to him.

The memory was not pleasant.

The bird perched on the windowsill, staring into his room with bright yellow eyes. The eyes blinked slowly, rhythmically; otherwise, the owl never moved.

Watching the owl watching him, paralyzed with fear without understanding why, unable to call for his mother and, afterward, the sick feeling all over, nauseated, dizzy, feverish, and the jittery, unnerving sensation of being watched that lingered for days.

When he turned thirteen, the dreams stopped. He had awakened; there was no need to hide the truth anymore. When the time came, his awakened self would need the gifts that the "owl" had given. He understood the dreams' purpose because his purpose had been revealed.

Make ready. Prepare the way.

The owl had been a lie to protect the tender psyche of his host body. After he awakened, another lie took its place: his life. His humanity was a lie, a mask, like the dream of owls in the dark.

Now he was dying. And the lie was dying with him.

There was no pain. He did not feel the bitter cold. His body seemed to float on a warm, boundless sea. The alarm signals from his nerves to the pain centers of his brain had been shut down.

This gentle, painless easing of his human body into oblivion would be the final gift.

And then, after the last human being was dead: rebirth.

A new human body unburdened by the memory of being human. He would not remember the past eighteen years. Those memories and the emotions attached to them would be forever lost—and there was nothing that could be done about the agony attending that knowledge.

Lost. Everything lost.

The memory of her face. *Lost.* The time with her. *Lost.* The war declared between what he was and what he pretended to be. *Lost.*

In the quiet of the winter-draped woods, floating on a boundless sea, he reached for her, and she slipped away.

He knew what would come of it. He had always known. Once he found her imprisoned in snow and carried her back and made her whole, his death would be the price. Virtues are vices now, and death is the cost of love. Not the death of his body. His body was the lie. True death. The death of his humanity. The death of his soul.

In the woods, in the bitter cold, on the surface of a boundless sea, whispering her name, entrusting her memory to the wind, to the embrace of the silent sentinel trees and to the care of the faithful stars, her namesake, pure and everlasting, the uncontained universe contained in her:

Cassiopeia.

16

HE WOKE TO PAIN.

Blinding pain in his head, his chest, his hands, his ankle. His skin was on fire. He felt as if he'd been dipped in boiling water.

A bird perched on a tree branch above him, a crow, regarding him with regal indifference. The world belonged to the crows now, he thought. The rest were interlopers, short-timers.

Smoke curled in the bare branches overhead: a campfire. And the smell of meat sizzling in a pan.

He was propped up against a tree, covered by a heavy wool blanket, with a rolled-up winter parka for a pillow. Slowly, he lifted his head an inch and realized immediately that any movement at all was a very bad idea.

A tall woman came into view carrying an armload of wood, then vanished from sight for a moment while she fed the fire.

"Good morning." Her voice was low-pitched, lilting, and vaguely familiar.

She sat beside him, pulled her knees to her chest, and wrapped her long arms around her legs. Her face was familiar, too. Fair-skinned, blond, Nordic features, like a Viking princess.

"I know you," he whispered. His throat burned. She pressed the mouth of her canteen against his raw lips, and he drank for a long time.

"That's good," she said. "You were talking nonsense last night. I was worried you'd suffered something a little more serious than a concussion."

She stood up and disappeared from view again. When she came

back, she was holding a frying pan. She sat next to him, placing the pan on the ground between them. She was studying him with the same haughty indifference as the crow.

"I'm not hungry," he said.

"You have to eat." Not pleading. Stating a fact. "Fresh rabbit. I made a stew."

"How bad is it?"

"Not bad. I'm a good cook."

He shook his head and forced a smile. She knew what he meant.

"It's pretty bad," she said. "Sixteen broken bones, skull fracture, second-degree burns over most of your body. Not your hair, though. You still have your hair. That's the good news."

The woman dipped a spoon into the stew, brought the spoon to her lips, blew gently, swiped her tongue slowly around the edge.

"What's the bad news?" he asked.

"Your ankle is fractured. Fairly badly. That's going to take some time. The rest . . ." She shrugged, sipped the stew, pursed her lips. "Needs salt."

He watched her dig into her rucksack, searching for the salt. "Grace," he said softly. "Your name is Grace."

"One of them," the woman said. Then she said her real name, the one she bore for ten thousand years. "I have to be honest. I like Grace better. So much easier to pronounce!"

She swirled the soup with the spoon. Offered him a sip. His lips tightened. The thought of food . . . She shrugged and took another sip. "I thought it was debris from the explosion," she went on. "I never expected to find one of the escape pods—or you in it. What happened to the guidance system? Did you disarm it?"

He thought carefully before he answered. "Malfunction."

"Malfunction?"

"Malfunction," he said louder. His throat was on fire. She held the canteen for him while he drank.

"Not too much," she cautioned him. "You'll get sick."

Water dribbled down his chin. She wiped it for him.

"The base was compromised," he said.

She seemed surprised. "How?"

He shook his head. "Not sure."

"Why were you there? That's the curious thing."

"I followed someone in." This was not going well. For a person whose entire life had been a lie, lying did not come easily to him. He knew Grace would not hesitate to terminate his current body if she suspected that the "compromise" extended to him. They all understood the risk in donning the human mantle. Sharing a body with a human psyche carried with it the danger of adopting human vices—as well as human virtues. And far more dangerous than greed or lust or envy or any of those things—or anything—was love.

"You . . . followed someone? A human?"

"I didn't have a choice." That much was true at least.

"The base was compromised. By a *human*." She shook her head with wonder. "And you abandoned your patrol to stop it."

He closed his eyes. Perhaps she'd think he passed out. The smell of the stew made his stomach roll.

"Very curious," Grace said. "There was always risk of a compromise, but from *within* the processing center. How could a human in your sector know anything about the cleansing?"

Playing possum wasn't going to work. He opened his eyes. The crow had not moved. The bird stared at him, and he remembered the owl on the sill and the little boy in the bed and the fear. "I'm not sure she did."

"She?"

"Yes. It was a . . . a female."

"Cassiopeia."

He looked sharply at her, couldn't help it. "How do you . . . ?"

"I've heard it a lot over the past three days."

"Three days?"

His heart quickened. He had to ask. But how could he? Asking might make her more suspicious than she already was. It would be foolish to ask. So he said, "I think she might have escaped."

Grace smiled. "Well, if she did, I'm sure we'll find her."

He let his breath out slowly. Grace would have no reason to lie. If she had found Cassie, she would have killed her and had no reservations in telling him. Though Grace not finding her was no proof of life: Cassie still may not have survived.

Grace reached into her rucksack again and took out a bottle of cream. "For the burns," she explained. Gingerly, she pulled the blanket down, exposing his naked body to the freezing air. Above them, the crow cocked its polished black head and watched.

The cream was cold. Her hands were warm. Grace had brought him out of fire; he had brought Cassie out of ice. He'd carried her through the undulating sea of white to the old farmhouse, where he removed her clothes and plunged her freezing body into warm water. As Grace's hands, slick with salve, roamed his body, his fingers had worked through the ice encrusted in Cassie's thick hair. Removing the bullet as she floated in the water stained pink by her blood. The bullet meant for her heart. His bullet. And, after he pulled her from the water and bandaged the wound, carrying her to his sister's bed, averting his eyes as he dressed her in his sister's gown; Cassie would have been mortified when she realized he'd seen her unclothed.

Grace's eyes fixed on him. His eyes fixed on the teddy bear on the pillow. He pulled the covers to Cassie's chin. Grace pulled the blanket to his.

You're going to live, he told Cassie. More of a prayer than a promise.

"You're going to live," Grace told him.

You have to live, he said to Cassie. "I have to," he said to Grace.

The way she cocked her head as she looked at him, like the crow in the tree, the owl on the sill.

"We all have to," Grace said, nodding slowly. "It's why we came."

She leaned forward and kissed him gently on the cheek. Warm breath, cool lips, and the faint odor of wood smoke. Her lips slid from his cheek toward his mouth. He turned his head.

"How did you know her name?" she whispered in his ear. "Cassiopeia. How did you know Cassiopeia?"

"I found her camp. Abandoned. She kept a journal . . ."

"Ah. And that's how you knew she planned to storm the base."

"Yes."

"Well, it all makes perfect sense, then. Did she say in her journal *why* she was storming the base?"

"Her brother . . . taken from a refugee camp to Wright-Patterson . . . she escaped . . ."

"That's remarkable. Then she overcomes our defenses and destroys the entire command center. That's even more remarkable. It borders on the unbelievable."

She picked up the pan, slung the contents into the brush, and rose to her feet. She towered over him, a six-foot blond colossus. Her cheeks were flushed, perhaps from the cold, perhaps from the kiss.

"Rest," she said. "You're well enough to travel now. We're leaving tonight."

"Where're we going?" Evan Walker asked.

She smiled. "My place."

17

AT SUNSET, Grace killed the fire, slipped the backpack and rifle over her shoulder, and scooped Evan from the ground for the sixteen-mile hike to her station house on the southern outskirts of Urbana. She would keep to the highway to make better time. There was little risk in it at this stage of the game: She hadn't seen a human being in weeks. Those she hadn't killed had been taken by the buses or had taken refuge against the onslaught of winter. This was the in-between time. In another year, perhaps two, though no more than five, there would be no need for stealth, because there would be no more prey to stalk.

The temperature plunged with the sun. Ragged clouds raced across the indigo sky, driven by a north wind that toyed with her bangs and playfully flipped the collar of her jacket. The first stars appeared, the moon rose, and the road shone ahead, a silver ribbon twisting across the black backdrop of dead fields and empty lots and the gutted shells of houses long abandoned.

She stopped once to rest and drink and spread more salve over Evan's burns.

"There's something different about you," she mused. "I can't put my finger on it." Putting her fingers all over him.

"I didn't have an easy awakening," he said. "You know that."

She grunted softly. "You're a brooder, Evan, and a very sore loser." She wrapped him back up in the blanket. Ran her long fingers through his hair. Looked deeply into his eyes. "There's something you're not telling me."

He said nothing.

"I felt it," she said. "The first night, when I hauled you out of the wreckage. There's a . . ." She searched for the right words. "A hidden room that wasn't there before."

His voice sounded hollow to him, empty as the wind. "Nothing is hidden."

Grace laughed. "You should never have been integrated, Evan Walker. You feel far too much for them to be one of them."

She picked him up as easily as a mother her newborn child. She lifted her face to the night sky and gasped. "I see her! Cassiopeia, the queen of the night." She pressed her cheek against the top of his head. "Our hunt is over, Evan."

18

GRACE'S STATION WAS an old, one-story wooden frame house on Highway 68, located at the exact center of her assigned six-square-mile patrol sector. Aside from boarding up the broken windows and repairing the exterior doors, she'd left the house as she found it. Family portraits on the walls, heirlooms and mementos too large to carry easily, smashed furniture and open drawers and the thousand pieces of the occupants' lives deemed worthless by looters were scattered in every room. Grace did not bother to clean up the mess. When spring arrived and the 5th Wave rolled out, she would be gone.

She carried Evan to the second bedroom at the rear of the house, the kids' room, with bright blue wallpaper and toys littering the floor and a mobile of the solar system hanging dejectedly from the ceiling. She laid him in one of the twin beds. A child had scratched his initials into the headboard: *K.M.* Kevin? Kyle? The tiny room smelled like the plague. There wasn't much light—Grace had boarded the window in here, too—but his eyesight was much more acute than an ordinary human's, and Evan could see the dark splotches of blood that had been flung on the blue walls during someone's death throes.

She left the room, returning after a few minutes with more salve and a roll of bandages. She worked quickly wrapping the burns, as if she had pressing business elsewhere. Neither spoke until she had covered him again.

"What do you need?" Grace asked. "Something to eat? Bathroom?"

"Clothes."

She shook her head. "Not a good idea. A week on the burns. Two, maybe three on the ankle."

I don't have three weeks. Three days is too long.

For the first time, he thought it might be necessary to neutralize Grace.

She touched his cheek. "Call if you need anything. Stay off that ankle. I have to get some supplies; I wasn't expecting company."

"How long will you be gone?"

"No more than a couple hours. Try to sleep."

"I'll need a weapon."

"Evan, there isn't anyone within a hundred miles." She smiled. "Oh. You're worried about the saboteur."

He nodded. "I am."

She pressed her pistol into his hand. "Don't shoot me."

He wrapped his fingers around the grip. "I won't."

"I'll knock first."

He nodded again. "That would be a good idea."

She paused by the door. "We lost the drones when the base fell."

"I know."

"Which means we're both off the grid. If something should happen to one of us—or any of us . . ."

"Does it matter now? It's almost over."

Grace nodded thoughtfully. "Do you think we'll miss them?"

"The humans?" He wondered if she was making a joke. He'd never heard her try before; joking wasn't in her character.

"Not the ones out there." She gestured beyond the walls, at the wider world. "The ones in here." Hand to her chest.

"You can't miss what you don't remember," he said.

"Oh, I think I'll keep her memories," Grace said. "She was a happy little girl."

"Then there'll be nothing to miss, will there?"

She folded her arms over her chest. She was leaving and now she wasn't. Why didn't she leave?

"I won't keep all of them," she said, meaning the memories. "Only the good ones."

"That's been my worry from the beginning, Grace: The longer we play at being human, the more human we become."

She looked at him quizzically and said nothing for a very long, very uncomfortable moment.

"Who's playing at being human?" she asked.

19

HE WAITED UNTIL her footfalls faded. Wind whistled in the cracks between the plywood and the window frame; otherwise, he heard nothing. Like his eyesight, his hearing was exquisitely acute. If Grace was sitting on the porch combing her hair, he would hear it.

First the gun. He pulled the magazine from the frame. Just as he suspected: no bullets. He thought the gun had been too light. Evan allowed himself a quiet laugh. The irony was too much. Their primary mission had not been to kill, but to sow mistrust among the survivors and drive them like frightened sheep to slaughterhouses like Wright-Patterson. What happens when the sowers of mistrust become its reapers? *Reapers.* He fought back a hysterical giggle.

He took a deep breath. This was going to hurt. He sat up. The room spun. He closed his eyes. No. That made it worse. He opened his eyes and willed himself to remain upright. His body had been augmented in preparation for his awakening. That was the truth the dream of the owl disguised. The secret that the screen memory kept him from seeing and therefore from remembering: While he and Grace and tens of thousands of children like them had slept, gifts had been delivered in the night. Gifts they would need in the years to come. Gifts that would turn their bodies into finely tuned weapons, for the designers of the invasion had understood a simple, though counterintuitive, truth: Where the body went, the mind followed.

Give someone the power of the gods and he will become as indifferent as the gods.

The pain subsided. The dizziness eased. He slid his legs off the edge of the bed. He needed to test the ankle. The ankle was the key. The other injuries were serious but inconsequential; he could manage those. Gently, he applied pressure to the ball of his foot, and a lightning bolt of agony rocketed up his leg. He fell onto his back, gasping. Overhead, dusty planets were frozen in orbit around a dented sun.

He sat up and waited for his head to clear. He wasn't going to find a way around the pain. He would have to find a way through it.

He eased himself onto the floor, using the side of the bed to support his weight. Then he forced himself to rest. No need to rush. If Grace returned, he could explain that he fell out of bed. Slowly, by inches, he scooted his butt along the carpet until he was flat on his back, seeing the solar system behind a shower of white-hot meteors that cascaded across his field of vision. The room was freezing, but he was sweating profusely. Out of breath. Heart racing. Skin on fire. He focused on the mobile, the faded blue of the Earth, the dusky red of Mars. The pain came in waves; he floated now in a different kind of sea.

The slats beneath the bed were nailed into place and weighed down by the heavy frame and mattress. No matter. He wiggled into the tight space beneath, the bodies of decayed insects crunching under his weight, and there was a toy car on its back and the twisted limbs of a plastic action figure from the time when heroes populated children's daydreams. He broke the board free with three hard whacks of the heel of his hand, scooched back the way he came, and broke the other end free. Dust settled into his mouth. He coughed, sending another tsunami of pain across his chest, down his side, to curl anaconda-like around his stomach.

Ten minutes later he was contemplating the solar system again, worried that Grace would find him passed out, clutching a four-by-six bed slat to his chest. That might be a little more difficult to explain.

The world spun. The planets held still.

There's a hidden room . . . He had crossed the threshold into that room, where a simple promise threw a thousand bolts: *I'll find you.* That promise, like all promises, created its own morality. To keep it, he would have to cross a sea of blood.

The world unloosed. The planets bound.

20

NIGHT HAD FALLEN by the time Grace returned, her arrival presaged by the glow of a lamp expanding in the hall outside. She set the lamp on the bedside table, and the light threw shadows that engulfed her face. He did not protest when she drew down the covers, unwrapped the bandages covering his wounds, and exposed his body to the frigid air.

"Did you miss me, Evan?" she murmured, fingertips slick with salve sliding over his skin. "I don't mean today. How old were we then? Fifteen?"

"Sixteen," he answered.

"Hmm. You asked me if I was afraid of the future. Do you remember?"

"Yes."

"Such a . . . human question."

The fingers of one hand massaging him while the fingers of the other slowly unbuttoned her shirt.

"Not as much as the other one I asked."

She tilted her head inquisitively. Her hair fell over her shoulder. Her face lost in shadow and her shirt falling open like a curtain drawn back.

"What was that?" she whispered.

"If you'd not been, for a very long time, inexpressibly lonely."

The coolness of her fingers. The heat of his seared flesh.

"Your heart is beating very fast," she breathed.

She stood up. He closed his eyes. *For the promise.* Just outside the circle of light, Grace stepped out of the pants that pooled around her ankles. He did not watch.

"Not so lonely," Grace said, her breath caressing his ear. "Being locked in these bodies does have its compensations."

For the promise. And Cassie the island he swam toward, rising from a blood-filled sea.

"Not so lonely, Evan," Grace said. She touched his lips with her fingers, his neck with her lips.

He had no choice. His promise afforded none. Grace would never let him go; she would not hesitate to kill him if he tried. There could be no outrunning her or hiding from her. *No choice.*

He opened his eyes, reached up with his right hand and ran his fingers through her hair. His left hand slid beneath the pillow. Above them, he could see the lonely sun stripped of its offspring, shining in the lamplight. He thought Grace might notice the planets were missing. He expected her to ask why he needed to remove them, though it wasn't the planets he needed.

It was the wire.

But Grace hadn't noticed. Her mind had been on other things. "Touch me, Evan," she whispered.

He rolled hard to his right and smashed his left forearm into her jaw. She stumbled backward as he came off the bed, driving his shoulder into her midsection. She sank her nails deep into the burns on his back and ripped. The room went black for a moment, but he didn't need to see—he just needed to be close.

She may have seen the makeshift garrote of broken wood and mobile wire in his hand, or she might have been just lucky, but her fist closed around the wire and pushed as he drew it tight. He swept her leg with the outside of his good ankle and took her to the floor, following her body down, crushing his knee into her lower back on impact.

No choice.

He summoned every ounce of augmented strength that remained into tightening the wire, until it sliced through her palm and hit bone.

She bucked against his weight. He swung his right knee around and ground it into her head. Tighter. *Tighter.* He smelled blood. His. Hers.

The room spun around.

Sinking deep into blood, his, hers, Evan Walker held still.

21

WHEN IT WAS DONE, he crawled to the bed and pulled out the broken slat. A little long for a crutch—he had to hold the board at a difficult angle—but it would have to do. He hobbled to the other bedroom, where he found men's clothing: a pair of jeans, a plaid shirt, a hand-knit sweater, and a leather jacket with the name of the owner's bowling team, *The Urbana Pinheads*, emblazoned on the back. The fabric scraped and rubbed against his raw skin, making every movement a study in pain. Then he shuffled into the living room, where he found Grace's rucksack and rifle. He threw both over his shoulder.

Hours later, resting in the nestlike mangle of metal in the middle of an eight-car pileup on Highway 68, he opened the sack to take inventory and found dozens of plastic baggies labeled with black marker, each bag containing clippings of human hair. At first he was puzzled. Whose hair was this and why was it in baggies, each neatly marked with dates? Then he understood: Grace was taking trophies from her kills.

Where the body went, the mind followed.

He fashioned a splint for his ankle from two pieces of broken metal and the rest of the bandage roll. He drank a few sips of water. His body ached for sleep, but he would not sleep again until he kept his promise. He lifted his face to the pinpricks of pure light fixed above him in the limitless dark. *Don't I always find you?*

The headlamp of the car beside him exploded in a shower of pulverized glass and plastic. He dove beneath the nearest vehicle, dragging the rifle behind him.

Grace. It had to be. Grace was alive.

He left too quickly. He assumed too much, hoped too much. And now he was trapped, pinned down with no way out, and Evan realized in that moment how promises can be kept in the most unexpected of ways: He'd found Cassie by becoming her.

Wounded, trapped beneath a car, unable to run, unable to rise, at the mercy of a faceless, merciless hunter, a Silencer engineered to snuff out the human noise.

22

HE MET—*found* would be more accurate—Grace the summer they both turned sixteen, at the Hamilton County Fair. Evan was standing outside the exotic petting zoo tent with his little sister, Val, who had been demanding to see the white tiger since they arrived early that morning. It was August. The line was long. Val was tired and grouchy and sticky with sweat. He'd put her off. He didn't like to see animals in captivity. When he looked into their eyes, something in their eyes looked back at him.

He found Grace first, standing beside the funnel cake trailer, a dripping wedge of watermelon in her hand. Blond hair that fell to the middle of her back, cool, nearly arctic features, especially the ice-blue eyes, and the cynical turn of her mouth, glistening with juice. She turned toward him and he quickly looked away, to the face of his baby sister, who would be dead in less than two years. A fact he carried within him, locked away in a different kind of hidden room. Sometimes it was hard to shake—the knowledge that every face he saw was the face of a corpse-to-be. His world was peopled with living ghosts.

"What?" Val asked.

He shook his head. *Nothing.* He took a deep breath and glanced toward the trailer again. The tall blond girl was gone.

Inside the tent, behind a steel mesh fence, the white tiger panted in the heat. Small children crowded in front. Behind them, cameras and smartphones clicked. The tiger remained regally indifferent to the attention.

"Beautiful," a husky voice murmured in Evan's ear. He did not turn. He knew, without looking, it was the girl with the long blond hair and lips that glistened with watermelon juice. The exhibit was packed; her bare arm brushed against his.

"And sad," Evan said.

"No," Grace said. "He could tear through that fence in two seconds. Rip off a kid's face in three. He's *choosing* to be there. That's the beautiful thing."

He looked at her. Her eyes were even more startling up close. They bored into his, and in a knee-weakening instant, he *knew* the entity hiding inside Grace's body.

"We should talk," Grace whispered.

23

AT DUSK, the lights of the Ferris wheel were switched on and the tinny music was turned up and the crowd swelled along the midway, cutoff shorts and flip-flops and the smell of coconut-scented sunscreen and the waddle of big-bellied men in John Deere caps with deeply callused hands and wallets attached to belt loops bulging in back pockets. He handed Val off to their mother, then headed for the Ferris wheel to wait nervously for Grace. She materialized out of the crowd, holding a large stuffed animal: a white Bengal tiger, plastic bright blue eyes only slightly darker than hers.

"I'm Evan," he said.

"I'm Grace."

They watched the giant wheel turn against the purple sky.

"Do you think we'll miss it when it's gone?" he asked.

"I won't." Her nose crinkled. "The smell of them is horrible. I can't get used to it."

"You're the first I've met since . . ."

She nodded. "Me too. Do you think it's an accident?"

"No."

"I wasn't coming today, but this morning when I woke up, there was this little voice. *Go*. Did you hear it?"

He nodded. "Yes."

"Good." She sounded relieved. "For three years I've been wondering if I'm crazy."

"You're not."

"You don't wonder?"

"Not anymore."

She smiled archly. "Do you want to go for a walk?"

They wandered over to the deserted show grounds and sat on the bleachers. The first stars appeared. The night was warm, the air moist. Grace wore a pair of shorts and a sleeveless white blouse with a lace collar. Sitting close to her, Evan could smell licorice.

"This is it," he said, nodding at the empty corral with its mangled floor of sawdust and manure.

"What?"

"The future."

She laughed as if he'd made a joke. "The world ends. The world ends and the world begins again. It's always been that way."

"You're never afraid of what's coming? Never?"

"Never." Hugging the stuffed tiger in her lap. Her eyes seemed to take on the color of whatever she looked at. Now she was looking up at the darkening sky, and her eyes were a bottomless black.

They spoke for a few minutes in their native language, but it was difficult and they gave up quickly. Too many words were unpronounceable. He noticed that she was much calmer afterward, and he realized it wasn't the future that frightened her; it was the past, the fact that she feared the entity inside her body was a figment of a young human girl's shattered mind. Meeting Evan validated her existence.

"You're not alone," he told her. He looked down and discovered her hand in his. One hand for him, the other for the tiger.

"That's been the worst part," she agreed. "Feeling as if you're the only person in the universe. That the whole thing is *here,*" touching her chest, "and nowhere else."

Years later, he would read something quite similar in the diary of another sixteen-year-old girl, the one he found and lost, found, then lost again:

Sometimes I think I might be the last human on Earth.

24

THE CAR'S UNDERCARRIAGE against his back. The cold asphalt against his cheek. The useless rifle clutched in his hand. He was trapped.

Grace had several options. He had two.

No. If there was any hope of keeping his promise, he had just one:

Cassie's choice.

She had made a promise, too. A hopeless, suicidal promise to the one person on Earth who still mattered to her—mattered to her more than her own life. She stood up that day to face the faceless hunter because her death was nothing compared to the death of that promise. If there was any hope left, it lay in love's hopeless promises.

He crawled forward, past the front bumper, into the open air, and then, like Cassie Sullivan, Evan Walker stood up.

He tensed, waiting for the finishing round. When Cassie stood up that cloudless autumn afternoon, her Silencer had run. He did not think Grace would run. Grace would finish what she began.

But no finish came. No silencing bullet, connecting Grace to him as if by a silver cord. He knew she was there. Knew she could see him standing crookedly in front of the car. And he realized there was no escaping the past, no dodging inevitable consequences: Cassie's terror, her uncertainty and pain, they belonged to him now.

Overhead, the stars. Straight ahead, the road that shone in the stars' light. The tight grip of the freezing air and the medicinal smell of the ointment Grace had spread over his burns. *Your heart is beating very fast.*

She's not going to kill you, he told himself. *Not the goal. If killing you was the goal, she wouldn't have missed that shot.*

There could be only one answer: Grace intended to follow him. He was a riddle to her and following him was the way to solve the riddle. He had escaped the trap only to sink deeper into the pit. Keeping his promise now was not being faithful; it was an act of betrayal.

He couldn't outrun her, not with the bad ankle. He couldn't reason with her—he could barely articulate his own reasons anymore. He could wait her out. Stay here, do nothing . . . and risk Cassie being discovered by soldiers of the 5th Wave or abandoning the hotel before his stalemate with Grace ended. He could force a confrontation, but he'd failed once and the odds were he would again. He was too weak, too hurt. He needed time to heal and there was no time.

He leaned against the hood of the car and looked up at the star-encrusted sky, undimmed by human lights, scrubbed clean of contaminants, and these the same stars that shone on the world before humankind walked upon it. For billions of years, these same stars, and what was time to them?

"Mayfly," Evan whispered. "Mayfly."

He shouldered the rifle and wormed his way through the pileup back to the backpack of supplies, which he threw over the other shoulder. Tucked the makeshift crutch beneath his arm. The going would be slow, painfully slow, but he would force Grace to choose between letting him go and following him, deserting her assigned territory at the moment when desertion could mean a serious setback in the carefully constructed timetable. He would swing north of the hotel—north toward the nearest base. North where the enemy had fled and retrenched and waited for spring to launch the final, finishing assault.

That's where hope lay—where all hope had been from the beginning—on the shoulders of the brainwashed child-soldiers of the 5th Wave.

25

LATER THAT EVENING on the day they met, Evan and Grace walked along the midway beneath the lights that beat back the dark, weaving their way through the crowd, past the ring toss and balloon dart game and basketball free throw. Music blared from speakers mounted on the light poles, and bubbling beneath the music was the sound of a thousand conversations, like an undercurrent, and the flow of the crowd was like a river, too, eddying and swirling, swift here, languid there. Tall and lissome and striking in their good looks, Evan and Grace drew attention from the passersby, which made him uncomfortable. He never liked crowds, preferring the solitude of the woods and the fields of the family farm, an inclination that would serve him well when the time of cleansing arrived.

Time. Above them, the stars turned like the points of light on the Ferris wheel that loomed above the fairgrounds, though too slowly for the human eye to register, the hands of the universal clock that was winding down, that had been winding down from the beginning, and the faces that passed marking the time, like the stars themselves, prisoners to it. Evan and Grace were not. They had conquered the unconquerable, denied the undeniable. The last star would die, the universe itself would pass away, but they would go on and on.

"What are you thinking?" she asked.

"'My spirit will not contend with humans forever, for they are mortal.'"

"What?" She was smiling.

"It's from the Bible."

She shifted the stuffed tiger to her other hand so she could take his. "Don't be morbid. It's a beautiful night and we won't see each other again until it's over. Your problem is you don't know how to live in the moment."

She tugged him from the main concourse into the shadows between two tents, where she kissed him, pressing her body tightly against his, and something opened inside him. She entered into him and the terrible loneliness he'd felt since his awakening eased.

Grace pulled away. Her cheeks were flushed, her eyes burning with a pale fire. "I think about it sometimes. The first kill. What it will be like."

He nodded. "I think about it, too. Mostly, though, I think about the last one."

26

HE LEFT THE HIGHWAY, cutting through open fields, crossing lonely country lanes, pausing to refill his canteen with water from an icy stream, navigating as the ancients did, by the North Star. His injuries forced him to rest often, and each time he saw Grace in the distance. She didn't bother to hide. She wanted him to know she was there, just outside the range of the rifle. By dawn he had reached Highway 68, the major artery connecting Huber Heights and Urbana. In a small stand of trees bordering the road, he gathered wood for a fire. His hands were shaking. He felt feverish. He worried the burns had become infected. His bodily systems had been augmented, but an enhanced body could reach a tipping point from which there was no return. His ankle was swollen to twice its normal size, the skin hot to the touch, and the wound throbbed with each beat of his heart. He decided to spend a day here, maybe two, and keep the fire burning.

A beacon to draw them into the trap. If they were out there. If they could be drawn.

The road before him. The woods behind him. He would remain in the open. Grace would stay in the woods. She would wait with him. Out of her assigned territory, fully committed now, no going back.

He warmed himself by the fire. Grace made no fire. His the light and warmth. Hers the dark and cold. He shrugged out of the jacket, pulled off the sweater, slipped off the shirt. Already the burns were scabbing over, but they had begun to itch horribly.

To distract himself, he whittled a new crutch from a tree branch salvaged from the woods.

He wondered if Grace would risk sleep. She knew his strength grew with each passing hour and every hour she delayed, her chances of success waned.

He saw her at midafternoon on the second day, a shadow among shadows, as he gathered more wood for the fire. Fifty yards into the trees, holding a high-powered sniper's rifle, a bloody bandage wrapped around her hand, another around her neck. In the subzero air, her voice seemed to carry into the infinite.

"Why didn't you finish me, Evan?"

He didn't answer at first. He continued gathering kindling for the beacon. Then he said, "I thought I did."

"No. You couldn't have thought that."

"Maybe I'm sick of murder."

"What does that mean?"

He shook his head. "You wouldn't understand."

"Who is Cassiopeia?"

He rose to his full height. The light was weak in the trees beneath a sheet of iron-gray clouds. Even so, he could see the cynical set of her lips and the pale blue fire of her eyes.

"The one who stood up when anyone else would have stayed down," Evan said. "The one I couldn't stop thinking about before I even knew her. The last one, Grace. The last human being on Earth."

She didn't say anything for a long time. He remained. She remained.

"You're in love with a human." Her voice was full of wonder. And then the obvious: "That's not possible."

"We used to think the same about immortality."

"It would be like one of them falling in love with a sea slug." Smiling now. "You're mad. You've gone insane."

"Yes."

He turned his back to her, inviting the bullet. He was mad, after all, and madness came with its own armor.

"It can't be that!" she shouted after him. "Why won't you tell me what's really going on?"

He stopped. The kindling clattered to the frozen ground. The crutch toppled from his side. He turned his head but did not turn around.

"Take cover, Grace," he said softly.

Her finger twitched on the trigger. Normal human eyes might have missed it. Evan's did not. "Or—what?" she demanded. "You'll attack me again?"

He shook his head. "I'm not going to attack you, Grace. They are."

She cocked her head at him, like the bird in the tree when he awakened in her camp.

"They're here," Evan said.

The first bullet struck her upper thigh. She rocked backward but remained upright. The next round punched into her left shoulder and the rifle slipped from her hand. The third round, most likely from a second shooter, exploded in the tree directly beside him, missing his head by millimeters.

Grace dove to the ground.

Evan ran.

27

RAN WAS AN EXAGGERATION. More like a frantic hop, swinging his bad leg wide to keep most of his weight on the good one, and each time his heel hit the ground, pinwheels of bright light exploded in his vision. Past the smoldering campfire, the beacon that had burned for two days, the sign he'd hung in the woods, *Here we are!* Snatching the rifle from the ground in stride; he had no intention of standing his ground. Grace would draw their fire—a patrol of at least two recruits, perhaps more. He hoped more. More would keep Grace busy for a while.

How far? Ten miles? Twenty? He wouldn't be able to maintain this pace, but as long as he kept moving, he should be close to the hotel by dawn the next day.

He could hear the firefight behind him. Sporadic pops, not continuous fire, which meant that Grace was being methodical. The soldiers would be wearing the eyepieces, evening the playing field a bit. Not much, but a bit.

He abandoned any attempt at stealth and hit the highway, loping down the center of the road, a solitary figure under the immensity of a leaden sky. A murder of crows a thousand strong whipped and wheeled over him, heading north. He kept moving, grunting with pain, every stride a lesson, every jolting footfall a reminder. His temperature soared, his lungs burned, his heart slammed in his chest. The friction from the clothes tore open the delicate scabs and soon he was bleeding. Blood plastered his shirt to his back, soaked through the jeans. He was pushing it, he knew.

The system installed to maintain his life past all human endurance could crash.

He collapsed when the sun did beneath the dome of the sky, a slow-motion stumbling kind of fall, hitting shoulder first and rolling to the edge of the road, where he came to rest flat on his back, arms spread wide, numb from the waist down, shaking uncontrollably, burning hot in the bitter air. Darkness rolled over the face of the Earth, and Evan Walker tumbled down to the lightless bottom, to a hidden room that danced in light and her face the source of that light, and he had no explanation for it, how her face illumed the lightless place inside. *You're mad. You've gone insane.* He'd thought so, too. He fought to keep her alive while every night he left her to kill the rest. Why should one live though the world itself will perish? She illumined the lightless—her life the lamp, the last star in a dying universe.

I am humanity, she had written. Self-centered, stubborn, sentimental, childish, vain. *I am humanity.* Cynical, naïve, kind, cruel, soft as down, hard as tungsten steel.

He must get up. If he can't, the light will go out. The world will be consumed by the crushing dark. But the totality of the atmosphere pushed him down and held him under, five quadrillion tons of bone-breaking force.

The system had crashed. Taxed past its limits, the alien technology installed inside his human body when he was thirteen had shut down. There was nothing to sustain or protect him now. Burned and broken, his human body was no different from his former prey's. Fragile. Delicate. Vulnerable. Alone.

He was not one of them. He was completely one of them. Wholly Other. Fully human.

He rolled onto his side. His back spasmed. Blood rushed into his mouth. He spat it out.

Onto his stomach. Then knees. Then hands. His elbows quivered, his wrists threatened to buckle under his own weight. Self-centered, stubborn, sentimental, childish, vain. *I am humanity.* Cynical, naïve, kind, cruel, soft as down, hard as tungsten steel.

I am humanity.

He crawled.

I am humanity.

He fell.

I am humanity.

He got up.

28

A LIFETIME LATER, from his hiding place beneath the highway overpass, Evan watched the dark-haired girl sprint across the hotel parking lot, cross the interstate access ramp, trot a few hundred yards north on Highway 68, then pause beside an SUV to look back at the building. He followed her gaze to a second-story window, where a shadow flitted for an instant, then was gone.

Mayfly.

The dark-haired girl vanished into the trees bordering the highway. Why she had left and where she was going were unknown. Perhaps the group was splitting up—it would increase the chance of survival a little—or perhaps she was scouting a more secure hiding place to ride out the winter. Whichever the case, he had the sense he'd found them just in time.

The dark-haired girl was one, leaving at least four inside, the ones he had seen manning the windows. He did not know if any of them had survived the explosion. He wasn't even sure it had been Cassie's shadow in the window.

Not that it mattered. He'd made a promise. He had to go in.

He couldn't approach openly. The situation was complicated by too many unknowns. What if it wasn't Cassie but a squad of 5th Wave soldiers cut off when the base blew—like the squad he'd left in Grace's care? He'd be dead before he crossed a dozen feet. The risk was nearly as great even if it was Cassie and a group of survivors: They might drop him before they realized who he was.

Going in now, though, posed its own set of risks. He didn't know how many there were inside. Didn't know if he could manage two, much less four, heavily armed trigger-happy kids jacked up on adrenaline, ready to blow away anything that moved. The system that augmented his body had crashed. *I'm fully human,* he'd told Cassie. Now that was literally true.

He was still weighing the options when a tiny figure appeared in the parking lot. A child wearing 5th Wave fatigues. Not Sam—Sam had been dressed in the white jumpsuit of the underaged and newly processed—but young. Six or seven, he guessed. Following the same route as the dark-haired girl, even pausing by the same SUV to look back at the hotel. This time he saw no shadow in the window; whoever had been there was gone.

That made two. Were they abandoning the hotel one at a time? Tactically, it made some sense. Shouldn't he simply wait, then, for Cassie to come out, rather than risk his life going in?

And the stars spun overhead, marking the time winding down.

He started to get up, then sank back. Another one exited the hotel, much larger than the one before, a big kid with a large head, toting a rifle. Three now, none of them Cassie or Sam or the friend from Cassie's high school—what was his name? Ken? With each exodus, the odds of Cassie not being in this group increased. Should he even attempt entry?

His instinct said *go*. No answers, no weapons, and hardly any strength. Instinct was all he had left.

He went.

29

FOR OVER FIVE YEARS he'd relied on the gifts that made him superior to humans in almost every way. Hearing. Eyesight. Reflexes. Agility. Strength. The gifts had spoiled him. He'd forgotten what normal felt like.

He was getting a crash course now.

He slipped into a ground-floor room through a broken-out window. Hobbled to the door and pressed his ear against it, but all he could hear was the thundering of his heart. Easing the door open, sliding into the hall, listening, waiting in vain for his eyes to adjust to the dark. Down the hall and into the lobby. His own breath, frosting in the frigid air, otherwise silence. Apparently the ground floor was deserted. He knew someone was standing at the small hallway window upstairs; he caught a glimpse of him as he maneuvered his way into the building.

Stairwell. Two flights. By the time he reached the second landing, he was dizzy from the pain and out of breath from the effort. He tasted blood. There was no light. He was entombed in utter darkness.

If there was only one person on the other side of this door, he had seconds. More than one and time didn't matter; he was dead. Every instinct said wait.

He went.

In the hall on the other side of the door was a small kid with extraordinarily large ears and a mouth flying open in astonishment the moment before Evan locked him in the chokehold, pressing his forearm hard against the kid's carotid, cutting off the blood supply to his brain. He dragged his squirming catch back into the black pit of the stairwell. The kid went limp before the door clicked shut again.

Evan waited for a few seconds on the other side. The hall had been empty, the snatch quick and relatively quiet. It could be a while before the others—if there were others—realized their sentry was gone. He dragged the kid to the bottom of the stairs and tucked his unconscious body into the small space between the steps and the wall. Went back up. Cracked open the door. Halfway down the hall, another door opened and two shadowy figures emerged. He watched them cross the hall and enter another room. They reappeared a moment later and went to another door.

They were checking each room. The stairs would be next. Or the elevator; he'd forgotten about the elevator. Would they drop down the shaft and take the stairs from below?

No. If there're only two, they'll split up. One for the stairs, one down the shaft, and meet up in the lobby.

He watched them come out of the last room, then go to the elevator, where one held the doors while the other dropped out of sight into the shaft. The one who remained had trouble standing, holding his stomach and grunting softly from the effort, favoring one side as he limped toward Evan.

He waited. Twenty feet. Ten. Five. Holding the rifle in his right hand, his gut with his left. Standing on the other side of the door, Evan smiled. *Ben. Not Ken. Ben.*

Found you.

Too dangerous to trust that Ben would recognize him and not shoot him on the spot. He burst through the door and rammed his fist as hard as he could into Ben's wounded stomach. The blow knocked the breath out of him, but Ben refused to go down. Rocking back, he brought his rifle up. Evan slung it to one side and hit him again, same spot, and this time Ben went down, dropping to his knees at Evan's feet. His head fell back. Their eyes met.

"I knew you weren't for real," Ben gasped.

"Where's Cassie?"

He knelt, grabbed two fistfuls of the yellow hoodie Ben was wearing, and brought their faces close.

"Where's Cassie?"

If he had been his old self, if the system hadn't crashed, he would have seen the blur of the blade as it came around, heard the infinitesimally small whistle of it cutting through the air. Instead, he wasn't aware of the knife until Ben had buried it in his thigh.

He fell back, dragging Ben with him. Hurled him to one side as Ben ripped the knife free. Evan slammed his knee down on Ben's wrist to neutralize the threat and clamped both hands over Ben's face, covering his nose and mouth and pushing hard. Time spun out. Beneath him, Ben thrashed and kicked, whipped his head from side to side, his free hand clawing for the rifle less than an inch from his fingertips, and time froze.

Then Ben went still and Evan fell away, gulping air, drenched in blood and sweat and feeling as if his body might burst into flames. No time to recover, though: Down the hall, through a crack in the door, a small, heart-shaped face turned his way.

Sam.

He pushed himself to his feet, lost his balance, careened into the wall, fell. Back up again, convinced now it was Cassie who had dropped into the shaft, but he had to secure Sam first, except the kid had slammed the door and was now screaming obscenities through it, and then, as Evan dropped his hand on the knob, he opened fire.

He threw himself against the wall next to the door while Sam emptied the magazine. When the pause came, he didn't hesitate. Sam had to be neutralized before he could reload.

Evan had a choice: kick open the door with the bad foot or put all his weight on it while he kicked with the other. Neither option was good. He chose to kick with the broken one; he couldn't risk losing his balance.

Three hard, sharp kicks. Three kicks that produced pain as he'd never experienced it before. But the lock broke with a loud wallop and the door slammed into the wall on the other side. He fell into the room and there was Cassie's brother crab-crawling toward the window and somehow Evan remained upright, something held him up and propelled him toward the child, hand outstretched, *I'm here, remember me? I saved you before; I'll save you again . . .*

And then, behind him, the last one, the final star, the one he carried across an infinite sea of white, the one thing he'd found worth dying for, opened fire.

And the bullet connected them when it wedded bone, binding them together as if by a silver cord.

IV

MILLIONS

30

THE BOY STOPPED talking the summer of the plague.

His father had disappeared. Their supply of candles ran low and he left one morning to find more. He never came back.

His mother was sick. Her head hurt. She ached all over. Even her teeth hurt, she told him. The nights were the worst. Her fever shot up. Her tummy couldn't hold anything down. The next morning she would feel better. Maybe I'll get over it, she said. She refused to go to the hospital. They'd heard stories, terrible stories, about the hospitals and walk-in clinics and emergency shelters.

One by one, families fled the neighborhood. Looting was getting bad and gangs roamed the streets at night. The man who lived two doors down was killed, shot in the head, for refusing to share his family's drinking water. Sometimes a stranger wandered into the neighborhood and told stories of earthquakes and walls of water five hundred feet high, flooding the land as far east as Las Vegas. Thousands dead. Millions.

When his mother became too weak to get out of bed, the baby became his responsibility. They called him the baby, but he was actually almost three. Don't bring him near me, his mother told him. He'll get sick. The baby wasn't that much work. He slept a lot. He played only a little. He was just a tiny kid; he didn't know. Sometimes he would ask where his daddy was or what was the matter with Mommy. Most of the time, he asked for food.

They were running out of food. But his mother wouldn't let

him leave. It's too dangerous. You'll get lost. You'll get abducted. You'll get shot. He would argue with her. He was eight and very big for his age, the target of school-yard taunts and cruel insults since he was six. He was tough. He could handle himself. But she wouldn't let him go. I can't keep anything down and you could stand to lose a little weight anyway. She wasn't being cruel; she was trying to be funny. He didn't think it was funny, though.

Then they were down to their last can of condensed soup and wrapper of stale crackers. He heated the soup in the fireplace, over a fire he fed with pieces of broken-up furniture and his father's old hunting magazines. The baby ate all the crackers but said he didn't want the soup. He wanted mac and cheese. We don't have mac and cheese. We have soup and crackers, and that's all we have. The baby cried and rolled on the floor in front of the fireplace, screaming for mac and cheese.

He brought a cup of the soup to his mother. Her fever was bad. The night before, she had started throwing up the lumpy black stuff, which was the lining of her stomach mixed with blood, though he didn't know that then. She watched him come into the room with dead, expressionless eyes, the fixed stare of the Red Death.

What do you think you're doing? I can't eat that. Take it away.

He took it away and ate it standing at the kitchen sink while his baby brother rolled on the floor and screamed and his mother sank deeper into mindlessness, the virus spreading into her brain. In the final hours, his mother would disappear. Her personality, her memory, the *who* of who she was, surrendering before her body. He ate the lukewarm soup and then licked the bowl clean. He would have to leave in the morning. There was no more food.

He would tell his little brother to stay inside no matter what and he wouldn't come back until he found something for them to eat.

He snuck out the next morning. He looked in abandoned groceries and convenience stores. He looked in looted restaurants and fast-food places. He found Dumpsters reeking of decaying produce and overflowing with torn-open garbage bags where many hands before his had searched. By late afternoon, he'd found only one edible morsel: a small cake about the size of his palm, still in its plastic wrapper, underneath an empty shelf in a gas station. It was getting late; the sun was going down. He decided to go home and return the next morning. Maybe there were more cakes and other kinds of food stashed or lost and he needed to look harder.

When he got home, the front door was ajar. He remembered closing it behind him, so he knew something was wrong. He ran inside. He called for the baby. He went room to room. He looked under beds and inside closets and in the cars that sat cold and useless in the garage. His mother called him into her room. Where had he been? The baby wouldn't stop crying for him. He asked his mother where the baby was and she snapped at him, Can't you hear him?

But he heard nothing.

He went outside and yelled the baby's name. He checked the backyard, walked over to the neighbor's house and banged on the door. He banged on every door on the street. Nobody answered. Either the people inside were too scared to come out or they were sick or dead or just gone. He walked several blocks one way, then several more the other way, calling his brother's name until he was hoarse. An old woman tottered out onto her porch and screamed at him to go away; she had a gun. He went home.

The baby was gone. He decided not to tell his mother. What would she do about it? He didn't want her to think he was bad for leaving. He should have brought him along, but he thought it was safer at home. Your home is the safest place on Earth.

That night, his mother called to him. Where is my baby? He told her the baby was asleep. It was the worst night yet. Bloody tissues wadded on the bed. Bloody tissues crowding the nightstand, littering the floor.

Bring me my baby.

He's asleep.

I want to see my baby.

You might make him sick.

She cursed him. She told him to go to hell. She spat bloody phlegm at him. He stood in the doorway, hands nervously fiddling in his pockets, and the cake wrapper crackled, the plastic damaged by the heat.

Where have you been?

Looking for food.

She gagged. Don't say that word!

Watching him with bright red, bloody eyes.

Why were you looking for food? You don't need any food. You're the most disgusting piece of pig lard I've ever seen. You could live till winter on just your belly fat.

He didn't say anything. He knew it was the plague talking, not his mother. His mother loved him. When the teasing at school got bad, she went to the principal and said she would file a lawsuit if the bullying didn't stop.

What's that noise? What's that horrible noise?

He told her he didn't hear anything. She got very angry. She started to curse again and bloody spittle spattered on the headboard.

It's coming from you. What are you playing with in your pocket?

There was nothing he could do. He had to show her. He pulled out the cake and she screamed for him to put it away and never take it out again. No wonder he was so fat. No wonder his baby brother was starving while he ate cakes and candies and all the mac and cheese. What sort of monster was he that he ate all his baby brother's mac and cheese?

He tried to defend himself. But every time he started talking, she screamed at him to shut up, shut up, shut UP. His voice made her sick. *He* made her sick. He did it. He did something to her husband and he did something to his baby brother and he did something to *her,* made her sick, poisoned her, he was *poisoning* her.

And every time he tried to speak, she screamed at him. Shut up, shut up, shut UP.

She died two days later.

He wrapped her in a clean sheet and carried her body into the backyard. He doused the body with his father's charcoal lighter fluid and set it on fire. He burned his mother's body and all the bedding, too. He waited another week for his baby brother to come home, but he never did. He searched for him—and for food. He found food, but not his brother. He stopped calling for him. He stopped talking altogether. He shut up.

Six weeks later, he was walking down a highway dotted with stalled-out cars and wrecks of cars and trucks and motorcycles when he saw black smoke in the distance and, after a few minutes, the source of the smoke, a yellow school bus full of children. There were soldiers on the bus and the soldiers asked his name and where he was from and how old he was, and later he remembered nervously stuffing his hands in his pockets and finding the old piece of cake, still in its wrapper.

Pig lard. Live till winter on your belly fat.

What's the matter, kid? Can't you talk?

His drill sergeant heard the story of how he came to camp with nothing but the clothes on his back and a piece of cake in his pocket. Before he heard the story, the drill sergeant called him Fatboy. After he heard the story, the drill sergeant renamed him Poundcake.

I like you, Poundcake. I like the fact that you're a born shooter. I bet you popped out of your momma with a gun in one hand and a doughnut in the other. I like the fact that you got the looks of Elmer Fudd and the goddamned heart of Mufasa. And I *especially* like the fact that you don't talk. Nobody knows where you're from, where you've been, what you think, how you feel. Hell, I don't know and I don't give a shit, and you shouldn't, either. You're a mute-assed, stone-cold killer from the heart of darkness with a heart to match, aren't you, Private Poundcake?

He wasn't.

Not yet.

V
THE PRICE

31

THE FIRST THING I planned to do when he woke up was kill him.

If he woke up.

Dumbo wasn't sure that would happen. "He's messed up bad," he told me after we stripped him down and Dumbo got a good look at the damage. Stabbed in one leg, shot in the other, covered in burns, bones broken, shaking with a high fever—though we piled covers on him, Evan still shook so violently that it looked like the bed was vibrating.

"Sepsis," Dumbo muttered. He noticed me staring dumbly at him and added, "When the infection gets into your bloodstream."

"What do we do?" I asked.

"Antibiotics."

"Which we don't have."

I sat on the other bed. Sam scooted to the foot, clutching the empty pistol. He refused to give it up. Ben was leaning on the wall, cradling his rifle and eyeing Evan warily, like he was sure any second Evan would bolt out of bed and make another attempt to take us out.

"He didn't have a choice," I told Ben. "How could he just stroll up in the dark without somebody shooting him?"

"I want to know where Poundcake and Teacup are," Ben said through gritted teeth.

Dumbo told him to get off his feet. He'd repacked the bandages, but Ben had lost a lot of blood. Ben waved him away. He pushed himself from the wall, limped to Evan's bedside, and whacked him across the cheek with the back of his hand.

"Wake up!" *Whack*. "Wake up, you son of a bitch!"

I shot from the bed and grabbed Ben's wrist before he could pop Evan again.

"Ben, this won't—"

"Fine." He yanked his arm away and lurched toward the door. "I'll find them myself."

"Zombie!" Sam called out. He popped up and ran to his side. "I'll come, too!"

"Cut it out, both of you," I snapped. "Nobody's going anywhere until we—"

"What, Cassie?" Ben yelled. "Until we what?"

My mouth opened and no words came out. Sam was tugging on his arm: *Come on, Zombie!* My five-year-old brother waving around an empty gun; there's a metaphor for you.

"Ben, listen to me. Are you listening to me? You go out there now—"

"I am going out there now—"

"—and we might lose you, too!" Shouting over him. "You don't know what happened out there—Evan probably knocked them out like he did you and Dumbo. But maybe he didn't—maybe they're on the way back right now, and going out there is a stupid risk—"

"Don't lecture me about stupid risks. I know all about—"

Ben swayed. The color drained from his face and he went down to one knee, Sam grabbing futilely on his sleeve. Dumbo and I pulled him up and got him to the empty bed, where he fell back, cussing us and cussing Evan Walker and cussing the whole fucked-up situation in general. Dumbo was giving me a deer-in-headlights look, like *You got the answers, right? You know what to do, right?*

Wrong.

32

I PICKED UP Dumbo's rifle and pushed it into the kid's chest.

"We're blind," I told him. "Stairway, both hall windows, east-side rooms, west-side rooms, keep moving and keep your eyes open. I'll stay here with the alpha males and try to keep them from killing each other."

Dumbo was nodding like he understood, but he wasn't moving. I put my hands on his shoulders and focused on his jiggly eyes. "Step up, Dumbo. Understand? Step up."

He jerked his head up and down, a human PEZ dispenser, and slumped out of the room. Leaving was the last thing he wanted to do, but we'd been at that point for a long time now, the point of doing the last thing we wanted to do.

Behind me, Ben growled, "Why didn't you shoot him in the head? Why the knee?"

"Poetic justice," I muttered. I sat next to Evan. I could see his eyes quivering behind the lids. He had been dead. I'd said goodbye. Now he was alive and I might not be able to say hello. *We're only about four miles from Camp Haven, Evan. What took you so long?*

"We can't stay here," Ben announced. "It was a bad call sending Ringer ahead. I knew we shouldn't've split up. We're bugging out of here in the morning."

"How are we going to do that?" I asked. "You're hurt. Evan is—"

"This isn't about him," Ben said. "Well, I guess it is to you—"

"He's the reason you're alive right now to bitch, Parish."

"I'm not bitching."

"Yes, you are. You're bitching like a junior miss beauty queen."

Sammy laughed. I don't think I'd heard my brother laugh since our mother died. It startled me, like finding a lake in the middle of a desert.

"Cassie called you a bitch," Sam informed Ben, in case he missed it.

Ben ignored him. "We waited here for him and now we're trapped here because of him. Do what you want, Sullivan. In the morning, I'm out of here."

"Me too!" Sams said.

Ben got up, leaned on the side of the bed for a minute to catch his breath, then hobbled to the door. Sam trailed after him, and I didn't try to stop either one of them. What would be the point? Ben cracked the door and called softly to Dumbo not to shoot him—he was coming out to help. Then Evan and I were alone.

I sat on the bed Ben had just abandoned. It was still warm from his body. I grabbed Sammy's bear and pulled it into my lap.

"Can you hear me?" I asked—Evan, not the bear. "Guess we're even now, huh? You shoot me in the knee; I shoot you in the knee. You see me butt naked; I see you butt naked. You pray over me; I—"

The room swam out of focus. I took Bear and popped Evan in the chest with it.

"And what was with that ridiculous jacket you were wearing? The Pinheads, that's about right. That nails it." I hit him again. "Pinhead." Again. "Pinhead." Again. "And now you're going to check out on me? Now?"

His lips moved and a word leaked out slowly, like air escaping from a tire.

"Mayfly."

33

HIS EYES OPENED. When I recalled writing about their warm, melted chocolateness, something in me went *gah*. Why did he have this knees-to-jelly effect on me? That wasn't me. Why did I let him kiss and cuddle and generally mope around after me like a forlorn little lost alien puppy? Who was this guy? From what warped version of reality did he transport into my own personal warped version of reality? None of it fit. None of it made sense. Falling in love with me might be like me falling in love with a cockroach, but what do you call my reaction to him? What's that called?

"If you weren't dying and all, I'd tell you to go to hell."

"I'm not dying, Cassie." Fluttery lids. Sweaty face. Shaky voice.

"Okay, then go to hell. You left me, Evan. In the dark, just like that, and then you blew up the ground beneath me. You could have killed all of us. You abandoned me right when—"

"I came back."

He reached out his hand. "Don't touch me." *None of your creepy Vulcan mind-meld tricks.*

"I kept my promise," he whispered.

Well, what snarky comeback did I have for that? A promise was what brought me to him in the beginning. Again I was struck by how really weird it was that he was where I had been and I was where he had been. His promise for mine. My bullet for his. Down to stripping each other naked because there's no choice; clinging to modesty in the age of the Others is like sacrificing a goat to make it rain.

"You almost got shot in the head, moron," I told him. "It didn't occur to you to just shout up the stairs, 'Hey, it's me! Hold your fire!'?"

He shook his head. "Too risky."

"Oh, right. Much more risky than chancing your head getting blown off. Where's Teacup? Where's Poundcake?"

He shook his head again. *Who?*

"The little girl who took off down the highway. The big kid who chased after her. You must have seen them."

Now he nodded. "North."

"Well, I know which direction they went . . ."

"Don't go after them."

That brought me up short. "What do you mean?"

"It isn't safe."

"Nowhere is safe, Evan."

His eyes were rolling back in his head. He was passing out. "There's Grace."

"What did you say? Grace? As in 'Amazing Grace' or what? What's that mean, 'There's grace'?"

"Grace," he murmured, and then he slipped away.

34

I STAYED WITH HIM till dawn. Sitting with him like he sat with me in the old farmhouse. He brought me to that place against my will and then my will brought him to this place, and maybe that meant we sort of owned each other. Or owed each other. Anyway, no debt is ever fully repaid, not really, not the ones that really matter. *You saved me,* he said, and back then I didn't understand what I had saved him from. That was before he told me the truth about who he was, and afterward I thought he meant I had saved him from that whole human genocide, mass-murderer thing. Now I was thinking he didn't mean I saved him from anything, but *for* something. The tricky part, the unanswerable part, the part that scared the crap out of me, was what that something might be.

He moaned in his sleep. His fingers clawed at the covers. Delirious. *Been there and done that, too, Evan.* I took his hand. Burned and bruised and broken, and I had wondered what took him so long to find me? He must have crawled here. His hand was hot; his face shone with sweat. For the first time it occurred to me that Evan Walker might die—so soon, too, after rising from the dead.

"You're going to live," I told him. "You have to live. Promise, Evan. Promise me you're going to live. Promise me."

I slipped a little. Tried not to. Couldn't help it:

"That'll complete the circle, then we're done; we're both done, me and you. You shot me and I lived. I shot you and you live. See? That's how it works. Ask anybody. Plus the fact that you're Mr. Ten-Centuries-Old Superbeing destined to save us pitiful humans from the intergalactic swarm. That's your job. What you were born to do. Or bred to. Whatever. You know, as plans to conquer the world go, yours has been pretty sucky. Almost a year into it and we're still here, and who's the one flat on his back like a bug with drool on his chin?"

Actually, he did have some drool on his chin. I dabbed it up with a corner of the blanket.

The door opened and big ol' Poundcake stepped into the room. Then Dumbo, grinning from big ear to big ear, then Ben, and finally Sam. Finally as in no Teacup.

"How is he?" Ben asked.

"Burning up," I answered. "Delirious. He keeps talking about grace."

Ben frowned. "Like 'Amazing Grace'?"

"Maybe saying grace, like before a meal," Dumbo suggested. "He's probably starving."

Poundcake lumbered over to the window and stared down at the icy parking lot. I watched him Eeyore-walk across the room, then turned to Ben. "What happened?"

"He won't say."

"Then make him say. You're the sarge, right?"

"I don't think he can."

"So Teacup's vanished and we don't know where or why."

"She caught up with Ringer," Dumbo guessed. "And Ringer decided to take her to the caverns, not waste any time bringing her back."

I jerked my head toward Poundcake. "Where was he?"

"Found him outside," Ben said.

"Doing what?"

"Just . . . hanging out."

"Just hanging out? Really? You guys ever wonder which team Poundcake might be playing for?"

Ben shook his head wearily. "Sullivan, don't start—"

"Seriously. The mute act could be just an *act.* Keeps you from having to answer any awkward questions. Plus the fact that it makes a lot of sense planting one of your own into each brainwashed squad, in case anybody starts to wise—"

"Right, and before Poundcake it was Ringer." Ben was losing it. "Next it'll be Dumbo. Or me. When the guy who admitted he was the enemy is lying right there, holding your hand."

"Actually, I'm holding *his* hand. And he isn't the enemy, Parish. I thought we covered this."

"How do we know he didn't kill Teacup? Or Ringer? How do we know that?"

"Oh, Christ, look at him. He couldn't kill a . . . a . . ." I tried to think of the proper thing he had the strength to kill, but the only thing my hungry, sleep-deprived brain could come up with was *mayfly,* which would have been a really, really bad choice of words. Like an inadvertent omen, if an omen can be inadvertent.

Ben whipped around to Dumbo, who flinched. I think he preferred Ben's wrath be directed at anybody but him. "Will he live?"

Dumbo shook his head, the tips of his ears growing bright pink. "It's bad."

"That's my question. How bad? How soon before he can travel?"

"Not for a while."

"Damn it, Dumbo, when?"

"A couple weeks? A month? His ankle's broke, but that's not the worst. The infection, then you've got the risk of gangrene . . ."

"A month? A month!" Ben laughed humorlessly. "He storms this place, takes you out, beats the crap out of me, and a couple hours later he can't move for a month!"

"Then go!" I shouted across the room at him. "All of you. Leave him with me, and we'll follow you as soon as we can."

Ben's mouth, which had been hanging open, snapped closed. Sam was hovering near Ben's leg, one tiny finger hooked into his big buddy's belt loop. Something in my heart gave a little at the sight. Ben told me they called my little brother "Zombie's dog" in camp, meaning ever faithfully by his side.

Dumbo was nodding. "Makes sense to me, Sarge."

"We had a plan," Ben said. His lips barely moved. "And we're sticking to the plan. If Ringer isn't back by this time tomorrow, we're bugging out." He glared at me. "All of us." He jabbed his thumb at Poundcake and Dumbo. "They can carry your boyfriend, if he needs to be carried."

Ben turned, bumped into the wall, pinballed off it, lurched through the door and into the hall.

Dumbo trailed after him. "Sarge, where're you . . . ?"

"Bed, Dumbo, bed! I gotta lie down or I'm gonna fall down. Take the first watch. Nugget—Sam—whatever your name is—what are you doing?"

"I'm coming with you."

"Stay with your sister. Wait. You're right. She's got her hands full—literally. Poundcake! Sullivan has the duty. Get some shut-eye, you big mute mother . . ."

His voice faded away. Dumbo came back to the foot of Evan's bed.

"Sarge is strung out," he explained, like I needed him to explain. "He's usually pretty chill."

"Me too," I said. "I'm the laid-back type. No worries."

He wouldn't go away. He was looking at me and his cheeks were as bright red as his ears. "Is he really your boyfriend?"

"Who? No, Dumbo. He's just a guy I met one day while he was trying to kill me."

"Oh. Good." He seemed relieved. "He's like Vosch, you know."

"He's nothing like Vosch."

"I mean he's one of them." Lowering his voice like he was sharing a dark secret. "Zombie says they're not like these tiny bugs in our brains, but somehow they downloaded themselves into us like a computer virus or something."

"Yeah. Something like that."

"That's weird."

"Well, I guess they could have downloaded themselves into house cats, but going that route would've made our extermination more time-consuming."

"Only by a month or two," Dumbo said, and I laughed. Like Sammy's, mine surprised me. If you wanted to separate humans from their humanity, I thought, killing laughter would be a good place to start. I was never very good at history, but I was pretty sure douchebags like Hitler didn't laugh very much.

"I still don't get it," he went on. "Why one of them would be on our side."

"I'm not sure he completely understands the answer to that question."

Dumbo nodded, squared his shoulders, took a deep breath. He was dead on his feet. We all were. I called softly to him before he stepped outside.

"Dumbo." Ben's question, unanswered. "Is he going to make it?"

He didn't say anything for a long time. "If I were an alien and

I could pick any body I wanted," he said slowly, "I'd pick a really strong one. And then, just to make sure I'd live through the war, I'd like, I don't know, make myself immune to every virus and bacteria on Earth. Or at least resistant. You know, like getting your dog vaccinated for rabies."

I smiled. "You're pretty smart, you know that, Dumbo?"

He blushed. "That's a nickname based on my ears."

He left. I had the eerie feeling of being watched. Because I was being watched: Poundcake stared at me from his post by the window.

"And you," I said. "What's your story? Why don't you talk?"

He turned away, and his breath fogged the window.

35

"CASSIE! CASSIE, wake up!"

I bolted upright. I'd been curled up next to Evan, my head pressed against his, my hand in his, and how the hell did that happen? Sam was standing beside the bed, pulling on my arm.

"Get up, Sullivan!"

"Don't call me that, Sams," I mumbled. The light was bleeding from the room; it was late afternoon. I'd slept through the day. "What . . . ?"

He put one finger to his lips and pointed at the ceiling with another. *Listen.*

I heard it: the unmistakable sound of a chopper's rotors—faint but growing louder. I jumped from the bed, grabbed my rifle, and followed Sam into the hall, where Poundcake and Dumbo huddled around Ben, the former quarterback squatting on his haunches, calling the play.

"Might be just a patrol," he was whispering. "Not even after us. There were two squads out there when the camp blew. Might be a rescue mission."

"They'll pick up our signatures," Dumbo said, panicking. "We're done, Sarge."

"Maybe not," Ben said hopefully. He'd gotten back some of his mojo. "Hear it? Fading already . . ."

Not his imagination: The sound was fainter. You had to hold your breath to hear it. We hung there in the hall for another ten minutes until the sound disappeared. Waited another ten and it didn't come back. Ben blew out his cheeks.

"Think we're good . . ."

"For how long?" Dumbo wanted to know. "We shouldn't stay here tonight, Sarge. I say we head for the caverns now."

"And chance missing Ringer on her way back?" Ben shook his head. "Or risk that chopper coming back while we're exposed? No, Dumbo. We stick to the plan."

He pushed himself to his feet. His eyes fell on my face. "What's up with Buzz Lightyear? No change?"

"His name is Evan and no. No change."

Ben smiled. I don't know, maybe imminent peril made him feel more alive somehow, for the same reason zombies are carnivores with only one item on the menu. You never heard of undead vegetarians. Where's the challenge in attacking a plate of asparagus?

Sams giggled. "Zombie called your boyfriend a space ranger."

"He isn't a space ranger—and why is everyone calling him my boyfriend?"

Ben's smile broadened. "He's not your boyfriend? But he kissed you . . ."

"Full on?" Dumbo asked.

"Oh, yeah. Twice. That's what I saw."

"With tongue?"

"Ewww." Sammy mouth's formed a sour lemon pout.

"I have a gun," I announced, only half joking.

"I didn't see any tongue," Ben said.

"Want to?" I stuck my tongue out at him. Dumbo laughed. Even Poundcake smiled.

That's when the girl appeared, stepping into the hallway from the stairwell, and then everything got very strange, very fast.

36

A MUD-(or it could have been blood-)stained, tattered pink Hello Kitty T-shirt. A pair of shorts that once had been tan, maybe, faded to a dirty white. Grungy white flip-flops with a couple stubborn rhinestones clinging to the straps. A narrow, pixieish face dominated by huge eyes, topped by a mass of tangled dark hair. And young, around Sammy's age, though she was so thin, her face looked like a little old lady's.

Nobody said anything. We were shocked. Seeing her at the far end of the hall, teeth chattering, knobby knees knocking in the freezing cold, was another Camp Ashpit, yellow-school-bus-pulling-up-when-school-would-never-exist-again moment. Something that simply could not be.

Then Sammy whispered, "Megan?"

And Ben said, "Who the hell is Megan?" Which was very much what the rest of us were thinking.

Sam took off before anybody could grab him. Pulled up halfway to her. The little girl didn't move. Didn't hardly blink. Her eyes seemed to shine in the dwindling light, bright and birdlike, like a wizened owl's.

Sam turned to us and said, "Megan!" As if he were pointing out the obvious. "It's Megan, Zombie. She was on the bus with me!" He turned back to her. "Hi, Megan." Casually, like they were meeting up at the monkey bars for a playdate.

"Poundcake," Ben said softly. "Check the stairs. Dumbo, take the windows. Then sweep the first floor, both of you. There's no way she's alone."

She spoke, and her voice came out in a high-pitched, scratchy whine that reminded me of fingernails scraping across a blackboard.

"My throat hurts."

Her big eyes rolled back in her head. Her knees buckled. Sam raced toward her, but he was too late: She went down hard, smacking the thin carpeting with her forehead a second before Sam could reach her. Ben and I rushed over, and he bent down to pick her up. I pushed him away.

"You shouldn't be lifting anything," I scolded him.

"She doesn't *weigh* anything," he protested.

I picked her up. He was nearly right. Megan weighed little more than a sack of flour; bones and skin and hair and teeth and that's about it. I carried her into Evan's room, put her in the empty bed, and piled six layers of blankets over her quaking little body. I told Sam to fetch my rifle from the hall.

"Sullivan," Ben said from the doorway. "This doesn't fit."

I nodded. Worse than the odds of her lucking into this hotel at random were the odds of her surviving this weather in her summer outfit. Ben and I were thinking the same thing: Twenty minutes after our hearing the chopper, Li'l Miss Megan appeared on our doorstep.

She didn't wander in here on her own. She was delivered.

"They know we're here," I said.

"But instead of firebombing the building, they drop her in. Why?"

Sam came back with my rifle. He said, "That's Megan. We met on the bus on the way to Camp Haven, Cassie."

"Small world, huh?" I pushed him away from the bed, toward Ben. "Thoughts?"

He rubbed his chin. I rubbed my neck. Too many thoughts skittering around both our heads. I stared at him rubbing his chin and he stared at me rubbing my neck, and that's when he said, "Tracker. They've implanted her with a pellet."

Of course. That must be why Ben's in charge. He's the Idea Man. I massaged the back of Megan's pencil-thin neck, probing for the telltale lump. Nothing. I looked at Ben and shook my head.

"They know we'd look there," he said impatiently. "Search her. Every inch, Sullivan. Sam, you come with me."

"Why can't I stay?" Sam whined. After all, he'd just reunited with a long-lost friend.

"You want to see a naked girl?" Ben made a face. "Gross."

Ben pushed Sam out the door and backed out of the room. I dug my knuckles into my eyes. Damn it. Goddamn it. I pulled the covers to the foot of the bed, exposing her wasted body to the dying light of a midwinter's evening. Covered in scabs and bruises and open sores and layers of dirt and grime, whittled down to her bones by the horrible cruelty of indifference and the brutal indifference of cruelty, she was one of us and she was all of us. She was the Others' masterwork, their magnum opus, humanity's past and its future, what they had done and what they promised to do, and I cried. I cried for Megan and I cried for me and I cried for my brother and I cried for all the ones too stupid or unlucky to be dead already.

Suck it up, Sullivan. We're here, then we're gone, and that was true before they came. That's always been true. The Others didn't invent death; they just perfected it. Gave death a face to put back in our face, because they knew that was the only way to crush us. It won't end on any continent or ocean, no mountain or plain, jungle or desert. It will end where it began, where it had been from the beginning, on the battlefield of the last beating human heart.

I stripped her of the filthy, threadbare summer clothes. I spread her arms and legs like the Da Vinci drawing of the naked dude inside the box, contained within the circle. I forced myself to go slowly, methodically, starting with her head and moving down her body. I whispered to her, "I'm sorry, I'm so sorry," pressing, kneading, probing.

I wasn't sad anymore. I thought of Vosch's finger slamming down on the button that would fry my five-year-old brother's brains, and I wanted to taste his blood so badly, my mouth began to water.

You say you know how we think? Then you know what I'm going to do. I'll rip your face off with a pair of tweezers. I'll tear your heart out with a sewing needle. I'll bleed you out with seven billion tiny cuts, one for each one of us.

That's the cost. That's the price. Get ready, because when you crush the humanity out of humans, you're left with humans with no humanity.

In other words, you get what you pay for, motherfucker.

37

I CALLED BEN into the room.

"Nothing," I told him. "And I checked . . . everywhere."

"What about her throat?" Ben said quietly. He could hear the residual rage in my voice. He got that he was talking to a crazy person and had to tread lightly. "Right before she fainted, she said her throat hurt."

I nodded. "I looked. There's no pellet in her, Ben."

"Are you positive? 'My throat hurts' is a very weird thing for a freezing, malnourished kid to say the minute she shows up."

He sidled over to the bed, I don't know, maybe because he was concerned I might jump him in a moment of misplaced fury. Not that *that's* ever happened. He gingerly pressed one hand to her forehead while prying her mouth open with the other. Stuck his eye close. "Hard to see anything," he muttered.

"That's why I used this," I said, handing him Sam's camp-issued penlight.

He shone the light down her throat. "It's pretty red," he observed.

"Right. Which is why she said it hurt."

Ben scratched his stubble, worrying over the problem. "Not 'help me' or 'I'm cold' or even 'resistance is futile.' Just 'my throat hurts.'"

I crossed my arms over my chest. "'Resistance is futile'? Really?"

Sam was hovering in the doorway. Big brown saucer eyes. "Is she okay, Cassie?" he asked.

"She's alive," I said.

"She swallowed it!" Ben said. The Idea Man. "You didn't find it because it's in her stomach!"

"Those tracking devices are the size of a grain of rice," I reminded him. "Why would swallowing one hurt her throat?"

"I'm not saying the device hurt her throat. Her throat has nothing to do with it."

"Then why are you so worried about it being sore?"

"Here's what I'm worried about, Sullivan." He was trying very hard to stay calm, because clearly somebody had to be. "Her showing up out of the blue like this could mean a lot of things, but none of those things could be a good thing. In fact, it can only be a bad thing. A very bad thing made even badder by the fact that we don't know the reason she was sent here."

"Badder?"

"Ha-ha. The dumb jock who can't talk the Queen's English. I swear to God, the next person who corrects my grammar gets punched in the face."

I sighed. The rage was leaching out of me, leaving me a hollow, bloodless, human-shaped lump.

Ben looked at Megan for a long moment. "We have to wake her up," he decided.

Then Dumbo and Poundcake crowded into the room. "Don't tell me," Ben said to Poundcake, who of course wouldn't. "You didn't find nothing."

"Anything," Dumbo corrected him.

Ben didn't punch him in the face. But he did hold out his hand.

"Give me your canteen." He unscrewed the cap and held the container over Megan's forehead. A drop of water hung quivering on the lip for an eternity.

Before eternity ended, a croaky voice spoke up behind us. "I wouldn't do that if I were you."

Evan Walker was awake.

38

EVERYBODY FROZE. Even the drop of water, swelling at the edge of the canteen's mouth, held still. From his bed, Evan watched us with red, fever-bright eyes, waiting for someone to ask the obvious question, which Ben finally did: "Why?"

"Waking her like that could make her take a very deep breath, and that would be bad."

Ben turned to face him. The water dribbled onto the carpet. "What the hell are you talking about?"

Evan swallowed, grimacing from the effort. His face was as white as the pillowcase beneath it. "She is implanted—but not with a tracking device."

Ben's lips tightened into a hard, white line. He got it before the rest of us. He whipped on Dumbo and Poundcake. "Out. Sullivan, you and Sam, too."

"I'm not going anywhere," I told him.

"You should," Evan said. "I don't know how finely it's been calibrated."

"How finely what's been calibrated to what?" I demanded.

"The incendiary device to CO_2." His eyes cut away. The next words were hard for him. "Our breath, Cassie."

Everybody understood by that point. But there's a difference between understanding and accepting. The idea was unacceptable. After all we had experienced, there were still places our minds simply refused to go.

"Get downstairs now, all of you," Ben snarled.

Evan shook his head. "Not far enough. You should leave the building."

Ben grabbed Dumbo's arm with one hand and Poundcake's with the other and slung them toward the door. Sam had backed into the bathroom entrance, tiny fist pressed against his mouth.

"Also, somebody should open that window," Evan gasped.

I pushed Sam into the hall, trotted over to the window, and pushed hard against the frame, but it wouldn't budge, probably frozen shut. Ben pushed me out of the way and smashed out the glass with the butt of his rifle. Freezing air rushed into the room. Ben strode back to Evan's bed and considered him for a second before grabbing a handful of his hair and yanking him forward.

"You son of a bitch . . ."

"Ben!" I put my hand on his arm. "Let him go. He didn't—"

"Oh, right. I forgot. He's a good evil alien." He let go. Evan fell back; he didn't have the strength to stay up. Then Ben suggested he do something to himself that was anatomically impossible.

Evan's eyes cut over to me. "In her throat. Suspended directly above the epiglottis."

"She's a bomb," Ben said, his voice quavering with rage and disbelief. "They took a child and turned her into an IED."

"Can we remove it?" I asked.

Evan shook his head. "How?"

"That's what she's asking you, dipshit," Ben barked.

"The explosive is connected to a CO_2 detector imbedded in her throat. If the connection's lost, it detonates."

"That doesn't answer my question," I pointed out. "Can we remove it without blowing ourselves into orbit?"

"It's feasible . . ."

"Feasible. *Feasible.*" Ben was laughing this weird, hiccupping kind of laugh. I was worried that he might be falling over the proverbial edge.

"Evan," I said as softly and calmly as I could. "Can we do it without . . ." I couldn't say it, and Evan didn't make me.

"The odds of it not detonating are a lot better if you did."

"Do it without . . . what?" Ben was having a hard time following. Not his fault. He was still flailing in the unthinkable place like a poor swimmer caught in a riptide.

"Killing her first," Evan explained.

39

BEN AND I CONVENED the latest oh-we're-screwed planning meeting in the hallway. Ben ordered everybody else to go across the parking lot and hide in the diner until he gave them the all-clear—or the hotel blew up, whichever came first. Sam refused. Ben got stern. Sam teared up and pouted. Ben reminded him that he was a soldier and a good soldier follows orders. Besides, if he stayed, who was going to protect Poundcake and Dumbo?

Before he left, Dumbo said, "I'm the medic." He'd figured out what Ben was up to. "I should do it, Sarge."

Ben shook his head. "Get out of here," he said tersely.

Then we were alone. Ben's eyes would not stay still. The trapped cockroach. The cornered rat. The falling man, off the cliff and no scrawny shrub to grasp.

"Well, I guess the big riddle's been answered, huh?" he said. "What I don't get is why they didn't just waste us with a couple of Hellfire missiles. They know we're here."

"Not their style," I said.

"Style?"

"Hasn't it ever struck you how personal it's been—from the beginning? There's something about killing us that gets them off."

Ben looked at me with sick wonder. "Yeah. Well. I can see why you'd want to date one of them." Not the thing to say. He realized it immediately and quickly backed off. "Who're we kidding, Cassie? There's nothing really to decide, except who's going to do it. Maybe we should flip a coin."

"Maybe it should be Dumbo. Didn't you tell me he trained in field surgery at the camp?"

He frowned. "Surgery? You're kidding, right?"

"Well, how else are we . . . ?" Then I understood. Couldn't accept, but understood. I was wrong about Ben. He had dropped farther than me into that unthinkable place. He was five thousand fathoms down.

He read the look on my face and dropped his chin toward his chest. His face was flushed. Not embarrassed so much as angry, intensely angry, the anger that's past all words.

"No, Ben. We can't do that."

He lifted his head. His eyes shone. His hands shook. "I can."

"No, you can't." Ben Parish was drowning. He was so far under, I wasn't sure I could reach him, wasn't sure I had the strength to pull him back to the surface.

"I didn't ask for this," he said. "I didn't ask for any of this!"

"Neither did she, Ben."

He leaned close and I saw a different kind of fever burning in his eyes. "I'm not worried about her. An hour ago, she didn't exist. Understand? She was nothing, literally nothing. I had you, and I had your little brother, and I had Poundcake and Dumbo. She was theirs. She belongs to *them.* I didn't take her. I didn't trick her into getting on a bus and tell her she was perfectly safe and then stuff a bomb down her throat. This isn't my fault. It isn't my responsibility. My job is to keep my ass and your ass alive for as long as possible, and if that means somebody else who is nothing to me dies, then I guess that's what it means."

I wasn't holding up well. He was too deep, there was too much pressure, I couldn't breathe.

"That's it," he said bitterly. "Cry, Cassie. Cry for her. Cry for all the children. They can't hear you and they can't see you and they can't feel how really bad you feel, but cry for them. A tear for each of them, fill up the fucking ocean, cry.

"You know I'm right. You know I don't have a choice. And you know Ringer was right. It's about the risk. It's always been about the risk. And if one little girl has to die so six people can live, then that's the price. That's the price."

He pushed past me and limped down the hall to the broken door, and I couldn't move, I couldn't speak. I didn't lift a finger or frame an argument to stop him. I'd reached the end of words, and gestures seemed pointless.

Stop him, Evan. Please, stop him, because I can't.

In the safe room underground, their faces lifted up to me, and my silent prayer, my hopeless promise: *Climb onto my shoulders, climb onto my shoulders, climb onto my shoulders.*

He wouldn't shoot her. Because of the risk. He'd smother her. Place a pillow over her face and press until he didn't need to press anymore. He wouldn't leave her body there: the risk. He would carry it outside, but he wouldn't bury it or burn it: the risk. He would take it far into the woods and toss it on the frozen ground like so much trash for the buzzards and crows and insects. The risk.

I sank down the wall and drew my knees to my chest, ducked my head, and covered it up with my arms. I stopped my ears. I closed my eyes. And there was Vosch's finger slamming down on the button, Ben's hands holding the pillow, my finger on the trigger. Sam, Megan. The Crucifix Soldier. And Ringer's voice, speaking out of the silent dark: *Sometimes you're in the wrong place at the wrong time and what happens is nobody's fault.*

And when Ben came out, all torn up and empty, I would get up and I would go to him and I would comfort him. I would take the hand that murdered a child and we would grieve for ourselves and the choices we made that weren't choices at all.

Ben came out. He sat against the wall ten doors down. After a minute, I got up and went to him. He didn't look up. He rested his forearms on his upraised knees and bowed his head. I sat next to him.

"You're wrong," I said. He twirled his hand: *Whatever.* "She did belong to us. They all belong to us."

His head fell back against the wall. "Hear them? Those mother-effing rats."

"Ben, I think you need to go. Now. Don't wait till morning.

Take Dumbo and Poundcake and get to the caverns as fast as you can." Maybe Ringer could help him. He listened to her, always seemed a little intimidated by her, even awed.

He laughed from a spot deep in his gut. "I'm kind of busted up right now. Broke. I'm broke, Sullivan." He looked at me. "And Walker is in no shape to do it."

"No shape to do what?"

"Cut the damn thing out. You're the only one here who has half a chance."

"You didn't . . . ?"

"I couldn't."

He laughed again. His head broke the surface and he took a deep, life-giving breath.

"I couldn't."

40

THE ROOM WHERE she lay was colder than a walk-in freezer, and Evan was sitting up now, watching me as I walked in. A pillow on the floor where Ben had dropped it, and me picking it up and sitting at the foot of Evan's bed. Our breaths congealing and our hearts beating and the silence thickening between us.

Until I said, "Why?"

And he said, "To blow apart what remains. To break the final, unbreakable bond."

I hugged the pillow to my chest and rocked slowly back and forth. *Cold. So cold.*

"No one can be trusted," I said. "Not even a child." The cold bored down to my bones and curled inside the marrow. "What are you, Evan Walker? *What are you?*"

He wouldn't look at me. "I told you."

I nodded. "Yes, you did. Mr. Great White Shark. I'm not, though. Not yet. We're not going to kill her, Evan. I'm going to pull it out, and you're going to help me."

He didn't argue. He knew better.

Ben helped me gather the supplies before he left to join the others in the diner across the parking lot. Washcloth. Towels. A can of air freshener. Dumbo's field kit. We said good-bye at the stairway door. I told him to be careful, there were some slippery rat guts on the way down.

"I lost it back there," he said, lowering his eyes and scrubbing his foot across the carpet like an embarrassed little boy caught in a lie. "That wasn't cool."

"Your secret is safe with me."

He smiled. "Sullivan . . . Cassie . . . in case you don't . . . I wanted to tell you . . ."

I waited. I didn't push him.

"They made a major mistake," he blurted out, "the dumb bastards, when they didn't start by killing you first."

"Benjamin Thomas Parish, that was the sweetest and most bizarre compliment anyone's ever given me."

I kissed him on the cheek. He kissed me on the mouth.

"You know," I whispered, "a year ago, I would have sold my soul for that."

He shook his head. "Not worth it." And, for one–ten thousandth of a second, all of it fell away, the despair and grief and anger and pain and hunger, and the old Ben Parish rose from the dead. The eyes that impaled. The smile that slayed. In another moment, he would fade, slide back into the new Ben, the one called Zombie, and I understood something I hadn't before: He *was* dead, the object of my schoolgirl desires, just as the schoolgirl who desired him was dead.

"Get out of here," I told him. "And if you let anything happen to my little brother, I'll hunt you down like a dog."

"I may be dumb, but I'm not that dumb."

He disappeared into the absolute dark of the stairwell.

I went back to the room. I couldn't do this. I had to do this. Evan scooted back in the bed until his butt touched the headboard. I slid my arms beneath Megan and slowly lifted her, turned, and then lowered her carefully onto Evan, leaning her head back into his lap. I picked up the spray can of air freshener (*A Delicate Blend of Essences!*) and saturated the washcloth. My hands were shaking. No way could I do this. No way I couldn't.

"A five-pronged hook," Evan said quietly. "Embedded beneath the right tonsil. Don't try to pull it out. Get a good grip on the wire, make the cut as close to the hook as you can, then pull the hook out—slowly. If the wire comes loose from the capsule . . ."

I nodded impatiently. "*Kaboom.* I know. You already told me that."

I opened the med kit and took out a pair of tweezers and surgical scissors. Small, but they seemed huge. I clicked on the penlight and stuck the butt end between my teeth.

I handed Evan the washcloth reeking of pine. He pressed the cloth over Megan's nose and mouth. Her body jerked, her eyelids fluttered open, her eyes rolled to the back of her head. Her hands, folded primly in her lap, twitched, became still. Evan dropped the cloth onto her chest.

"If she wakes up while I'm in there . . ." I said around the flashlight, sounding like a very bad ventriloquist: *Eh chee wecks uh . . .*

Evan nodded. "A hundred ways it can go wrong, Cassie."

He tilted her head back and forced her mouth open. I stared down a glistening red tunnel the width of a razor and a mile deep. Tweezers in my left hand. Scissors in my right. Both hands the size of footballs.

"Can you open it any wider?" I asked.

"If I open it any wider, I'll dislocate her jaw."

Well, in the grand scheme of things, a dislocated jaw was better than being able to pick up our pieces with this pair of tweezers. But *whatever.*

"This one?" Touching the tonsil gently with the end of the tweezers.

"I can't see."

"When you said right tonsil, you meant her right, not my right, right?"

"Her right. Your left."

"Okay," I breathed. "Just wanted to make sure."

I couldn't see what I was doing. I had the tweezers down her throat but not the scissors, and I didn't know how I was going to stuff both in the tiny mouth of this little girl.

"Hook the wire with the end of the tweezers," Evan suggested. "Then very slowly lift it up so you can see what you're doing. Don't yank. If the wire disconnects from the capsule—"

"Dear Jesus Christ, Walker, you don't have to warn me every two minutes what happens if the freaking wire disconnects from the freaking capsule!" I felt the tip of the tweezers catch on something. "Okay, I think I've got it."

"It's very thin. Black. Shiny. Your light should reflect—"

"Please be quiet." Or, in penlight speak: *Pweez be qwiwet.*

My whole body was shaking but my hands, miraculously, had become rock steady. I forced my right hand into her mouth by pushing against the inside of her cheek, maneuvering the tips of the scissors into position. Was that it? Did I actually have it? The wire, if that was the wire shining in my light, was as thin as a strand of human hair.

"Slowly, Cassie."

"Shut. Up."

"If she swallows it—"

"I am going to kill you, Evan. Seriously." I had the wire now, pinched between the tines of the tweezers. I could see the tiny hook embedded in her enflamed flesh as I tugged. *Slow, slow, slow. Make sure you cut on the right end of the wire. The claw end.*

"You're too close," he warned me. "Stop talking and don't breathe directly into her mouth . . ."

Right. So instead, I think I'm going to punch you directly in yours.

A hundred ways it could go wrong, he said. But there's wrong ways, really wrong ways, and really *really* wrong ways. When Megan's eyes flipped open and her body bucked beneath mine, we went down a really *really* one.

"She's awake!" I yelled unnecessarily.

"Don't let go of the wire!" he shouted back, necessarily.

Her teeth clamped down hard on my hand. Her head whipped from side to side. My fingers were trapped inside her mouth. I tried to hold the tweezers still, but one hard tug and the capsule would pull free . . .

"Evan, *do* something!"

He fumbled for the rag soaked in air freshener.

I shouted, "No, hold her head still, moron! Don't let her—"

“Let go of the wire,” he gasped.

“*What?* You just said *don’t* let go of the . . .”

He pinched her nose shut. Let go? Don’t let go? If I let go, the wire might twist around the tweezers and pull free. If I don’t let go, all the turning and twisting and whipping around might yank it free. Megan’s eyes rolled in her head. Pain and terror and confusion, the constant mix the Others never failed to deliver. Her mouth flew open and I jammed the scissors down her throat.

“I hate you right now,” I breathed at him. “I hate you more than I hate anyone else in the world.” I felt like he needed to know that before I snapped the scissors closed. In case we were vaporized.

“Do you have it?” he asked.

“I have no freaking clue if I have it!”

“Do it.” Then he smiled. Smiled! “Cut the wire, Mayfly,” he said.

I cut the wire.

41

“IT’S A TEST,” Evan said.

The green liquid-gelcap-looking thing lay on the desk, safely—we hoped—sealed inside a clear plastic baggie, the kind your mom used in the long-gone good old days to keep your sandwich and chips fresh for lunch period.

“What, like human IEDs are still in the R-and-D phase?” Ben asked. He was leaning on the sill of the busted-out window, shivering, but someone had to watch the parking lot, and he wasn’t letting anyone else take the risk. At least he had changed out of the blood-soaked, hideous (it was hideous before it was blood-soaked) yellow hoodie and into a black sweatshirt that almost brought him back to his pre-Arrival, buffed-out period.

From the bed, Sam giggled hesitantly, unsure if his beloved Zombie leader was making a joke. I'm no shrink, but I guessed Sams had undergone some transference due to seriously unresolved daddy issues.

"Not the bomb," Evan answered. "Us."

"Great," Ben growled. "First test I've passed in three years."

"Cut it out, Parish," I said. Who passed the law that said jocks had to act stupid to be cool? "I know for a fact you were a National Merit Finalist last year."

"Really?" Dumbo's ears perked up. Okay, I shouldn't make remarks about his ears, but he did appear to be dumbfounded.

"Yes, really," Ben said with a patented Parish smile. "But it was a very weak year. Aliens invaded." He looked at Evan. His smile died, which his smile usually did when he looked at Evan. "What are they testing us *for*?"

"Knowledge."

"Yeah, that would be the purpose of a test. You know what would be really helpful right now? If you'd knock off the enigmatic alien routine and get the fuck real. Because every second that goes by and that thing doesn't go off"—nodding to the baggie—"is a second that doubles our risk. Sooner or later, and I'm leaning toward *sooner,* they're coming back and blowing our asses to Dubuque."

"Dubuque?" Dumbo squeaked. He didn't get the reference and that frightened him. What was wrong in Dubuque?

"Just a town, Dumbo," Ben said. "A random town."

Evan was nodding. I glanced over at Poundcake filling the

doorway, his mouth hanging open slightly as his big head ping-ponged to follow the conversation.

"They will come back," Evan said. "Unless we fail the test so they don't have to."

"Fail it? We passed, didn't we?" Ben turned to me. "I feel as if we passed. How about you?"

"Failing means we took her in, all fat, dumb, and happy," I explained, "and then got our asses blown back to Dubuque."

"Dubuque," Dumbo echoed, mystified.

"The absence of detonation can mean only one of three things," Evan said. "One, the device malfunctioned. Two, the device was incorrectly calibrated. Or three . . ."

Ben held up his hand. "Or three, someone in the hotel knows about the bomb-children and was able to remove it, put it in a plastic baggie, and conduct a seminar on how to instill panic and paranoia among the dopey humans. The test is to see if we have a Silencer among us."

"We do!" Sam yelled. He jabbed his finger at Evan. "*You're* a Silencer!"

"Something you absolutely can't know for sure if you vaporize the joint with a couple of well-placed Hellfire missiles," Ben finished.

"Which raises the question," Evan said quietly. "Why would they suspect such a thing?"

A silence settled over the room. Ben drummed his fingers on his forearm. Poundcake's mouth snapped closed. Dumbo tugged on an earlobe. I rocked back and forth in the chair, plucking at Bear's paw. I didn't know how I came into possession of Bear. Maybe I grabbed him while Poundcake was moving Megan into the adjacent room. I remembered his getting knocked to the floor but didn't remember picking him up.

"Well, it's obvious," Ben said. "They must have a way of knowing you're here. Right? Otherwise, you run the risk of taking out your own players."

"If they knew I was here, there would be no need for a test. They *suspect* I'm here."

Then I got it. And getting it did not bring me any comfort.

"Ringer."

Ben's head whipped toward me. The slightest breath of wind would have toppled him from his perch.

"She's been captured," I said. "Or Teacup. Or both." I turned to Evan, because the look on Ben's face was too much to bear.

"That makes the most sense," Evan agreed.

"Bullshit! Ringer would never give us up," Ben barked at him.

"Not willingly," Evan said.

"Wonderland," I breathed. "They've downloaded her memories . . ."

Ben came off the sill then, lost his balance, staggered forward, knocked against the edge of Sammy's bed. He was shaking, and not from the cold. "Oh no. No, no, no. Ringer has *not* been captured. She's *safe* and Teacup's safe and we are *not* going there . . ."

"No," Evan said. "We're already there."

I slid out of the chair and went to Ben. One of those moments when you know you have to do something but you have no idea what. "Ben, he's right. The reason we're alive right now is the same reason they sent Megan."

"What is it with you?" Ben demanded. "You buy into everything he says like he's Moses come down from the mountaintop. If they think he's here, for whatever reason, then they know he's a *traitor* and would *still* send us packing to Dubuque."

Everybody looked at Dumbo, waiting for it.

"They don't want to kill me," Evan said finally. He had a sad, sick look on his face.

"That's right, I forgot," Ben said. "That would be me." He pulled away from me and shuffled back to the window, leaned his hands on the sill and studied the night sky. "Stay here, we're done. Bug out, we're done. We're like five-year-olds playing chess with Bobby Fischer." He swung back around to Evan. "You could have been spotted by a patrol, followed here." He pointed at the baggie. "That doesn't mean they have Ringer or Cup. All it means is we're out of time. Can't hide, can't run, so the question circles back to same question it's always been: not *if* we're gonna die, but *how*. How are we going to die? Dumbo, how do you want to die?"

Dumbo stiffened. His shoulders squared, his chin came up. "Standing up, sir."

Ben looked at Poundcake. "Cake, do you want to die standing up?"

Poundcake had come to attention, too. He nodded smartly.

Ben didn't have to ask Sam. My little brother simply stood up and very slowly and deliberately gave his commanding officer a salute.

42

OH, BROTHER. *Guys.*

I tossed Bear on the desk. "I've been here before," I told the Macho Brigade. "Run equals die. Stay equals die. So before we go all O.K. Corral on this, let's consider the third option: *We* blow it up."

That suggestion sucked all the air from the room. Evan got it first, nodding slowly, but clearly not happy with the idea. Lots of variables. A thousand ways it can go wrong, only one way right.

Ben cut right to the gooey guts of the problem: "How? Who has the duty of breathing on it and getting vaporized?"

"I'll do it, Sarge," Dumbo said. His ears had turned red, like he was embarrassed by his own courage. He smiled shyly. He'd finally gotten it: "I've always wanted to see Dubuque."

"Human breath isn't the only source of CO_2," I pointed out to the National Merit Finalist.

"Coke!" Dumbo fairly shouted.

"Good luck finding one of those," Ben said. It was true. Along with anything alcoholic, soft drinks were one of the first casualties of the invasion.

"A can or a bottle, yes," Evan said. "Cassie, didn't you tell me there was a diner next door?"

"The CO_2 canisters for the fountain drinks," I started.

"Are probably still there," he finished.

"Attach the bomb to the canister . . ."

"Rig the canister to dispense the CO_2 . . ."

"A slow leak . . ."

"In a confined space . . ."

"The elevator!" we said in unison.

"Wow," Ben breathed. "Brilliant. But I'm a little unclear on how this solves the problem."

"They'll think we're dead, Zombie," Sam said. The five-year-old understood, but he lacked Ben's burden of experience in outwitting Vosch and company.

"Then they check it out, they find no bodies, they know," Ben said.

"But it will buy us time," Evan pointed out. "And my guess is by the time they realize the truth, it'll be too late."

"Because obviously we're just too darn clever for them?" Ben asked.

Evan smiled grimly. "Because we're going to the last place they'd think to look."

43

THERE WAS NO TIME for more debate; we had to pull the trigger on Operation Early Checkout before the 5th Wave pulled the trigger on us. Ben and Poundcake left to fetch a CO_2 canister from the diner. Dumbo took hall patrol. I told Sam he had to watch Megan, her being a pal from the old days on the school bus. He asked for the gun back. I reminded him that having the gun didn't help so much the last time: He'd emptied the magazine without even nicking the target. I tried to give him Bear. He rolled his eyes. *Bear was* so *six months ago.*

Then Evan and I were alone. Just him, me, and a little green bomb made three.

"Spill it," I ordered him.

"Spill what?" Eyes all big and innocent as Bear's.

"Your guts, Walker. You're holding back."

"Why do you—?"

"Because that's your style. Your modus operandi. Like an iceberg, three-quarters under the surface, but there's no way I'm letting you turn this hotel into the *Titanic.*"

He sighed, avoiding my glare. "Pen and paper?"

"What? Time for a tender love poem?" That was his style, too: Every time I edged too close to something, he deflected by telling me how much he loved me or how I saved him or some other swoony, pseudo-profound observation about the nature of my magnificence. But I grabbed the pad and pen from the desk and handed them over because, at the end of the day, who minds getting a tender love poem?

Instead he drew a map.

"Single-story, white—or used to be white—wood frame, I don't remember the address, but it's right on Highway 68. Next to a service station. Has one of those old metal signs hanging out front, Havoline Oil or something like that."

He tore off the sheet and pressed it into my hand.

"And why is this the last place they'd look for us?" I was falling for the deflecting technique again, not that Havoline Oil had anything cloyingly poetical about it. "And why are you drawing me a map when you're coming with us?"

"In case something happens."

"To you. What if something happens to both of us?"

"You're right. I'll make five more."

He started on the next one. I watched for two seconds, then grabbed the pad out of his hand and threw it at his head.

"You son of a bitch. I know what you're doing."

"I was drawing a map, Cassie."

"Rigging a detonator from a soda fountain *Mission: Impossible* style, really? While we all run like hell for the Havoline sign with you in the lead on your broken ankle and stabbed leg, sporting a hundred-and-six-degree temperature . . ."

"If I had a hundred-and-six-degree temperature, I'd be dead," he pointed out.

"No, and you want to know why? *Because dead people have no temperature!*"

He was nodding thoughtfully. "God, I've missed you."

"There! There it is, right there! Just like the Walker homestead, just like Camp Ashpit, just like Vosch's death camp. Whenever I've got you cornered . . ."

"You had me cornered the minute I laid—"

"*Stop it.*"

He stopped. I sat on the bed next to him. Maybe I was going about this all wrong. You catch more flies with honey, my grandmother always said. The problem was that womanly wiles weren't something I carried in my wheelhouse. I took his hand. I looked deeply into his eyes. I considered unbuttoning my shirt a bit, but decided he might see through that little ploy. Not that my ploys were *that* little.

"I'm not letting you pull another Camp Haven on me," I said, adding what I hoped to be an alluring purr to the timbre. "That isn't going to happen. You're coming with us. Poundcake and Dumbo can carry you."

He reached up with his other hand and touched my cheek. I knew that touch. I'd missed it. "I know," he said. The expression in his chocolatey (*gah*) eyes was infinitely sad. I knew that look, too. I'd seen it before, in the woods when he confessed who he really was. "But you don't know everything. You don't know about Grace."

"Grace," I echoed, pushing his hand from my cheek, forgetting all about the honey. I liked his touch too much, I decided. I needed to work on not liking it so much. And also work on not liking the way he looked at me as if I were the last person on Earth, which I actually thought I was before he found me. That's a terrible thing, an awful burden to put on someone. You make your whole existence dependent on another human being and you're asking for a world of trouble. Think of every tragic love story ever written. And I didn't want to play Juliet to anybody's Romeo, not if I could help it. Even if the only candidate available was willing to die for me and sitting right beside me holding my hand and looking deeply into my eyes with the *not-so-gah-now* eyes the color of melted chocolate. Plus being practically naked under those covers and possessing the body of a Hollister dude . . . but I'm not getting into all that.

"Grace again. You kept mentioning grace after I shot you," I told him.

"You don't know Grace."

Well, that stung. I never knew he was so religious—or judgmental. The two usually go hand in hand, still . . .

"Cassie, I have to tell you something."

"You're a Baptist?"

"That day on the highway after I—let you get away, I was very afraid. I didn't understand what happened, why I couldn't . . . do what I came to do. Do what I was born to do. It didn't make sense to me. And in a lot of ways, it still doesn't make sense. You think you know yourself. You think you know the person you see in the mirror. I found you, but in finding you, I lost myself. Nothing was clear anymore. Nothing was simple."

I nodded. "I remember that. I remember simple."

"In the beginning, after I brought you back, I really didn't know if you were going to make it. And I would sit there with you and I'd think, *Maybe she shouldn't.*"

"Gee, Evan. That's so romantic."

"I knew what was coming," he said, and *that* sure was something clear and simple. He grabbed both my hands and pulled me close, and I fell a thousand miles into those damn eyes, which is why the honey technique doesn't fit me: I'm more the fly when I'm around him. "I know what's coming, Cassie, and until now I thought the dead were the lucky ones. But I see it now. I see it."

"What? What do you see, Evan?" My voice quivering. He was scaring me. Maybe it was the fever talking, but Evan was acting very un-Evanish.

"The way out. The way to finish it. The problem is Grace. Grace is too much for you—for any of you. Grace is the doorway and I'm the only one who can walk through it. I can give you that. And time. Those two things, Grace and time, and then *you can finish it.*"

44

THEN DUMBO, with perfect timing, popped his head into the room. "They're back, Sullivan. Zombie said—" He stopped. Obviously he'd interrupted an intimate moment. Thank God I hadn't unbuttoned my shirt. I pulled my hands from Evan's and stood up.

"Did they find a canister?"

Dumbo nodded. "They're putting it in the elevator now." He looked at Evan. "Zombie said anytime you're ready."

Evan nodded slowly. "Okay." But he didn't move. I didn't move. Dumbo stood there for a few seconds.

"Okay," he said. Evan didn't say anything. I didn't say anything.

Then Dumbo said, "See you guys later—in Dubuque! Heh-heh." He backed out of the room.

I whirled on Evan. "All right. Remember what Ben said about the enigmatic alien thing?"

Then Evan Walker did something I'd never seen him do—or heard him say, to be accurate.

"Shit," he said.

Dumbo was back in the doorway, slack-jawed, red-eared, and in the grasp of a tall girl with a cascade of honey-blond hair and striking Norwegian-model-type features, piercing blue eyes, full, pouty, collagen-packed lips, and the willowy figure of a runway fashion princess.

"Hello, Evan," *Cosmo* Girl said. And of course her voice was deep and slightly scratchy like every seductive villainess ever conceived by Hollywood.

"Hello, Grace," Evan said.

45

GRACE: A PERSON, not a prayer or anything close to being connected to God. And armed to the teeth: She had Dumbo's M16 in addition to the hefty sniper rifle hanging from her back. She shoved the kid into the room and then blew out my eyesight with her megawatt smile.

"And you must be Cassiopeia, queen of the night sky. I'm surprised, Evan. She's nothing like I pictured. Kind of a ginger. Didn't know that was your type."

I looked at Evan. "Who the hell is this person?"

"Grace is like me," Evan said.

"We go way back. Ten centuries, give or take. Speaking of taking . . ." Grace motioned for my rifle. I tossed it at her feet. "Sidearm, too. And that knife strapped to your ankle, under the fatigues."

"Let them go, Grace," Evan said. "We don't need them."

Grace ignored him. She gave my rifle a little kick and told me to toss it out the window with the Luger and the knife. Evan nodded at me as if to say, *Better do it.* So I did. My head was spinning. I couldn't grab hold of a single coherent thought. Grace was a Silencer like Evan—that one I could hug tight. But how did she know my name and why was she here and how did Evan know she was coming and what did he mean by *Grace is the doorway*? The doorway to *what*?

"I knew she was human." Grace was back on Evan's favorite subject. "But I never imagined how *completely* human she was."

Evan knew it was coming, but he tried to stop it anyway. "Cassie . . ."

"Fuck you and the horse you rode in on, you fucking alien motherfucker."

"Colorful. Imaginative. Nice." Grace motioned with Dumbo's rifle for me to sit.

Again, Evan shot me a look: *Do it, Cassie.* So I sat on the bed next to his, beside Dumbo, who was breathing through his mouth like an asthmatic. Grace remained in the doorway so she could keep an eye on the hall. Maybe she didn't know about Sam and Megan in the next room or Ben and Poundcake waiting for Evan in the elevator downstairs. I understood Evan's strategy then: *Stall. Buy time.* When Ben and Poundcake came up to see what the hell was going on, that would be our chance. I remembered

Evan taking out an entire squad of 5th Wavers, outgunned and outnumbered, in pitch darkness, and thought, *No, when they show up, that will be* her *chance.*

I studied her, the way she leaned against the jamb with one ankle thrown casually over the other, golden tresses flowing over one shoulder, her head turned slightly to display for our admiration her stunning Nordic profile, and I thought, *Sure, makes sense. If you can download yourself into any sort of human body, why not pick an impeccable one? Evan, too.* In that sense, he was nothing but a big phony. And that's weird to think about. Deep down, the dude who gave me the Jell-O knees was an effigy, a mask over a faceless face that probably ten thousand years ago looked like a squid or something.

"Well, they *did* tell us there was risk, living so long as humans among humans," Grace said. "Tell me something, Cassiopeia: Don't you think he's perfectly *perfect* in bed?"

"Why don't you tell me," I shot back. "You extraterrestrial slut."

"Feisty," Grace said to Evan with a smile. "Like her namesake."

"They have nothing to do with this," Evan said. "Let them go, Grace."

"Evan, I'm not even sure I understand what *this* is." She left her post and floated—there's no other word for it—to his bedside. "And nobody is going anywhere until I do." She leaned over and took his face in her hands and kissed him long and lingering on the lips. He fought her—I could see that—but she immobilized him with her otherworldly überwiles, which she carried in spades in *her* wheelhouse. "Did you tell her, Evan?" she murmured against his cheek, though she made sure I could hear. "Does she know how all of this ends?"

"Like this," I said, and launched myself at her, leading, as I usually did, with my head, aiming the hard crown part of it at the soft temple part of hers. The impact knocked her sideways into the closet doors. I ended up sprawled across Evan's lap. *Perfectly perfect,* I thought, a little incoherently.

I pushed myself up and Evan wrapped his arms around my waist and yanked me back down. "*No, Cassie.*"

But he was weak and I was strong and I ripped free easily and jumped from the bed onto her back. That was a big mistake: She grabbed my arm and hurled me across the room. I smashed against the wall beside the window and plopped straight down on my ass, sending a hot jolt of pain up my back. From the hallway, I heard a door fly open, and I shouted, "Get out, Sam! Get Zombie! Get—"

She was gone before I got the second *get* out. The last time I saw someone move that fast was at Camp Ashpit, when the phony soldiers from Wright-Patterson spotted me hiding in the woods. Like, cartoon fast, which might be humorous if not for the reason she bolted.

Oh no you don't, bitch. Not my little brother.

I raced past Dumbo, past Evan, who had thrown off the covers and was struggling to swing his badly wounded self out of bed, into the hall, which was empty, not a good thing, not good at all, then two steps to Sam's room, and when my fingers touched the handle, a wrecking ball smashed into the back of my head and my nose smacked into the wood. Something went *crunch,* and it wasn't the wood. I stepped backward, blood pouring down my face. I could taste my blood and somehow it was the taste that kept me upright—I didn't know till then that rage had a taste and it tasted like your own blood.

Cold fingers locked around my neck and I watched my feet leave the ground through a shower of red rain. Then I was soaring down the length of the hallway, coming down hard on my shoulder, and rolling to a stop a foot from the window at the far end.

Grace: "*Stay there.*"

She was standing by Sammy's door, a lithe shadow down a dimly lit tunnel, shimmering on the other side of the tears that welled uncontrollably and spilled down my cheeks to mix with blood.

"Leave. My. Brother. Alone."

"That adorable little boy? He's your brother? I'm sorry, Cassiopeia, I didn't know." Shaking her head in mock sadness. Like they mocked every decent human thing.

"He's already dead."

46

THREE THINGS HAPPENED then, all at the same time. Four, if you counted my heart blowing apart.

I ran—not *away* but *toward*. I was going to rip her cover-model face off. I was going to tear her pseudo-human heart from between her perfectly shaped human boobs. I was going to open her up with my fingernails.

That was the first thing.

The second was the stairway door flying open and Poundcake entering the hall in anything but Eeyore fashion, shoving me back with one arm as the other brought his rifle to bear on Grace. Not an easy shot by any means, but Poundcake was the squad's best marksman after Ringer, according to Ben.

The third thing was a shirtless, boxer-shorts-wearing Evan Walker, crawling out of the room behind Grace. Expert marksman or not, if Poundcake missed . . . or if Grace dived out of the way at the last second . . .

So I did the diving, wrapping my arms around the kid's ankles. He toppled forward, his rifle discharged, and then I heard the stairway door again and Ben shouting, "*Freeze!*" just like they used to in the movies, but nobody froze, not me, not Poundcake, and not Evan—and certainly not Grace, who was gone. She was there and then she wasn't. Ben hopped over me and Poundcake and limped down the hall to the room opposite Sam's.

Sam.

I jumped up and raced down the hall. Ben was motioning to Poundcake, saying, "She's in there."

I yanked on the handle. Locked. *Thank you, God!* I pounded on the door. "Sam! Sam, open up! It's me!"

And from the other side, a voice no louder than a mouse's squeak: "It's a trick! You're tricking me!"

I lost it. Pressed my bloody cheek against the door and had a good, solid, and very satisfying mini-breakdown. I'd let my guard down. I'd forgotten how cruel the Others could be. Not enough to punch a hole through my heart with a bullet. No, first you have to pummel it and stomp on it and crush it in your hands until the tissue oozes from between your fingers like Play-Doh.

"Okay, okay, okay," I whimpered. "Stay in there, okay? No matter what, Sam. Don't come out till I come back."

Poundcake was standing to one side of the door across the hall. Ben was helping Evan to his feet—or trying to. Every time he loosened his grip, Evan's knees buckled. Ben finally decided to lean him against the wall, where Evan rocked, gasping for air, his skin the color of the ashes at the camp where my father died.

Evan looked over at me and he hardly had the breath for the words: "Get out of this hallway. *Now.*"

The drywall in front of Poundcake blew apart in a rain of fine white dust and chunks of moldy wallpaper. He staggered backward. His rifle fell from his limp fingers. He knocked into Ben, who grabbed him by the shoulder and threw him into the room with Dumbo. Ben reached for me next, but I slapped his hand away and told him to grab Evan before picking up Poundcake's rifle and opening up on Grace's door. The sound was deafening in the narrow hall. I emptied the magazine before Ben got hold of me and pulled me back.

"Don't be an idiot!" he shouted. He slapped a full magazine into my hand and told me to watch the door but *stay down.*

The scene played out like a TV show going on in another room: just voices. I was flat on my stomach, resting my upper body on my elbows, the rifle trained on the door directly across from me. *Come on, ice maiden. I have a little something for you.* Running my tongue over my bloody lips, hating the taste, loving the taste. *Come on, you creepy Swede.*

Ben: Dumbo, how is it? Dumbo!

Dumbo: It's bad, Sarge.

Ben: How bad?

Dumbo: Pretty bad . . .

Ben: Oh, Christ. I can freaking see that it's bad, Dumbo!

Evan: Ben—listen to me—you have to listen to me—we have to get out of here. Now.

Ben: Why? We got her contained—

Evan: Not for long.

Ben: Sullivan can handle her. Who the hell is she, anyway?

Evan: (*unintelligible*)

Ben: Well, sure. The more the merrier. Guess we're well into Plan B. I've got you, Walker. Dumbo, you have Poundcake. Sullivan will take the kids.

Ben eased down beside me, placing his hand on the small of my back. He nodded toward the door.

"We can't bug out until the threat's neutralized," he whispered. "Hey, what happened to your nose?"

I shrugged. *Swipe, swipe* went the tongue. "How?" I sounded like I had a bad head cold.

"Pretty simple. Somebody takes the door, one low, one high, one to the right, one to the left. Worst part the first two and a half seconds."

"What's the best part?"

"The last two and a half seconds. Ready?"

"Cassie, wait." Evan, on his knees behind us like a pilgrim at the altar. "Ben doesn't know what he's dealing with—but you do. Tell him. Tell him what she's capa—"

"Shut up, lover boy," Ben growled. He tugged on my shirt. "Let's roll."

"She's not even in there anymore—I guarantee you," Evan said, raising his voice.

"What? She jumped two stories?" Ben laughed. "That's great. I'll pop her broken-legged ass when I get down there."

"She probably has jumped—but she didn't break anything. Grace is like me." Evan was talking to both of us but looking desperately at me. "Like me, Cassie."

"But you're human—I mean, your body is," Ben said. "And no human body could—"

"*Her* body could. Not mine anymore. Mine has . . . crashed."

"You getting all this?" Ben asked me. "Because to me, this sounds like more of Mr. E.T.'s bullshit."

"What do you suggest we do, Evan?" I asked. Despite the mighty tasty blood in my mouth, the rage was draining out of me, replaced by the very uncomfortable and, by now, very familiar feeling of being in five thousand fathoms over my head.

"Get out. Now. It isn't you she wants."

"Sacrificial goat," Ben said with a nasty smile. "I like it."

"She'll just let us walk away," I said, shaking my head. My sense of drowning was growing more acute. Could Ben be right? What was I thinking, trusting Evan Walker with my life and the life of my brother? Something was off here. Something was wrong. "Just like that."

"I don't know," Evan answered, which was a point in his favor. He could have said, *Sure, she's an okay person once you get past her itsy-bitsy sadism problem.* "But I do know what will happen if you stay."

"Good enough for me," Ben announced. He backed into the room. "Change of plans, boys. I'll handle Poundcake. Dumbo, you take Megan. Sullivan's got her brother. Drop your trunk and grab your junk, we're goin' to a party!"

"Cassie." Evan scooted beside me. He turned my face toward his, ran his thumb over my bloody cheek. "It's the only way."

"I'm not leaving you, Evan. And I'm not letting you leave me. Not again."

"And Sam? You made a promise to him, too. You can't keep both. Grace is my problem. She . . . she belongs to me. Not the way that Sam belongs to you; I don't mean that . . ."

"Really? I'm surprised, Evan. You're usually so clear about everything."

I sat up, took a deep breath, and slapped his beautiful face. I could have shot him but decided to let him off easy.

And that's when we heard it, like the slap was the signal it had been waiting for: the sound of an attack helicopter, coming in fast.

47

THE SPOTLIGHT HIT NEXT: Brilliant bright light flooded the hall, poured into the room, flung hard-edged shadows against the walls and floor. Ben raced over and yanked me to my feet; I grabbed Evan's arm and tugged. He pulled free, shaking his head.

"Just leave a gun with me."

"You got it, pal," Ben said, handing over his sidearm. "Sullivan, get your brother."

"What's the matter with you guys?" I said. I couldn't believe it. "We can't run now."

"What's *your* plan?" Ben shouted. He had to shout. The roar of the chopper smashed down anything softer—by the angle of light and the sound, directly over the hotel now.

Evan wrapped his fingers around the splintered doorjamb and heaved himself to his feet—or to his foot; he couldn't put any weight on the other one. I shouted in his ear, "Just tell me one thing, and for once in your ten-thousand-year-old life be honest. You never intended to rig a bomb and escape with us. You knew Grace was coming and you were planning to blow both of—"

At that moment, Sammy banged out of his room, one hand locked around Megan's wrist. At some point, the little girl had acquired Bear. Sams probably gave it to her—he was always passing that bear to someone in need. "Cassie!" He barreled into me, hitting me hard in the gut with his head. I hauled him onto my hip, swayed, *Jesus, he's getting heavy,* and grabbed Megan's hand.

A maelstrom of icy wind roared through the broken window, and I heard Dumbo scream, "They're landing on the roof!"

I heard him because he was practically climbing into my back pocket trying to get into the hall. Ben was right behind him, Poundcake leaning against his side, the big kid's arm draped around his shoulder.

"Sullivan!" Ben shouted. "Move it!"

Evan locked his fingers around my elbow. "*Wait.*" He looked up at the ceiling. His lips moved soundlessly, or maybe there was sound and I just couldn't hear it.

"Wait?" I hollered. The general sense of panic had become quite specific. "Wait for *what*?"

Eyes still heavenward: "Grace."

A banshee howl rose over the thrumming of the rotors, increasing in volume and pitch until it became an ear-piercing, unearthly scream. The whole building shook. A crack raced down the ceiling. The horrible hotel prints in their cheap frames toppled from the walls. The spotlight winked out, and a second later, the explosion, and a superheated blast of air rumbled into the room.

"She got the pilot," Evan said with a nod. He pulled me, Sams, and Megan into the hall and said over his shoulder to Ben, "*Now* you go." Then to me: "The house on the map. It's Grace's now, but it won't be after tonight. Don't leave it. There's food and water and plenty of supplies to last through the winter." Speaking very quickly now, almost out of time—the 5th Wave might not be coming, but Grace was. "You'll be safe there, Cassie. At the equinox . . ."

Ben, Dumbo, and Poundcake had reached the stairs. Ben was frantically waving at us, *Come on!*

"Cassie! Are you listening? At the equinox, the mothership will send a pod to extract Grace from the safe house . . ."

"Sullivan! Now!" Ben bellowed.

"If you can figure out a way to rig it . . ." He was pressing something into my stomach, but my hands were full. I watched wide-eyed as my little brother snatched the plastic baggie holding the bomb from Evan's hand.

Then Evan Walker cupped my face in his hands and kissed me hard on the mouth.

"You can end it, Cassie. You. And that's the way it should be. It should be you. *You.*"

Kissing me again, and my blood marking his face, his tears marking mine.

"I can't make any promises this time," he hurried on. "But you can. Promise me, Cassie. Promise me you'll end it."

I nodded. "I'll end it." And the promise a sentence handed down, a cell door slamming shut, a stone around my neck to carry me down to the bottom of an infinite sea.

48

I PAUSED FOR a half second at the stairway door, knowing I might be seeing him for the last time or, more accurately, for the *second* last time. Then the plunge into pitch dark, not unlike the *first* last time, and whispering to Megan to watch out for rat guts, and then into the lobby, where the boys who brought me to this party hung by the front doors, their bodies silhouetted in the dusky orange glow of the burning chopper. Fleeing through the main entrance was a brilliantly counterintuitive move, I thought. Grace probably assumed we were barricaded in a room upstairs and would *Matrix*-hop her way up a wall to the busted-out window on the other side of the building.

"Cassie," Sam said in my ear. "Your nose is really *big.*"

"That's because it's broken." *Like my heart, kid. It's a set.*

Poundcake was no longer leaning against Ben with his arm around his neck. His whole big *body* was draped over Ben's in a fireman's carry. And Ben did not look like he was enjoying it.

"That isn't going to work, you know," I informed him. "You won't get a hundred yards."

Ben ignored me. "Bo, you've got Megan duty. Sam, you're gonna have to climb down; your sister's taking the point. I've got the rear."

"I need a gun!" Sammy said.

Ben ignored him, too. "*Stages*. Stage One: the overpass. Stage Two: the trees on the other side of the overpass. Stage Three—"

"East," I said. I set Sammy on the ground and pulled the crumpled map from my pocket. Ben was looking at me like I'd lost my mind. "We're going here." Pointing at the tiny square representing Grace's safe house.

"Noooo, Sullivan. We're going to the caverns to meet up with Ringer and Teacup."

"I don't care where we go, as long as it's not Dubuque!" Dumbo cried.

Ben shook his head. "You're killing it, Dumbo. Just killing it. Okay, here we go."

We went. A light snow was falling, the tiny crystals ignited in the orange light spinning, and you could smell the oily stench of the fuel burning and feel the heat pressing down on your head, and I took the lead as Ben suggested—well, ordered—Sammy hanging on to a belt loop and Dumbo right behind with Megan, who hadn't spoken a word, and who could blame her? She was in shock, probably. Halfway across the parking lot, nearing the strip of dirt that separated it from the interstate on-ramp, I glanced behind me in time to see Ben go down under the weight of his burden. I slung Sammy toward Dumbo and skidded across the slick pavement to Ben. On the roof of the hotel, I could see the mangled metal remains of the Black Hawk.

"I told you this wouldn't work!" I whisper-yelled at him.

"I'm not leaving him . . ." Ben was on all fours, gasping, retching. His lips shone crimson in the firelight; he was coughing up blood.

Then Dumbo was standing beside me. "Sarge. Hey, Sarge . . . ?"

Something in Dumbo's voice grabbed his attention. He looked up at Dumbo, who shook his head slowly: *He's not going to make it.*

And Ben Parish slammed his open hand onto the frozen ground, arching his back and yelling incoherently, and I'm thinking, *Oh*

God, oh God, not the time for an existential crisis. We're done if he loses it. We are so done.

I knelt beside Ben. His face was contorted by pain and fear and rage, the anger rooted in the unchangeable, ever-present past, where his sister cried for him and he still abandoned her to death. He abandoned her but she would not abandon him. She would always be with him. She would be with him until he took his last breath. She was with him now, bleeding out a foot away, and there was nothing he could do to save her.

"Ben," I said, running my fingers over the back of his head. His hair shimmered, dotted in crystalline snow. "It's over."

A shadow flitted past us, racing toward the hotel. I jumped up and took off after it, because the shadow was attached to my baby brother and he was hauling ass toward the front doors. I caught him and yanked him off the ground, and he commenced kicking and squirming and generally going berserk, and I was sure Dumbo was going to pop next, and three lunatics were too many for any person to manage.

I was worried for nothing, though. Dumbo had Ben on his feet and Megan by the hand, urging both toward the road, having an easier time of it than I was with Sammy hooked under my arm facedown, arms and legs flailing, yelling, "We gotta go back, Cassie! We gotta go back!"

Across the on-ramp, down the steep hill to the overpass, Stage One complete, and then I deposited Sammy on the ground and whacked him hard on the butt and told him to knock it off or he'd get us all killed.

"What's the matter with you, anyway?" I asked.

"I was trying to *tell* you!" he sobbed. "But you wouldn't listen. You *never* listen! I dropped it!"

"You dropped—?"

"The bag, Cassie. Running out, I . . . I dropped it!"

I looked over at Ben. Hunched over, head down, forearms resting on his upraised knees. I looked at Dumbo. Slump-shouldered, wide-eyed, hand holding Megan's.

"I have a bad feeling about this," he whispered.

The world went breathless. Even the snow seemed to hang suspended in the air.

The hotel blew apart in a blinding fireball of neon green. The ground shuddered. Air rushed into the vacuum, knocking the four of us off our feet. Then the debris roaring toward us, and I threw myself over Sammy. A wave of concrete, glass, wood, and metal particles (and—yes—bits of Ben's effing rats) no larger than grains of sand barreled down the hill, a gray boiling mass that engulfed us.

Welcome to Dubuque.

VI

THE TRIGGER

49

HE DIDN'T LIKE being around the smallest kids at the camp. They reminded him of his baby brother, the one he lost. The one that was there the morning he went out looking for food and wasn't there when he returned. The one he never found. At camp, when he wasn't training or eating or sleeping or washing down the barracks or shining his boots or cleaning his rifle or pulling KP duty or working in the P&D hangar, he was volunteering in the children's housing or working the buses as they came in. He didn't like being around the little kids, but he did it anyway. He never lost hope that one day he'd find his baby brother. That one day he would walk into the receiving hangar and find him sitting in one of the big red circles painted on the floor, or see him swinging from the old tire hung from the tree in the makeshift playground next to the parade grounds.

But he never found him.

At the hotel, when he discovered the enemy was planting bombs in children, he wondered if that's what happened to his brother. If they found him and took him and made him swallow the green capsule and sent him out again to be found by someone else. Probably not. Most children were dead. Only a handful were saved and brought to the camp. His brother probably didn't live many days past the day he disappeared.

But he could have been taken. He could have been forced to swallow the green capsule. He could have been thrown back out into the world and left to wander until he stumbled onto a group of survivors who would take him in and feed him and fill the room with their breath. It could have happened that way.

What's bothering you? Zombie wanted to know. They had gone across the parking lot to find a CO_2 canister in the old diner. Zombie had given up talking to him unless he was giving an order, and he'd given up trying to get him to talk. When he asked the question, Zombie really didn't expect an answer.

I can always tell when something's bothering you. You get like this constipated look. Like you're trying to crap a brick.

The canister wasn't that heavy, but Zombie was hurt and took the point on the way back. Zombie was nervous, jumping at every shadow. He kept saying there was something wrong. Something wrong about this Evan Walker and something wrong about the situation in general. Zombie thought they were being tricked.

Back in the hotel, Zombie sent Dumbo upstairs to get Evan. Then they waited inside the elevator for Evan to come down.

See, Cake, this goes back to my point, right back to it. EMPs and tsunamis and plagues and aliens in disguise and brainwashed kids and now kids with bombs inside them. Why are they making this so damn complicated? It's like they *want* a fight. Or want the fight to be interesting. Hey. Maybe that's it. Maybe you reach a certain point in evolution where boredom is the greatest threat to your survival. Maybe this isn't a planetary takeover at all, but a *game*. Like a kid pulling wings off flies.

As the minutes passed, Zombie got more nervous.

What now? Where the hell is he? Oh Christ, you don't think . . . ? Better get up there, Poundcake. Throw his ass over your shoulder and carry him down here if you have to.

Halfway up the stairs, he heard a heavy thump over his head, then a second, softer thump, and then he heard someone scream. He got to the door in time to see Cassie's body fly past and hit the floor. He followed her trajectory backward and saw the tall girl standing beside the room with the busted door. And he didn't hesitate, he burst into the hall and he knew the tall girl would not survive. He was a good shot, the best in his squad until Ringer came, and he knew that he would not miss.

Except Cassie tackled him and the tall girl slipped from his sights. He would have killed her if Cassie hadn't done that. He was sure of it.

Then the tall girl shot him through the wall.

Dumbo tore open his shirt and pressed a wadded-up sheet into the wound. He told him that it wasn't bad, that he was going to make it, but he knew he wasn't. He'd been around too much death. He knew what it smelled like, tasted like, felt like. He carried death inside him in the memories of his mother and the ten-foot pyres and the bones along the road and the conveyor belt carrying hundreds into the furnace of the power plant at camp, the dead burned to light their barracks and heat their water and keep them warm. Dying didn't bother him. Dying without knowing what happened to his brother bothered him.

Dying, he was taken downstairs. Dying, he was thrown over Zombie's shoulders. And then in the parking lot Zombie fell and the others gathered around and Zombie pounded the frozen pavement until the skin on his palms burst open.

They left him after that. He wasn't angry. He understood. He was dying.

And then he got up.

Not at first. At first, he crawled.

The tall girl was standing in the lobby when he dragged himself inside. She was beside the door that opened to the stairs, holding a pistol in both hands, bowing her head as if she were listening for something.

That's when he stood up.

The tall girl stiffened. She turned. She raised the gun and then she lowered it when she saw he was dying. She smiled and said hello. She was watching him beside the front doors and couldn't see the elevator or Evan dropping down into it from the escape hatch. Evan saw him and froze, like he didn't know what to do.

I know you. The tall girl was walking toward him. If she turned now, if she glanced behind her, she would see Evan, so he drew his sidearm to distract her, but the gun slipped from his hand and landed on the floor. He had lost a lot of blood. His blood pressure was dropping. His heart couldn't pump hard enough and he was losing feeling in his hands and feet.

He dropped to his knees and reached for the gun. She shot him in the hand. He fell onto his butt, jamming the wounded hand into his pocket as if that might protect it.

Gosh, you're a big, strong boy, aren't you? How old are you?

She waited for him to answer.

What's the matter? Cat got your tongue?

She shot him in the leg. Then she waited for him to scream or cry or say something. When he didn't, she shot him in the other leg.

Behind her, Evan dropped to his stomach and started to crawl toward them. He shook his head at Evan, gulping air. He felt numb all over. There was no pain, but a gray curtain had drawn down over his eyes.

The tall girl came closer. She was now halfway between him and Evan. She aimed the gun at the middle of his forehead.

Say something or I will blow your brains out. Where's Evan?

She started to turn. She might have heard Evan crawling toward her. So he stood up for the next to last time to distract her. He didn't stand up fast. It took over a minute, boots slipping on the tile wet from melted snow, rising up, flopping back down, the fact that he kept his hand in his pocket making it twice as hard. The tall girl smiled and chuckled, smirking the way the kids did at school. He was fat. He was clumsy. He was stupid. He was pig lard. When he finally got to his feet, she shot him again.

Please hurry up. I'm wasting ammo.

The plastic of the cake wrapper had been stiff and crinkly and always made a noise when he played with it in his pocket. That's how his mom knew he had it the day his brother disappeared. That's how the soldiers on the bus knew, too. And the drill sergeant called him Poundcake because he loved the story of the fat kid coming into camp with just the clothes on his back and a wrapper full of stale cake crumbs in his pocket.

The plastic sandwich bag that he found just outside the hotel doors didn't crinkle. It was much softer. There was no noise when he pulled it from his pocket. The bag slid out silently, as silent as he had been after he was told to shut up, shut up, shut UP.

The tall girl's smile went away.

And Poundcake started moving again. Not toward her and not toward the elevator, but toward the side door at the end of the hall.

Hey, what have you got there, big fella? Huh? What is that? I'm guessing it isn't a Tylenol.

The tall girl's smile came back. A different kind of smile, though. A nice smile. She was very pretty when she smiled like that. She was probably the prettiest girl he had ever seen.

You've got to be very careful with that. Do you understand? Hey. Hey, you know what? I'll make a deal with you. I'll put my gun down if you put that down, okay? How's that sound?

And then she did. She laid her gun on the floor. She took the rifle off her shoulder and laid that down, too. Then she held up her hands.

I can help you. Put that down and I'll help you. You don't have to die. I know how to fix you. I'm—I'm not like you. I'm definitely not as brave and strong as you, that's for sure. I can't believe you're still standing like that.

She was going to wait. She would wait until he passed out or fell over dead. All she had to do was keep talking and smiling and pretending she liked him.

He unzipped the bag.

The tall girl wasn't smiling now. She was running toward him, faster than he'd seen anyone run in his life. The gray veil shimmered as she came on. When she was close, her feet left the ground and she javelined into the spot where the first bullet hit him, hurling him backward and smashing him into the metal door frame. The baggie flew from his numb fingers and slid like a hockey puck across the tile. The gray veil turned black for a second. The tall girl pivoted as gracefully as a ballerina toward the bag. He hooked her ankle with his leg and sent her sprawling.

She was too quick and he was too hurt. She'd get there before him. So he picked up the gun that he had dropped and shot her in the back.

Then he got up for the last time. He tossed the gun away. He stepped over her writhing body, and that's as far as he got before falling for the last time.

He crawled toward the bag. She crawled after him. She couldn't stand up. The bullet had shattered her spinal cord. She was paralyzed from the waist down. But she was stronger than him and hadn't lost as much blood.

He scooped the plastic bag from the floor. Her hand fell on his arm and yanked him toward her as if he weighed nothing at all. She would finish him with a single punch to his dying heart.

But all he had to do was breathe.

He slapped the opening of the bag over his mouth.

And breathed.

— BOOK TWO —

VII

THE SUM OF ALL THINGS

50

I'M SITTING ALONE in a windowless classroom. Blue carpet, white walls, long white tables. White computer monitors with white keyboards. I'm wearing the white jumpsuit of new recruits. Different camp, same drill, down to the implant in my neck and a trip to Wonderland. I'm still paying for that trip. You don't feel empty after they drain your memories. You're sore as hell all over. Muscles retain memory, too. That's why they have to strap you down for the ride.

The door opens and Commander Alexander Vosch steps into the room. He carries a wooden box that he sets down on the table in front of me.

"You're looking well, Marika," he says. "Much better than I expected."

"My name is Ringer."

He nods. He understands exactly what I mean. More than once I've wondered if the information gathered by Wonderland flows both ways. If you can download human experience, why couldn't you upload it? It's possible the person who is smiling at me now contains the memories of every single human being who's been through the program. He may not be human—and I have my doubts about that—but he may also be the sum of all humans who have passed through Wonderland's gates.

"Yes. Marika is dead." He sits down across from me. "And now here you are, rising phoenixlike from her ashes."

He knows what I'm going to say. I can tell by the twinkling in his baby-blue eyes. Why can't he just tell me? Why do I have to ask?

"Is Teacup alive?"

"Which answer are you more likely to trust? *Yes* or *no*?"

Think before you respond. Chess teaches that. "*No*."

"Why?"

"*Yes* could be a lie to manipulate me."

He's nodding appreciatively. "To give you false hope."

"To gain leverage."

He cocked his head and looked down his narrow nose at me. "Why would someone like me need leverage over someone like you?"

"I don't know. There must be something you want."

"Otherwise . . . ?"

"Otherwise I'd be dead."

He doesn't say anything for a long moment. His stare pierces down to my bones. He gestures at the wooden box.

"I brought you something. Open it."

I look at the box. Look back at him. "I'm not going to do it."

"It's just a box."

"Whatever you want me to do, I won't. You're wasting your time."

"And time is the only currency we have left, isn't it? Time—and promises." Tapping the lid of the box. "I spent a great deal of that first precious commodity to find one of these." He nudges the box toward me. "*Open it.*"

I open it. He goes on. "Ben wouldn't play with you. Or little Allison—I mean Teacup; Allison is dead, too. You haven't played a game of chess since your father died."

I shake my head. Not in answer to his question. I shake my

head because I don't get it. The chief architect of the genocide wants to play chess with me?

I'm shivering in the paper-thin jumpsuit. The room is very cold. Smiling, Vosch is watching me. No. Not just watching. *This isn't like Wonderland. It isn't just your memories he knows. He knows what you're thinking, too.* Wonderland is a device. It records, but Vosch *reads.*

"They're gone," I blurt out. "They're not at the hotel. And you don't know where they are." That has to be it. I can think of no other reason why he hasn't killed me.

A crappy reason, though. In this weather and with his resources, how hard could it be to find them? I clamp my cold hands between my knees and force myself to breathe slowly and deeply.

He opens the lid, removes the board, and takes out the white queen. "White? You prefer white."

Long, nimble fingers set up the board. The fingers of a musician, a sculptor, a painter. He rests his elbows on the table and laces those fingers to make a shelf for his chin, like my father did every time *he* played.

"What do you want?" I ask.

He raises an eyebrow. "I want to play a game of chess."

Staring at me silently. Five seconds becomes ten. Ten becomes twenty. After thirty seconds, an eternity has passed. I think I know what he's doing: playing a game within a game. I just don't understand why.

I open with the Ruy Lopez. Not the most original opening in the history of the game; I'm a little stressed. As we play, he hums softly, tunelessly, and now I know he's deliberately mocking my father. My stomach rolls with revulsion. To survive I built walls, an emotional fortress that protected me and kept me sane in a world gone dangerously insane, but even the most open person has a private, sacred place where no one else may go.

I understand the game within the game now: There is nothing private, nothing sacred. There is no part of me hidden from him. My stomach churns with revulsion. He's violated more than my memories. He's molesting my soul.

The mouse and keyboard to my right are wireless. But the monitor beside him isn't. A lunge across the table, a wallop upside his head, and a wrap of the cord around his neck. Executed in four seconds, over in four minutes. Unless we're being watched, and we probably are. Vosch will live, Teacup and I will die. And even if I manage to take him out first, the victory will be Pyrrhic, assuming Evan Walker's claim is true. At the hotel, I pointed this out to Sullivan when she said Evan had sacrificed himself to blow up the base: If they can download themselves into human bodies, they can also make copies of themselves. The set of "Evans" and "Voschs" would be infinite. Evan could kill himself. I could kill Vosch. Wouldn't matter. By definition, the entities inside them are immortal.

You need to pay close attention to what I'm telling you, Sullivan said with exaggerated patience. *There's a human Evan who* merged *with the alien consciousness. He's not one or the other; he's both. So he* can *die.*

Not the important part.

Right, she snapped. *Just the insignificant human part.*

Vosch is leaning over the board. His breath smells like apples. I press my hands into my lap. He raises an eyebrow. *Problem?*

"I'm going to lose," I tell him.

He feigns surprise. "What makes you think so?"

"You know my moves before I make them."

"You're referring to the Wonderland program. But you're forgetting that we are more than the sum of our experiences. Human beings can be marvelously unpredictable. Your rescue of Ben Parish during the fall of Camp Haven, for example, defied logic and ignored the first prerogative of all living things: to continue living. Or your decision yesterday to give yourself up when you realized capture was the little girl's only chance to survive."

"Did she?"

"You already know the answer to that question." Impatiently, like a harsh teacher to a promising student. He gestures at the board: *Play.*

I wrap a hand around my fist and squeeze as hard as I can. Imagining my fist is his neck. Four minutes to choke the life out of him. Just four minutes.

"Teacup's alive," I tell him. "You know the threat to fry my brain won't make me do what you want me to do. But you know I'll do it for her."

"You belong to each other now, yes? Connected as if by a silver cord?" Smiling. "Anyway, besides the serious injuries from which she may not recover, you've given her the priceless gift of time. There is a saying in Latin. *Vincit qui patitur.* Do you know what it means?"

I'm beyond cold. I've reached absolute zero. "You know I don't."

"'He conquers who endures.' Remember poor Teacup's rats. What can they teach us? I told you when you first came to me; it isn't so much about crushing your capacity to fight as it is your will to fight."

The rats again. "A hopeless rat is a dead rat."

"Rats do not know hope. Or faith. Or love. You were right about those things, Private Ringer. They will not deliver humanity through the storm. You were wrong, however, about rage. Rage isn't the answer, either."

"What's the answer?" I don't want to ask, don't want to give him the satisfaction, but I can't help it.

"You're close to it," he says. "I think you might be surprised how close you are."

"Close to what?" My voice sounds as small as a rat's.

He shakes his head, impatient again. "Play."

"It's pointless."

"A world in which chess does not matter is not a world in which I wish to live."

"Stop doing that. Stop mocking my father."

"Your father was a good man in thrall to a terrible disease. You shouldn't judge him harshly. Nor yourself for abandoning him."

Please don't go. Don't leave me, Marika.

Long, nimble fingers clawing at my shirt, the fingers of an artist. Face sculpted by the merciless knife of hunger, the infuriated artist with the helpless clay, and red eyes rimmed in black.

I'll come back. I promise. You're going to die without it. I promise. I'll come back.

Vosch is smiling soullessly, a shark's smile or a skull's sneer, and if rage is not the answer, what is? I'm squeezing my fist hard enough to force my nails into my palm. *Here's how Evan described it,* Sullivan said, wrapping her fist in her hand. *This is Evan. This is the being inside.* My hand is the rage, but what is my fist? What is the thing wrapped up in rage?

"One move from mate," Vosch says softly. "Why won't you make it?"

My lips barely move. "I don't like to lose."

He pulls a silver device the size of a cell phone from his breast pocket. I've seen one before. I know what it does. The skin around the tiny patch of adhesive sealing the insertion point on my neck begins to itch.

"We're a little beyond that stage," he says.

Blood inside the fist that's within the hand clenching the fist. "Push the button. I don't give a shit."

He nods approvingly. "Now you're very close to the answer. But it is not *your* implant linked to this transmitter. Do you still want me to push it?"

Teacup. I look down at the board. *One move from mate.* The match was over before it began. When the game is fixed, how do you avoid losing?

A seven-year-old knew the answer to that question. I slide my hand beneath the board and hurl it toward his head. *I guess that's checkmate, bitch!*

He sees it coming and ducks easily out of the way. Pieces clatter on the table, roll lazily on the tabletop before falling off the edge. He shouldn't have told me that the device is linked to Teacup: If he pushes the button, he loses his leverage over me.

Vosch pushes the button.

51

MY REACTION IS months in the making. And instantaneous.

I leap across the table, drive my knee hard into his chest, and knock him straight back onto the floor. I land on top of him and smash the heel of my bloody hand into his aristocratic nose, rotating my shoulders into the blow to maximize the impact, textbook perfect, just like my trainers at Camp Haven taught me. Drill after drill after drill until there's no need to think: Muscles retain memory, too. His nose breaks with a satisfying *crunch*. This is the point, the instructors told me, when a wise soldier withdraws. Hand-to-hand is unpredictable and every second you remain engaged increases the risk. *Getting off the X* was the expression. *Vincit qui patitur.*

But there's no getting off this particular X. The clock's down to the final tick; I'm out of time. The door flies open and soldiers pour into the room. I'm taken down quick and hard, yanked off Vosch and thrown face-first onto the floor, a shin pressed against my neck. I smell blood. Not mine, his.

"You disappoint me," he whispers in my ear. "I told you rage wasn't the answer."

They pull me to my feet. The lower half of Vosch's face is covered in blood. It smears his cheeks like war paint. His eyes are already swelling, giving him a weird, piglike appearance.

He turns to the squad leader standing beside him, a slender, fair-skinned recruit with blond hair and soulful dark eyes.

"Prep her."

52

HALLWAY: LOW CEILINGS, flickering fluorescents, cinderblock walls. The press of bodies around me, one in front, one behind, two on either side holding my arms. The squeak of rubber-soled shoes against the gray concrete floor and the faint odor of sweat and the bittersweet smell of recycled air. Stairwell: metal rails painted gray like the floors, cobwebs fluttering in corners, dusty yellow lightbulbs in wire cages, descending into warmer, mustier air. Another hall: unmarked doors and large red stripes running down each gray wall and signs that read NO ACCESS and AUTHORIZED PERSONNEL ONLY. Room: small, windowless. Cabinets on one wall, a hospital bed in the middle, vital signs monitor beside it, screen dark. On either side of the bed, two people wearing white coats. A middle-aged man, a younger woman, forcing smiles.

The door clangs shut. I'm alone with the White Coats, except for the blond recruit standing at the door behind me.

"Easy or hard," the man in the white coat says. "Your choice."

"Hard," I say. I whip around and drop the recruit with a punch to the throat. His sidearm clatters onto the tile. I scoop it up and turn back to the White Coats.

"There's no escape," the man says calmly. "You know that."

I do know that. But escaping isn't the reason I need the gun. Not escaping in the sense he means it. I'm not taking hostages and I'm not killing anyone. Killing human beings is the enemy's goal. Behind me, the kid writhes on the floor, making hiccupping, gurgling sounds. I may have fractured his larynx.

I glance up at the camera mounted in the far corner of the room. Is he watching? Thanks to Wonderland, he knows me better than anyone on Earth. He must know why I took the gun:

I'm mated. And it's too late to resign the game.

I press the cold muzzle against my temple. The woman's mouth comes open. She takes a step toward me.

"Marika." Kind eyes. Soft voice. "She's alive because you are. If you aren't, she won't be."

It clicks then. He told me rage isn't the answer, and rage is the only explanation for him hitting the kill switch when I upended the board. That's what I thought when it happened. It never occurred to me that he might be bluffing.

And it should have. There's no way he'd give up his leverage. Why didn't I see that? I'm the one blinded by rage, not him.

I'm dizzy; the room won't stay still. Bluffs inside bluffs, feints within counterfeints. I'm in a game in which I don't know the rules or even the object. Teacup is alive because I am. I'm alive because she is.

"Take me to her," I say to the woman. I want proof that that one fundamental assumption is true.

"Not going to happen," the man says. "So now what?"

Good question. But the issue has to be pressed and pressed hard, as hard as I press the gun against my temple. "Take me to her or I swear to God I'll do it."

"You can't," the young woman says. Soft voice. Kind eyes. Hand outstretched.

She's right. I can't. It could be a lie; Teacup could be dead. But a chance remains that she's alive, and if I'm gone, there's no reason to keep her that way. The risk is unacceptable.

This is the bind. This is the trap. This is where the road of impossible promises dead-ends. This is the only possible outcome of the antiquated belief that the insignificant life of a seven-year-old kid still matters.

I'm sorry, Teacup. I should have finished this back in the woods.

I lower the gun.

53

THE MONITOR FLICKERS on. Pulse, blood pressure, breathing, temperature. The kid I took down is back up, leaning against the door, one hand massaging his throat, the other holding the gun. He glowers at me lying on the bed.

"Something to help you relax," the woman with the soft voice and kind eyes murmurs. "A little stick."

The bite of the needle. The walls disappear into colorless nothing. A thousand years pass. I am ground to dust beneath the heel of time. Their voices lumber, their faces expand. The thin foam beneath me dissolves. I am floating on an unbounded ocean of white.

A disembodied voice emerges from the fog. "And now let's return to the problem of rats, shall we?"

Vosch. I don't see him. His voice has no source. It originates from everywhere and nowhere, as if he's inside me.

"You've lost your home. And the lovely one—the *only* one—that you've found to replace it is infested with vermin. What can you do? What are your choices? Resign yourself to live peaceably with the destructive pests or exterminate them before they can destroy your new home? Do you say to yourself, 'Rats are disgusting creatures, but nevertheless they are living things with the same rights as me'? Or do you say, 'We are incompatible, these rats and I. If I am to live here, these vermin must die'?"

From a thousand miles away, I hear the monitor beeping, marking the beat of my heart. The sea undulates. I rise and fall with each roll of the surface.

"But it isn't really about the rats." His voice pounds, dense, thick as thunder. "It never was. The necessity of exterminating them is a given. It's the method that troubles you. The real issue, the fundamental problem, is rocks."

The white curtain peels away. I'm still floating, but now I'm far above the Earth in a black void awash with stars, and the sun kissing the horizon paints the planet's surface beneath me a shimmering gold. The monitor beeps frantically, and a voice says, "Oh, crap," and then Vosch's: "Breathe, Marika. You're perfectly safe."

Perfectly safe. So that's why they sedated me. If they hadn't, my heart probably would have stopped from shock. The effect is three-dimensional, indistinguishable from reality, except I would not be breathing in space. Or hearing Vosch's voice in a place where sound does not exist.

"This is the Earth as it was sixty-six million years ago. Beautiful, isn't it? Edenic. Unspoiled. The atmosphere before you poisoned it. The water before you fouled it. The land lush with life before you, rodents that you are, shredded it to pieces to feed your voracious appetites and build your filthy nests. It may have remained pristine for another sixty-six million years, unsullied by your mammalian gluttony, if not for a chance encounter with an alien visitor one-quarter the size of Manhattan."

It whizzes past me, pockmarked and craggy, blotting out the stars as it barrels toward the planet. When it breaks through the atmosphere, the lower half of the asteroid begins to glow. Bright yellow, then white.

"And thus the fate of the world is decided. By a rock."

Now I'm standing on the shores of a vast, shallow sea, watching the asteroid fall, a tiny dot, a pebble, insignificant.

"When the dust from the impact has settled, three-quarters of all life on Earth will be gone. The world ends. The world begins again. Humanity owes its existence to a bit of cosmic whimsy. To a rock. It really is remarkable when you think about it."

The ground shudders. A distant boom, then an eerie silence.

"And therein lies the conundrum, the riddle you've been avoiding, because confronting the problem shakes apart the very foundation, doesn't it? It defies explanation. It renders all that's happened impossibly discordant, absurd, nonsensical."

The sea roils; steam whips and swirls. The water is boiling away. A massive wall of dust and pulverized stone roars toward me, blotting out the sky. The air is filled with high-pitched screeching, like the screams of a dying animal.

"I don't have to state the obvious, do I? The question has been bothering you for a very long time."

I can't move. I know it isn't real, but my panic is as the thundering wall of steam and dust bears down. A million years of evolution has taught me to trust my senses, and the primitive part of my brain is deaf to the rational part that screams in a high pitch like a dying animal, *Not real not real not real not real.*

"Electromagnetic pulses. Giant metal rods raining from the sky. Viral plague . . ." His voice rises with each word and the words are like thunderclaps or the heel of a boot slamming down. "Sleeper agents implanted in human bodies. Armies of brainwashed children. What *is* this? *That's* the central question. The only one that really matters: Why bother with any of it when all you need is a very, very big *rock*?"

The wave rolls over me, and I drown.

54

I'M BURIED FOR MILLENNIA.

Miles above me, the world wakes. In the cool shadows pooling on the rain forest floor, a ratlike creature digs for tender roots. Its descendants will tame fire, invent the wheel, discover mathematics, create poetry, reroute rivers, level forests, build cities, explore deep space. For now, the only important business is finding food and staying alive long enough to make more ratlike creatures.

Annihilated in fire and dust, the world is reborn in a hungry rodent digging in the dirt.

The clock ticks. Nervously, the creature sniffs the warm, moist air. The metronomic beat of the clock speeds up, and I rise toward the surface. When I emerge from the dust, the creature has transformed: It's sitting in a chair beside my bed, wearing a pair of jeans stiff with dirt and a torn T-shirt. Stoop-shouldered, unshaven, hollow-eyed inventor of the wheel, inheritor, caretaker, prodigal.

My father.

The *beep-beep* of the monitor. The dripping IV and the stiff sheets and the hard pillow and the lines snaking from my arms. And the man sitting beside the bed, sallow and sweaty, covered with grime, restless, nervously plucking at his shirt, bloodshot eyes and wet, swollen lips.

"Marika."

I close my eyes. *It's not him. It's the drug Vosch pumped into you.*

Again: "Marika."

"Shut up. You're not real."

"Marika, there's something I want to tell you. Something you should know."

"I don't understand why you're doing this to me," I say to Vosch. I know he's watching.

"I forgive you," my father says.

I can't catch my breath. There's a sharp pain in my chest, like a knife driving home.

"Please," I beg Vosch. "Please don't do this."

"You had to leave," my father says. "You didn't have a choice, and anyway, what happened is my own damn fault. You didn't make me a drunk."

Instinctively, I press my hands against my ears. But his voice isn't in the room; it's in me.

"I didn't last long after you left," my father tries to reassure me. "Only a couple hours."

We made it as far as Cincinnati. A little over a hundred miles. Then his stash ran out. He begged me not to leave him, but I knew if I didn't find some alcohol fast, he'd die. I found some—a bottle of vodka tucked underneath a mattress—after breaking into sixteen houses, if you can call it breaking in, since every house was abandoned and all I had to do was step through a broken window. I was so happy to find that bottle, I actually kissed it.

But I was too late. He was dead by the time I made it back to our camp.

"I know you beat yourself up over that, but I would've died either way, Marika. Either way. You did what you thought you had to do."

There's no hiding from his voice. No running from it, either. I open my eyes and look straight into his. "I know this is a lie. You aren't real."

He smiles. The same smile as when I made a particularly good move in a match. The delighted teacher.

"That's what I've come to tell you!" He rubs his long fingers against his thighs, and I can see the dirt encrusted beneath the nails. "That's the lesson, Marika. That's what they want you to understand."

Warm hand against cool skin: He's touching my arm. The last time I felt his hand was against my cheek, in hard, stinging slaps while the other hand held me still. *Bitch! Don't leave me. Don't you ever leave me, bitch!* Each *bitch!* punctuated by a slap. His mind was gone. Seeing things that weren't there in the profound darkness that slammed down every night. Hearing things in the awful silence that threatened to crush you every day. On the night he died, he woke up screaming, clawing at his eyes. He could feel bugs inside them, crawling.

Those same swollen eyes staring at me now. And the claw marks beneath them still fresh. Another circle, another silver cord: Now I am the one seeing things, hearing things, feeling things that aren't there in awful silence.

"First they taught us not to trust them," he whispers. "Then they taught us not to trust each other. Now they're teaching us we can't even trust ourselves."

And I whisper back, "I don't understand."

He's fading away. As I drop deeper into lightless depths, my father fades into depthless light. He kisses me on the forehead. A benediction. A curse.

"You belong to them now."

55

THE CHAIR IS EMPTY AGAIN. I'm alone. Then I remind myself I was alone when the chair wasn't empty. I wait for the pounding of my heart to subside. I will myself to stay calm, to control my breathing. The drug will work its way through my system and I'll be fine. *You're safe,* I tell myself. *Perfectly safe.*

The blond recruit I punched in the throat comes in. He's carrying a tray of food: a slab of gray mystery meat, potatoes, a mushy pile of beans, and a tall glass of orange juice. He sets the tray by the bed, pushes the button to raise me to a sitting position, rotates the tray in front of me, then stands there, arms crossed, as if he's waiting for something.

"Let me know how it tastes," he whispers hoarsely. "I can't eat solid food for three more weeks."

His skin is fair, which makes his brown, deep-set eyes seem even darker. He isn't big, not buff like Zombie or blocky like Poundcake. He's tall and lean, a swimmer's body. There's a quiet intensity about him, in the way he carries himself but especially in the eyes, a carefully contained force coiled just beneath the surface.

I'm not sure what he expects me to say. "Sorry."

"Sucker punch." Drumming his fingers on his forearm. "You're not going to eat?"

I shake my head. "Not hungry."

Is the food real? Is the kid who brings the food real? The uncertainty of my own experience is crushing. I am drowning in an infinite sea. Sinking slowly, the weight of the lightless depths forcing me down, forcing the air from my lungs, squeezing the blood from my heart.

"Drink the juice," he scolds. "They said you should at least drink the juice."

"Why?" I manage to choke out. "What's in the juice?"

"A little paranoid?"

"A little."

"They just drained about a pint of blood from you. So they said make sure you drink the juice."

I have no memory of their taking my blood. Did that happen while I was "talking" to my father? "Why are they draining my blood?"

Dead-eyed stare. "Let's see if I can remember. They tell me everything."

"What did they tell you? Why am I here?"

"I'm not supposed to talk to you," he says. Then: "They told us you're a VIP. Very important prisoner." Shaking his head. "I don't get it. In the good old days, Dorothys just . . . disappeared."

"I'm not a Dorothy."

He shrugs. "I don't ask questions."

But I need him to answer some. "Do you know what happened to Teacup?"

"Ran away with the spoon, what I heard."

"That was the dish."

"I was making a joke."

"I don't get it."

"Well. Fuck you."

"The little girl who choppered in with me. Badly wounded. I need to know if she's alive."

Nodding seriously. "I'll get right on that."

I'm going about this wrong. I was never good with people. My nickname in middle school was Her Majesty Marika and a dozen variations of the same. Maybe I should establish a rapport beyond *eff-you*. "My name's Ringer."

"That's wonderful. You must be very satisfied with that."

"You look familiar. Were you at Camp Haven?"

He starts to say something. Stops himself. "I have orders not to talk to you."

I almost say *Then why are you?* But I catch myself. "It's probably a good idea. They don't want you to know what I know."

"Oh, I know what you know: It's all a lie, we've been tricked by the enemy, they're using us to wipe out survivors, blah, blah, blah. Typical Dorothy crap."

"I used to think all that," I admit. "Now I'm not so sure."

"You'll figure it out."

"I will." Rocks and rats and life-forms evolved beyond the need for physical bodies. I'll figure it out, but probably too late, though it's probably already too late. Why did they take my blood? Why is Vosch keeping me alive? What could I have that he could possibly need? Why do they need me, this blond kid, or any human? If they could genetically engineer a virus that kills nine out of ten people, why not ten out of ten? Or, as Vosch said, why bother with any of it, when all you need is a very big rock?

My head hurts. I'm dizzy. Nauseated. I miss being able to think clearly. It used to be my number one favorite thing.

"Drink your damn juice so I can go," he says.

"Tell me your name and I'll drink it."

He hesitates, then: "Razor."

I drink the juice. He picks up the tray and leaves. I got his name at least. A minor victory.

56

THE WOMAN IN the white lab coat shows up. She says her name is Dr. Claire. Dark, wavy hair pulled back from her face. Eyes the color of an autumn sky. She smells like bitter almonds, which is also the odor of cyanide.

"Why did you take my blood?"

She smiles. "Because Ringer is so sweet, we decided to clone a hundred of her." There is not a hint of sarcasm in her voice. She disconnects the IV and steps back quickly, as if she's afraid I'll leap from the bed and strangle her. Strangling her *did* occur to me, briefly, but I'd rather stab her to death with a pocketknife. I don't know how many stabs that would take. A lot, probably.

"That's another thing that doesn't make sense," I tell her. "Why download your consciousness into a human body when you can clone as many as you like in your mothership? Zero risk." Especially since one of your downloads can go all Evan Walker on you and fall in love with a human girl.

"That's a good point." Nodding seriously. "I'll bring that up at the next planning meeting. Maybe we need to rethink this whole hostile-takeover thingy." She motions toward the door. "March."

"Where?"

"You'll find out. Don't worry." Claire adds, "You're going to enjoy it."

We don't go far. Two doors down. The room is spare. A sink and a cabinet, a toilet and a shower stall.

"How long has it been since you've had a decent shower?" she asks.

"Camp Haven. The night before I shot my drill sergeant in the heart."

"Did you?" she asks casually, as if I'd told her I used to live in San Francisco. "Towel right there. Toothbrush, comb, deodorant in the cabinet. I'll be right on the other side of the door. Knock if you need anything."

Alone, I open the cabinet. Roll-on antiperspirant. A comb. A travel-sized tube of toothpaste. A toothbrush in a plastic wrapper. No floss. I'd hoped there'd be floss. I waste a couple of minutes wondering how long it would take to sharpen the end of the toothbrush into a proper cutting instrument. Then I slip out of the jumpsuit and step into the shower, and I think of Zombie, not because I'm naked in a shower, but remembering him talking about Facebook and drive-thrus and tardy bells and the endless list of all things lost, like greasy fries and musty bookstores and hot showers. I turn the temperature as high as I can stand it and let the water rain over me until my fingertips pucker. Lavender soap. Fruity shampoo. The hard lump of the tiny transmitter rolls beneath my fingers. *You belong to them now.*

I hurl the shampoo bottle against the shower wall. Slam my fist into the tile again and again until the skin on my knuckles splits open. My anger is greater than the sum of all lost things.

Vosch is waiting for me back in the room two doors down. He says nothing as Claire bandages my hand, silent until we're alone.

"What did you accomplish?" he asks.

"I needed to prove something to myself."

"Pain being the only true proof of life?"

I shake my head. "I know I'm alive."

He nods thoughtfully. "Would you like to see her?"

"Teacup is dead."

"Why do you think that?"

"There's no reason to let her live."

"That's correct, if we proceed from the assumption that the only reason to keep her alive is to manipulate you. Really, the narcissism of today's youth!"

He presses a button on the wall. A screen lowers from the ceiling.

"You can't force me to help you." Fighting down a rising sense of panic, of losing control of something I never had control over.

Vosch holds out his hand. In his palm is a shiny green object the size and shape of a large gel capsule. A hair-thin wire protrudes from one end. "This is the message."

The lights dim. The screen flickers to life. The camera soars over a winter-killed field of wheat. In the distance, a farmhouse and a couple of outbuildings, a rusty silo. A tiny figure stumbles from a stand of trees bordering the field and lurches through the dry and broken stalks toward the cluster of buildings.

"That is the messenger."

From this height, I can't tell if it's a boy or girl, only that it's a small child. Nugget's age? Younger?

"Central Kansas," Vosch goes on. "Yesterday at approximately thirteen hundred hours."

Another figure comes into view on the porch steps. After a minute, someone else comes out. The child begins to run toward them.

"That isn't Teacup," I whisper.

"No."

Crashing through the brittle chaff toward the adults who watch motionlessly, and one of them holds a gun, and there is no sound, which somehow makes it more terrible.

"It's the ancient instinct: In times of great danger, be wary of strangers. Trust no one outside your circle."

My body tenses. I know how this ends; I lived it. The man with the gun: me. The child crashing toward him: Teacup.

The child falls. Gets up. Runs. Falls again.

"But there's another instinct, far older, as old as life itself, nearly impossible for the human mind to override: Protect the young at all costs. Preserve the future."

The child breaks through the wheat into the yard and falls for the last time. The one with the gun doesn't lower it, but his companion races to the fallen child and scoops it off the frozen ground. The gunman blocks their way back into the house. The tableau holds for several seconds.

"It's all about risk," Vosch observes. "You realized that long ago. So of course you know who will win the argument. After all, how much risk does a little child pose? *Protect the young. Preserve the future.*"

The person carrying the child sidesteps the one with the gun and rushes up the steps into the house. The gunman drops his head as if in prayer, then lifts his head as if in supplication. Then he turns and goes inside. The minutes spin out.

Beside me, Vosch murmurs, "The world is a clock."

The farmhouse, the outbuildings, the silo, the brown fields, and the blur of numbers as the time display at the bottom of the screen ticks off the seconds by the hundredths. I know what's coming but still I flinch when the silent flash whites out the scene. Then roiling dust and debris and billowing smoke: The wheat is burning, consumed in a matter of seconds, tender fodder for the fire, and where the buildings used to be, a crater, a black hole bored into the Earth. The feed goes black. The screen retracts. The lights stay dim.

"I want you to understand," Vosch says gently. "You've wondered why we kept the little ones, the ones too young to fight."

"I don't understand." Tiny figure in acres of brown, dressed in denim overalls, barefoot, running through the wheat.

He misreads my confusion. "The device inside the child's body is calibrated to detect minute fluctuations in carbon dioxide, the chief component of human breath. When the CO_2 reaches a certain threshold, indicating the presence of multiple targets, the device detonates."

"No," I whisper. They brought him inside, wrapped him in a warm blanket, brought him water, washed his face. The group gathered around him, bathing him in their breath. "They'd be just as dead if you dropped a bomb."

"It isn't about the dead," he snaps impatiently. "It never was."

The lights come up, the door comes open, and Claire comes in wheeling a metal cart, followed by her white-coated buddy and Razor, who looks at me and then looks away. That got to me more than the cart with its array of syringes: He couldn't bring himself to look at me.

"It doesn't change anything." My voice rising. "I don't care what you do. I don't even care about Teacup anymore. I'll kill myself before I help you."

He shakes his head. "You're not helping me."

57

CLAIRE TIES a rubber strap around my arm and taps the inside of my elbow to bring up a vein. Razor stands on the other side of the bed. The man in the white coat—I never got his name—is by the monitor, holding a stopwatch. Vosch leans against the sink, watching me with bright, flinty eyes glittering, like the crows' in the woods on the day I shot Teacup, curious but curiously indifferent, and then I understand that Vosch is right: The answer to their arrival is not rage. The answer is rage's opposite. The only possible answer is the opposite of all things, like the pit where the farmhouse once stood: simply nothing. Not hate, not anger, not fear, not anything at all. Empty space. The soulless indifference of the shark's eye.

"Too high," murmured Mr. White Coat, looking at the monitor.

"First something to relax you." Claire slides the needle into my arm. I look at Razor. He looks away.

"Better," White Coat says.

"I don't care what you do to me," I tell Vosch. My tongue feels bloated, clumsy.

"It doesn't matter." He nods at Claire, who picks up the second syringe.

"Inserting the hub on my mark," she says.

The hub?

"Uh-oh," White Coat says. "Careful." Eyeing the monitor as my heart rate kicks up a notch.

"Don't be afraid," Vosch says. "It won't harm you." Claire gives him a startled look. He shrugs. "Well. We ran tests." He flicks his finger at her: *Get on with it.*

I weigh ten million tons. My bones are iron; the rest is stone. I don't feel the needle slide into my arm. Claire says, "*Mark,*" and White Coat clicks the stopwatch. The world is a clock.

"The dead have their reward," Vosch says. "It is the living—you and I—who still have work to do. Call it what you like, fate, luck, providence. You have been delivered into my hands to be my instrument."

"Appending to the cerebral cortex." From Claire. Her voice sounds muffled, as if my ears have been stuffed with cotton. I roll my head toward her. A thousand years go by.

"You've seen one before," Vosch says, a thousand miles away. "In the testing room, on the day you arrived at Camp Haven. We told you it was an infestation of an alien life-form attached to the human brain. That was a lie."

I can hear Razor breathing, loud, like a diver's breath through a regulator.

"It is actually a microscopic command hub affixed to the prefrontal lobe of your brain," Vosch says. "A CPU, if you will."

"Booting up," Claire says. "Looking good."

"Not to control *you* . . . ," Vosch says.

"Introducing first array." Needle glinting in fluorescent light. Black specks suspended in amber fluid. I feel nothing as she injects it into my vein.

"But to coordinate the forty thousand or so mechanized guests to which you will play host."

"Temp ninety-nine point six," White Coat says.

Razor beside me breathing.

"It took the prehistoric rats millions of years and a thousand generations to reach the current stage in human evolution," Vosch says. "It will take you days to achieve the next."

"Link with the first array complete," Claire says, bending over me again. Bitter almond breath. "Introducing second array."

The room is furnace-hot. I'm drenched in sweat. White Coat announces that my temperature is one hundred and two.

"It's a messy business, evolution," Vosch says. "Many false starts and blind alleys. Some candidates aren't suitable hosts. Their immune systems crash or they suffer from permanent cognitive dissonance. In layman's terms, they go mad."

I'm burning. My veins are filled with fire. Water flows from my eyes, trickles down my temples, pools in my ears. I see Vosch's face leaning over the surface of the undulating sea of my tears.

"But I have faith in you, Marika. You did not come through fire and blood only to fall now. You will be the bridge that connects what-was to what-will-be."

"We're losing her," White Coat calls out, tremble-voiced.

"No," Vosch murmurs, cool hand on my wet cheek. "We have saved her."

58

THERE IS NO DAY or night anymore, only the sterile glow of the fluorescent lights, and those lights never go out. I measure the hours by Razor's visits, three times a day to deliver meals I can't keep down.

They can't control my fever. Can't stabilize my blood pressure.

Can't subdue my nausea. My body is rejecting the eleven arrays designed to augment each of my biological systems, each array consisting of four thousand units, which makes a total of forty-four thousand microscopic robotic invaders coursing through my bloodstream.

I feel like shit.

After every breakfast, Claire comes in to examine me, tinker with my meds, and make cryptic remarks like, *You better start feeling better. The window of opportunity is closing.* Or snide ones like, *I'm starting to think the whole very-big-rock idea was the right way to go.* She seems to resent that I've reacted badly to her pumping me full of forty thousand alien mechanisms.

"It's not like there's anything you can do about it," she told me once. "The procedure is irreversible."

"There is one thing."

"What? Oh. Sure. Ringer the irreplaceable." She pulled the kill switch device from her lab coat pocket and held it up. "Got you keyed in. I'll push the button. Go ahead. Tell me to push the button." Smirking.

"Push the button."

She laughed softly. "It's amazing. Whenever I start wondering what he sees in you, you say something like that."

"Who? Vosch?"

Her smile faded. Her eyes went shark-eyed blank. "We will terminate the upgrade if you can't adjust."

Terminate the upgrade.

She peeled the bandages away from my knuckles. No scabs, no bruises, no scars. As if it hadn't happened. As if I'd never pounded my fist into the wall until the skin split down to the bone. I thought of Vosch appearing in my room completely healed, days after I smashed his nose and gave him two black eyes. And Sullivan, who told the story of Evan Walker torn apart by shrapnel and yet, somehow, hours later, able to infiltrate and take out an entire military installation by himself.

First they took Marika and made her Ringer. Now they've taken Ringer and "upgraded" her into someone completely different. Someone like *them.*

Or some*thing.*

There is no day or night anymore, only a constant sterile glow.

59

"WHAT HAVE THEY done to me?" I ask Razor one day when he carts in another inedible meal. I don't expect an answer, but he's expecting me to ask the question. It must strike him as weird that I haven't.

He shrugs, avoiding my gaze. "Let's see what's on the menu today. Oooh. Meat loaf! Lucky duck."

"I'm going to vomit."

His eyes widen. "Really?" He looks around for the plastic upchuck container, desperate.

"Please, take the tray away. I can't."

He frowns. "They'll pull the plug on you if you don't get your shit together."

"They could have done this to anyone," I say. "Why did they do it to me?"

"Maybe you're special."

I shake my head and answer as if he were serious. "No. I think it's because someone else is. Do you play chess?"

Startled: "Play what?"

"Maybe we could play. When I'm feeling better."

"I'm more of a baseball guy."

"Really? I would have guessed swimming. Or tennis."

He cocks his head. His eyebrows come together. "You must be feeling bad. Making conversation like you're halfway human."

"I *am* halfway human. Literally. The other half . . ." I shrug. It coaxes out a grin.

"Oh, the 12th System is definitely theirs," he says.

The 12th System? What did that mean exactly? I'm not sure, but I suspect it's in reference to the eleven normal systems of the human body.

"We found a way to yank them out of Teds' bodies and . . ." Razor trails off, gives the camera an abashed look. "Anyway, you have to eat. I overheard them talking about a feeding tube."

"So that's the official story? Like Wonderland: We're using their technology against them. And you believe that."

He leans against the wall, crosses his arms over his chest, and hums "Follow the Yellow Brick Road." I shake my head. Amazing. It isn't that the lies are too beautiful to resist. It's that the truth is too hideous to face.

"Commander Vosch is implanting bombs inside children. He's turning kids into IEDs," I tell him. He hums louder. "Little kids. Toddlers. They're separated when they come in, aren't they? They were at Camp Haven. Anyone younger than five is carted off and you never see them again. Have you seen any? Where are the children, Razor? Where are they?"

He stops humming long enough to say, "Shut up, Dorothy."

"And does that make sense: loading up a Dorothy with superior alien technology? If command decided to 'enhance' people for the war, do you really think it would pick the crazy ones?"

"I don't know. They picked you, didn't they?" He grabs the tray of untouched food and heads for the door.

"Don't go."

He turns, surprised. My face is hot. The fever must be spiking. That has to be it.

"Why?" he asks.

"You're the only honest person I have left to talk to."

He laughs. It's a good laugh, authentic, unforced; I like it, but I am feverish. "Who says I'm honest?" he asks. "We're all enemies in disguise, right?"

"My father used to tell this story about six blind men and an elephant. One man felt the elephant's leg and said an elephant must look like a pillar. Another felt the trunk and said an elephant must look like a tree branch. Blind guy number three felt the tail and said an elephant is like a rope. Fourth guy feels the belly: The elephant is like a wall. Fifth guy, ear: The elephant is shaped like a fan. Sixth guy, a tusk, so an elephant must be like a pipe."

Razor stares at me stone-faced for a long moment, then smiles. It's a good smile; I like it, too.

"That's a beautiful story. You should tell it at parties."

"The point is," I tell him, "from the moment their ship appeared, we've all been blind men patting an elephant."

60

IN THE CONSTANT sterile glow, I measure the days by the uneaten meals he brings. Three meals, one day. Six, two days. On the tenth day, after he sets the tray in front of me, I ask him, "Why do you bother?" My voice like his now, a throaty croak. I'm soaked in sweat, fever spiking, head pounding, heart racing. He doesn't answer. Razor hasn't spoken to me in seventeen meals. He seems jittery, distracted, even angry. Claire's gone silent, too. She comes twice a day to change my IV bag, look into my eyes with an otoscope, test my reflexes, change out the catheter bag, and empty the bedpan. Every sixth meal, I get a sponge bath. One day, she brings a tape measure and wraps it around my biceps, I guess to see how much muscle I've lost. I don't see anyone else. No Mr. White Coat. No Vosch or dead fathers pumped into my head by Vosch. I'm not so out of it that I don't know what they're doing: holding vigil, waiting to see if the "enhancement" kills me.

She's rinsing out the bedpan one morning when Razor comes in with my breakfast, and he waits silently until she's finished, and then I hear him whisper, "Is she dying?"

Claire shakes her head. Ambivalent: could be *no,* could be *your guess is as good as mine.* I wait till she's gone to say, "You're wasting your time."

He glances at the camera mounted in the ceiling. "I just do what they tell me."

I pick up the tray and hurl it onto the floor. His lips tighten, but he doesn't say anything. Silently, he cleans up the mess while I lie panting, exhausted from the effort, sweat pouring off me.

"Yeah, pick that up. Make yourself useful."

When my fever shoots up, something in my mind loosens, and I imagine I can feel the forty-four thousand microbots swarming in my bloodstream and the hub with its delicate lace of tendrils burrowed into every lobe, and I understand what my father felt in his dying hours as he clawed at himself to subdue the imaginary insects crawling beneath his skin.

"*Bitch,*" I gasp. From the floor, Razor looks up at me, startled. "Leave me, bitch."

"No problem," he mutters. On his hands and knees, using a wet rag to mop up the mess, and the tart smell of disinfectant. "Fast as I can."

He stands up. His ivory cheeks are flushed. Deliriously, I think the color brings out the auburn highlights in his blond hair. "It won't work," he tells me. "Starving yourself. So you better think of something else."

I've tried. But there's no alternative. I can barely lift my head. *You belong to them now.* Vosch the sculptor, my body the clay, but not my spirit, never my soul. Unconquered. Uncrushed. Uncontained.

I am not bound; they are. Languish, die, or recover, the game's over, the grand master Vosch mated.

"My father had a favorite saying," I tell Razor. "*We call chess the game of kings because, through chess, we learn how to rule kings.*"

"Again with the chess."

He drops the dirty rag into the sink and slams out the door. When he returns with the next meal, there's a familiar wooden box beside the tray. Without a word, Razor picks up the food and dumps it into the trash, tosses the metal tray into the sink, where it lands with a loud clang. The bed hums, maneuvering my body into a sitting position, and he slides the box in front of me.

"You said you didn't play," I whisper.

"So teach me."

I shake my head and say to the camera behind him, "Nice try. But stuff it up your ass."

Razor laughs. "Not their idea. But speaking of asses, you can bet yours I got permission first."

He opens the box, pulls out the board, fumbles with the pieces. "You got your queens and kings and the prawns and these guard-tower-looking things. How come every piece is like a person except those?"

"*Pawns,* not *prawns*. A prawn is a big shrimp."

He nods. "That's the name of a guy in my unit."

"Shrimp?"

"Prawn. Never knew what the hell it meant."

"You're setting it up wrong."

"That could be because I don't know how to freaking play. You do it."

"I don't want to do it."

"Then you're conceding defeat?"

"Resigning. It's called resigning."

"That's good to know. I have a feeling that'll come in handy." Smiling. Not the Zombie high-voltage type. Smaller, subtler, more ironic. He sits beside the bed and I catch a whiff of bubble gum. "White or black?"

"Razor, I'm too weak to even lift—"

"Then you point where you want to go and I'll move you."

He's not giving up. I didn't really expect him to. By this point, wafflers and wusses have been winnowed out. There are no pussies left. I tell him where to place the pieces and how each one moves. Describe the basic rules. Lots of nodding and *uh-huh*s, but I get the feeling there's a lot of agreeing and not much grasping. Then we play and I slaughter him in four moves. The next game, he falls into arguing and denying: *You can't* do *that! Tell me that isn't the stupidest damn rule ever.* Game three and I'm sure he's regretting the whole idea. My spirits aren't being lifted and his are being totally crushed.

"This is the dumbest-assed game ever invented," he pouts.

"Chess wasn't invented. It was discovered."

"Like America?"

"Like mathematics."

"I knew girls just like you in school." He leaves the point there and starts to set up the board again.

"That's all right, Razor. I'm tired."

"Tomorrow I'm bringing some checkers." Spoken like a threat.

He doesn't, though. Tray, box, board. This time he sets up the pieces in a strange configuration: the black king in the center facing him, the queen on the edge facing the king, three pawns behind the king at ten, twelve, and two o'clock, one knight on the king's right, another on his left, a bishop directly behind him and, next to the bishop, another pawn. Then Razor looks at me, wearing that seraphic grin.

"Okay." I'm nodding, not sure why.

"I've invented a game. Are you ready? It's called . . ." He taps on the bedrail to produce a drumroll. "Chaseball!"

"Chaseball?"

"Chess-baseball. Chaseball. Get it?" He plops a coin beside the board.

"What's that?" I ask.

"It's a quarter."

"I know it's a quarter."

"For the purposes of the game, it's the ball. Well, not really the ball, but it *represents* the ball. Or what happens *with* the ball. If you'd be quiet a second, I could explain all the rules."

"I wasn't talking."

"Good. You give me a headache when you talk. Name-calling and Yoda quotes about chess and cryptic elephant stories. You want to play or not?"

He doesn't wait for an answer. He places a white pawn just in front of the black queen, saying that's him, the batter.

"You should lead off with your queen. She's the most powerful."

"That's why she bats cleanup." He shakes his head. My ignorance is astounding. "Real simple: Defense, that's you, flips first. Heads, it's a strike. Tails, a ball."

"A coin won't work," I point out. "There are three possibilities: strike, ball, or a hit."

"Actually, there are *four,* counting fouls. You stick to chess; I'll handle baseball."

"Chaseball," I correct him.

"*Anyway.* If you flip a ball, that's a ball, and you flip again. Comes up heads, though, and then I get the coin. See, that gives me a chance to get a hit. Heads I connect, tails I miss. If I miss, strike one. And so on."

"I get it. And if you flip heads, I get the coin back to see if I can field it. Heads I throw you out . . ."

"Wrong! So wrong! No. First *I* flip, three times. Four times if I get a TT."

"TT?"

"Two tails. That's a triple. With a TT you get one more flip: heads is a home run; tails, just a triple. Heads-heads is a single; heads-tails is a double."

"Maybe we should just start playing and you can—"

"*Then* you get the coin back to see if you can field my *potential* single, double, triple, or homer. Heads, I'm out. Tails, I'm on base." He takes a deep breath. "Unless it's a home run, of course."

"Of course."

"Are you making fun of me? Because I don't know—"

"I'm just trying to absorb—"

"It kind of sounds like you are. You have no idea how long it took me to come up with this. It's pretty complicated. I mean, not like the game of kings, but you know what they call baseball, don't you? The national pastime. Baseball is called the national pastime because, by playing it, we learn how to master time. Or the past. One of 'em."

"Now you're the one making fun of me."

"Actually, I'm the *only* one making fun of you right now." He waits. I know what he's waiting for. "You never smile."

"Does it matter?"

"Once, when I was a kid, I laughed so hard, I peed my pants. We were at Six Flags. The Ferris wheel."

"What made you laugh?"

"I can't remember now." He slides his hand beneath my wrist and lifts my arm to press the quarter into my upturned palm. "Flip the damn coin so we can play."

I don't want to hurt his feelings, but the game isn't that

complicated. He gets very excited on his first hit, triumphantly fist pumping, then proceeding to move the black pieces around the board while he calls the play in a hoarse, high-pitched imitation of an announcer's voice, like a kid playing with action figures.

"It's a deep drive into center field!" The center-field pawn slides toward second base, the bishop second baseman and the pawn shortstop drop back, and the left-field pawn runs up, then cuts toward center. That's with one hand while the other manipulates the quarter, turning it in his fingers like a ball spinning in flight, lowering it as if in slow motion to land in center-left field. It's so ridiculous and childish that I would have smiled if I still smiled.

"He's *safe*!" Razor bellows.

No. Not childish. Childlike. Eyes fever bright, voice rising in excitement, he's ten again. Not all things are lost, not the important things.

His next hit is a blooper that drops between first base and right field. He creates a dramatic collision between my fielder and baseman, first base sliding back, right field sliding up, then *smack!* Razor cackles at the impact.

"Wouldn't that be an error?" I ask. "It's a catchable ball."

"Catchable ball? Ringer, it's just a dorky game I made up in five minutes with a bunch of chess pieces and a quarter."

Two more hits; he's three runs up at the top of the first. I've always sucked at games of chance. Always hated them for that reason. Razor must sense my enthusiasm waning. He amps up the commentary while sliding the pieces around (despite my pointing out they're *my* pieces, since I'm on defense). Another drive deep center-left. Another floater behind first base. Another impact of first baseman and outfielder. I don't know if he's repeating himself because he thinks it's funny or because he has a serious deficit in imagination. There's a part of me that feels as if I should be deeply affronted on behalf of chess players everywhere.

By the third inning, I'm exhausted.

"Let's pick it up again tonight," I suggest. "Or tomorrow. Tomorrow would be better."

"What? You don't like it?"

"No. It's fun. I'm just tired. Really tired."

He shrugs like it doesn't matter, which it does, or he wouldn't shrug. He slips the quarter back into his pocket and packs up the box, muttering under his breath. I catch the word *chess*.

"What did you say?"

"Nothing." Cutting his eyes away.

"Something about chess."

"Chess, chess, chess. Chess on the brain. Sorry chaseball has nothing on chess in the sheer thrill category."

He shoves the box under his arm and stomps to the door. One last parting shot before he goes: "I thought maybe I'd cheer you up a little, that's all. Thanks. We don't have to play anymore."

"Are you angry at me?"

"I gave chess a chance, didn't I? You didn't see me bitching."

"You didn't. And you did. A lot."

"Just think about it."

"Think about what?"

He shouts across the room: "Just *think* about it!"

He slams out the door. I'm out of breath, shaky, and can't figure out why.

61

I'M READY WITH an apology when the door opens that night. The more I think about it with my feverish mind, the more I feel like the bully at the beach who kicks over some little kid's sand castle.

"Hey, Razor, I'm—"

My mouth drops open. There's a stranger holding the tray, a kid around twelve or thirteen.

"Where's Razor?" I ask. Well, more like demand.

"I don't know," the kid squeaks. "They handed me the tray and said take it."

"Take it," I echo stupidly.

"Yeah. Take it. Take the tray."

They pulled Razor off Ringer duty. Maybe chaseball's against regs. Maybe Vosch got ticked, two kids acting like kids for a couple of hours. Despair is addictive, for the one watching it and the one experiencing it.

Or maybe Razor's the ticked party here. Maybe he asked to be reassigned, took his chaseball and went home.

I don't sleep well that night, if you can call it night under the constant sterile glow. My fever shoots up to a hundred and three as my immune system launches its final, desperate assault on the arrays. I can see the blurry green numbers on the monitor inching upward. I slip into a semi-delirious doze.

Bitch! Leave me. You know why they call it baseball, don't you? It's a deep drive into center field! I'm done. Take care of yourself.

The grungy silver turning in Razor's fingers. *It's a deep drive. A deep drive.* Lowering toward the board in slow motion, where the fielders come up, second base and shortstop go back, left goes right. *Blooper on the first-base line!* Fielder races up, baseman back, *boom.* Fielders up, infield back, cut to the right. First baseman back, right fielder up, *boom.* Up, back, cut. Back, up. *Boom.*

Over and over, *let's go to the instant replay,* up, back, cut. Back, up.

Boom.

Now I'm wide-awake, staring at the ceiling. No. Can't see it as well. Better with my eyes closed.

Center and left slash down. Left cuts across:

H

Right steps up. First base runs back:

I

Oh, come on. Ridiculous. *You're delusional.*

When I got back to our camp that night with the vodka, I found my dead father curled into a fetal position, his face covered in blood where he had clawed at the bugs born inside his mind. *Bitch,* he called me before I left to find the poison that would save him. He called me another name, too, the name of the woman who left us when I was three. He thought I was my mother, which was ironic. From the time I was fourteen, I was more like *his* mother, feeding him, washing his clothes, taking care of the house, making sure he didn't do something catastrophically stupid to himself. And every day I went to school in my perfectly pressed uniform and they called me Her Majesty Marika and said I thought I was better than everybody else because my father was a semi-famous artist, the reclusive genius type, when the truth was that most days my father didn't know what planet he was on. By the time I got home from school, he'd be full-on delusional. And I let people on the outside hold their delusions, too. I let them think I thought I was better, the way I let Sullivan think she was right about me. I didn't just foster the delusions. I lived them. Even after the world crashed around us, I clung to them. But after he died, I told myself no more. No more brave fronts or false hopes or pretending everything's okay when nothing is. I thought I was being tough by pretending, calling it being optimistic, brave, keeping my head up or whatever bullshit seemed to fit the moment. That's not tough. That's the very definition of soft. I was ashamed of his disease and angry at him, but I was just as guilty. I played right into the lies right up to the end: When he called me my mother's name, I didn't correct him.

Delusional.

In the corner, the camera's blank, soulless eye staring.

What did Razor say? *Just think about it!*

That's not all you said, is it? I ask him, looking blankly back at the blank, black eye. *That isn't everything.*

62

I HOLD MY BREATH when the door opens the next morning.

All night I seesawed between belief and doubt. I wallowed in every aspect of the new reality.

First option: Razor didn't invent chaseball any more than I invented chess. The game is Vosch's creation for reasons too murky to see clearly.

Second option: Razor, for reasons only clear to Razor, has decided to seriously mess with my head. It wasn't just the hard-hearted and resilient who survived the winnowing of the human race. A lot of sadistic assholes persisted, too. That's the way of every human catastrophe. The douchebag is nearly indestructible.

Third option: All of it is entirely in my head. Chaseball is a silly game made up by a kid to take my mind off the fact that I may be dying. There's no other point, no secret messages traced on a chessboard. My seeing letters where there are no letters is the human brain's tendency to find patterns, even where there are no patterns.

And I hold my breath for another reason: What if it's the squeaky-voiced kid again? What if Razor doesn't come back, *ever* come back? There's a real possibility that Razor is dead. If he was trying to secretly communicate with me and Vosch figured it out, I'm sure Vosch's response would be one thing and only one thing.

I let out my breath slow and steady when he steps into the room. The beeping of the monitor kicks up a notch.

"What?" Razor asks, narrowing his eyes at me. He senses something's up right away.

I say it. "Hi."

His eyes cut right, cut left. "Hi." Drawing the tiny word out slowly, as if he's not sure if he's with a lunatic. "Hungry?"

I shake my head. "Not really."

"You should try to eat this. You look like my cousin Stacey. She was a meth addict. I don't mean you *literally* look like a meth addict. Just . . ." Face turning red. "You know, like something is eating you from the inside."

He pushes the button beside the bed. I rise. He says, "You know what I'm addicted to? Sour Patch Kids. Raspberry. Not so crazy about the lemon. I have a stash. I'll bring you some if you want."

He sets the tray in front of me. Cold scrambled eggs, fried potatoes, a blackened, crusty thing that may or may not be bacon. My stomach clenches. I look up at him.

"Try the eggs," he suggests. "They're fresh. Free range, organic, chemical free. We raise them right here in camp. The chickens, not the eggs."

Dark, soulful eyes and that small, mysterious, beatific smile. What did his reaction mean when I said hi? Was he startled I offered him a halfway human greeting or was he startled because I had figured out the real point of chaseball? Or was he not startled at all and I'm picking up cues that aren't there?

"I don't see the box."

"What box? Oh. It was kind of a stupid game." He looks away and says softly to himself, "I miss baseball."

He's quiet for the next couple of minutes while I move the cold eggs around the plate. *I miss baseball.* A universe of loss in four syllables.

"No, I liked it," I tell him. "It was fun."

"Really?" A look: *Are you serious?* He doesn't know that I am 99.99999 percent of the time. "You didn't seem too down with it at the time."

"I guess I'm just not feeling well lately."

He laughs and then seems surprised at his own reaction. "Okay. Well, I left it in my quarters. I'll bring it someday if nobody swipes it."

The conversation meanders off the game. I discover Razor was the youngest of five kids, grew up in Ann Arbor, where his dad worked as an electrician and his mom as a middle school librarian, played baseball and soccer and loved Michigan football. Until he was twelve, his great ambition was to be the starting quarterback for the Wolverines. But he grew tall, not big, and baseball became his passion.

"Mom wanted me to be a doctor or a lawyer, but the old man didn't think I was smart enough . . ."

"Wait. Your dad didn't think you were smart?"

"Smart *enough*. There's a difference." Defending his father even in death. People die; love endures. "He wanted me to be an electrician like him. Dad was a big union guy, president of his local, stuff like that. That was the real reason he didn't want me to be a lawyer. *Suits,* he called them."

"He had a problem with authority."

Razor shrugs. "'Be your own man,' he always said. 'Don't be the Man's man.'" He shuffles his feet, embarrassed, like he's talking too much. "What about your old man?"

"He was an artist."

"That's cool."

"He was also a drunk. Did more drinking than painting." Though not always. Yellowed photographs of showings hanging crooked in dusty frames and the students buzzing in his studio nervously cleaning brushes and the cathedral hush that fell when he walked into a crowded room.

"What kind of shit did he paint?" Razor asks.

"Mostly that. Shit." Not always, though. Not when he was younger and I was small and the hand that held mine was stained with rainbow colors.

He laughs. "The way you joke. Like you don't even know it's a joke, and it's your own joke."

I shake my head. "I wasn't joking."

He nods. "Maybe that's why you don't know it."

63

AFTER THE EVENING meal I don't eat and the forced banter and the minuscule awkward silences that drop between our sentences, and after the board comes out of the wooden box and he's set up the pieces and we flip to see who's the home team and he wins, I tell him I think I can handle my own fielding, and he smirks, *Yeah, right, let's go, girl,* after he's sitting beside me on the edge of the bed and after weeks of learning to let go of my rage and embrace the howling emptiness and after years of erecting fortress walls around pain and loss and the feeling that I will never feel again, after losing my father and losing Teacup and losing Zombie and losing everything but the howling emptiness and that is nothing, nothing at all, I silently say the word:

HI

Razor nods. "Yeah." He taps his finger on the blanket. I feel the tap against my thigh. "Yeah." Tap. "Not bad, though it's cooler when you do it in slo-mo." He demonstrates. "Get it now?"

"If you insist." I sigh. "Yeah." I tap my finger on the bedrail. "Well, to be honest I don't really see the point."

"No?" Tap-tap on the blanket.

"No." Tap-tap on the rail.

The next word takes over twenty minutes to trace:

HLP

Tap. "Did I ever tell you about my summer job before there were no more summer jobs?" he asks. "Dog grooming. Worst part of the job? Expressing the anal glands . . ."

He's on a roll. Four runs and not a single out.

HOW

I won't get an answer for another forty minutes. I'm a little tired and more than a little frustrated. This is like texting with someone a thousand miles away using one-legged runners. Time slows down; events speed up.

PLN

I have no idea what that means. I look at him but he's looking at the board, moving the pieces back into position, talking, filling in the tiny silences that drop, stuffing the empty space with chatter.

"That's what they actually called it: *expressing,*" he says, still on the dogs. "Rinse, wash, rinse, express, repeat. So freaking boring."

And the black, soulless, unblinking eye of the camera, staring down.

"I didn't understand that last play," I tell him.

"Chaseball isn't some lame-ass game like chess," he says patiently. "There are intricacies. *Intricacies.* To win, you gotta have a *plan.*"

"And that's you, I guess. The man with the plan."

"Yes, that's me."

Tap.

64

I HADN'T SEEN Vosch in days. That changes the next morning.

"Let's hear it," he tells Claire, who's standing beside Mr. White Coat looking like a middle-schooler dragged into the principal's office for bullying the scrawny kid.

"She's lost eight pounds and twenty percent of her muscle mass. She's on Diovan for the high blood pressure, Phenergan for the nausea, amoxicillin and streptomycin to keep her lymphatic system tamped down, but we're still struggling with the fever," Claire reports.

"'Struggling with the fever'?"

Claire's eyes cut away. "On the upside, her liver and kidneys are still functioning normally. A bit of fluid in her lungs, but we're—"

Vosch waves her off and steps up to my bedside. Bright bird eyes glittering.

"Do you want to live?"

I answer without hesitating. "Yes."

"Why?"

The question takes me off guard for some reason. "I don't understand."

"You cannot overcome us. No one can. Not if you numbered seven times seven billion when it began. The world is a clock and the clock has wound to its final second—why would you want to live?"

"I don't want to save the world," I tell him. "I'm just hoping I might get the opportunity to kill you."

His expression doesn't change, but his eyes glitter and dance. *I know you,* his eyes say. *I know you.*

"Hope," he whispers. "Yes." Nodding: He's pleased with me. "Hope, Marika. Cling to your hope." He turns to Claire and Mr. White Coat. "Pull her off the meds."

Mr. White Coat's face turns the color of his smock. Claire starts to say something, then looks away. Vosch turns back to me.

"What is the answer?" he demands. "It isn't rage. What is it?"

"Indifference."

"Try again."

"Detachment."

"Again."

"Hope. Despair. Love. Hate. Anger. Sorrow." I'm shaking; my fever must be spiking. "I don't know. I don't know. I don't know."

"Better," he says.

65

IT GETS SO BAD that night, I can barely make it through four innings of chaseball.

XMEDS

"Heard a rumor going around they took you off your meds," Razor says, shaking the quarter in his closed fist. "True?"

"The only thing left in my IV bag is saline to keep my kidneys from shutting down."

He glances at my vitals on the monitor. Frowning. When Razor frowns, he reminds me of a little boy who's stubbed his toe and thinks he's too big to cry.

"So you must be getting better."

"Guess so." Tap-tap on the bedrail.

"Okay," he breathes. "My queen is up. Look out."

My back stiffens. My vision blurs. I lean to the side and empty my stomach, what little is inside my stomach, onto the white tile. Razor leaps up with a disgusted cry, toppling the board.

"Hey!" he shouts. Not at me. At the black eye above us. "Hey, a little help here!"

No help comes. He looks at the monitor, looks at me, and says, "I don't know what to do."

"I'm okay."

"Sure. You're fine, just fine!" He goes to the sink, wets a clean towel, and lays it across my forehead. "Fine, my ass! Why the hell did they take you off the meds?"

"Why not?" I'm fighting the urge to hurl again.

"Oh, I don't know. Maybe because you'll *die* without them." He glares at the camera.

"Maybe you should hand me that container over there."

He dabs at the crud sticking on my chin, refolds the cloth, grabs the container, and places it on my lap.

"Razor."

"Yeah?"

"Please don't put that back on my face."

"Huh? Oh. Shit. Yeah. Hang on." He grabs a clean towel and runs it under the water. His hands are shaking. "You know what it is? I know what it is. Why didn't I think of it? Why didn't *you* think of it? The meds must be interfering with the system."

"What system?"

"The 12th System. The one they injected into you, Sherlock. The hub and his forty thousand little friends to supercharge the other eleven." He puts the cool towel on my forehead. "You're cold. You want me to find another blanket?"

"No, I'm burning up."

"It's a war," he says. He taps his chest. "In here. You gotta declare a truce, Ringer."

I shake my head. "No peace."

He nods, squeezing my wrist beneath the thin blanket. Squats on the floor to gather the fallen chess pieces. Curses when he can't find the quarter. Decides he can't leave the vomit just lying there. Grabs the dirty towel he used to wipe my chin and swabs the deck on his hands and knees. He's still cursing when the door opens and Claire comes into the room.

"Good timing!" Razor barks at her. "Hey, can't you at least give her the anti-puke serum?"

Claire jerks her head toward the door. "Get out." She points at the box. "And take that with you."

Razor glowers at her, but he does it. I see again the tightly contained force behind his angelic features. *Careful, Razor. That's not the answer.*

Then we're alone, and Claire studies the monitor for a long, silent moment.

"Were you telling the truth earlier?" she asks. "You want to live so you can kill Commander Vosch? You're smarter than that." In the tone of a mother scolding a very young child.

"You're right," I answer. "I'll never get that chance. But I'm going to have the opportunity to kill you."

She looks startled. "Kill me? Why would you want to kill me?" When I don't answer, she says, "I don't think you're going to live through the night."

I nod. "And you're not going to live out the month."

She laughs. The sound of her laughter causes bile to rise into my throat. Burning. Burning.

"What are you going to do?" she says softly. She yanks the towel from my forehead. "Smother me with this?"

"No. I'm going to overcome the guard by smashing his head in with a heavy object, and then I'm going to take his gun and shoot you in the face."

She laughs through the whole thing. "Well, good luck with that."

"It won't be luck."

66

CLAIRE TURNS OUT to be wrong about me being dead by morning.

Nearly a month later, by my reckoning of three meals per day, and I'm still here.

I don't remember much. At some point they disconnected me from the IV and the monitor, and the silence that slammed down after the constant beeping was loud enough to crack mountains. The only person I saw during that time was Razor. He's my full-time caretaker now. Feeds me, empties my bedpan, washes my face and hands, turns me so I don't develop bedsores, plays chaseball in the hours when I'm not delirious, and talks non-stop. He talks about everything, which is another way of saying he talks about nothing. His dead family, his dead friends, his squad mates, the drudgery of winter camp, the fights borne of boredom and fatigue and fear (but mostly fear), the rumors that when spring comes the Teds are launching a major offensive, a last-ditch effort to purge the world of the human noise, of which Razor is very much an active part. He talks and talks and talks.

He had a girlfriend, her name was Olivia and her skin was dark like a muddy river and she played clarinet in the school band and was going to be a doctor and hated Razor's dad because he didn't think Razor could be a doctor. He lets it slip that his given name is Alex like A-Rod and his drill sergeant named him Razor not because he was slender but because he cut himself shaving one morning. *I have very sensitive skin.* His sentences are without periods, without commas, without paragraphs, or, to be accurate, it's all one long paragraph with no margins.

He shuts up just one time after nearly a month of the verbal diarrhea. He's going on about how he won first place in the fifth-grade science fair with his project about how to turn a potato into a battery when he stops in midsentence. His silence is jarring, like the stillness after a building implodes.

"What is that?" he asks, staring intently into my face, and nobody stares more intently than Razor, not even Vosch.

"Nothing." I turn my head away from him.

"Are you crying, Ringer?"

"My eyes are watering."

"No."

"Don't tell me no, Razor. I don't cry."

"Bullshit." A tap on the blanket.

Tap-tap on the railing. "Did it work?" I ask, turning back to him. What does it matter if he sees me cry? "The potato battery."

"Sure it worked. It's *science.* Never a doubt about it working. You plan it all out, follow the steps, and it can't go wrong." Squeezing my hand through the blanket: *Don't be scared. Everything's set. I won't let you down.*

It's too late to go back now anyway: His eyes wander to the food tray beside the bed. "You ate all the pudding tonight. You know how they make chocolate pudding without chocolate? You don't want to know."

"Let me guess. Ex-Lax."

"What's Ex-Lax?"

"Seriously? You don't know?"

"Oh, so sorry I don't know what Ex-Lax-who-gives-a-shit is."

"It's a chocolate-flavored laxative."

He makes a face. "That's sick."

"That's the point."

He grins. "The point? Oh God, did you just make a *joke*?"

"How would I know? Just promise me nobody slipped Ex-Lax into my pudding."

"Promise." *Tap.*

I last for a few hours after he leaves, long after lights-out in every other part of the camp, deep into the belly of the winter night, before the pressure becomes unbearable, and then, when I can't take it anymore, I start shouting for help, waving at the camera and then rolling over to press my chest against the cold metal railings, pounding my fist into the pillow in frustration and fury, until the door bursts open and Claire charges in, followed closely by a big bear of a recruit, whose hand immediately flies to cover his nose.

"What happened?" Claire says, though the smell should tell her all she needs to know.

"Oh, crap!" the recruit burbles behind his hand.

"Exactly," I gasp.

"Great. Just great," Claire says, throwing the blanket and sheet onto the floor and motioning for the recruit to help her. "Fine job, missy. I hope you're proud of yourself."

"Not yet," I whimper.

"What are you doing?" Claire shouts at the recruit. Gone is the soft voice. Vanished are the kind eyes. "Help me with this."

"Help you with what, ma'am?" He has a flattened nose and very small eyes and a forehead that bulges in the middle. His belly hangs over his belt and his pants are an inch too short. He's huge; he's got about a hundred pounds or more on me.

It won't matter.

"Get up," Claire snaps at me. "Come on. Get your legs under you." She takes one arm and Jumbo Recruit takes the other and together they haul me out of the bed. Big Recruit's smushed-in face is twisted with revulsion.

"Ah, God. It's everywhere!" he softly wails.

"I don't think I can walk," I tell Claire.

"Then I'll make you crawl," she snarls. "I should just leave you like this. It's so perfectly metaphorical."

They haul me two doors down and into the shower room. Big Recruit is coughing and gagging and Claire is bitching and I'm apologizing while she strips off the jumpsuit and throws it at Jumbo Recruit, telling him to wait outside. "Don't lean on *me.* Lean on the *wall,*" she orders harshly. My knees are buckling. I hang on to the shower curtain to keep upright; I haven't used my legs in a month.

With one hand locked around my left arm, Claire pushes me under the water, bending at the waist to stay dry. The spray is icy. She didn't bother to adjust the temperature. The slap of cold water against my body is like an alarm going off, snapping me from a long winter's hibernation, and I reach up and grab the showerhead pipe coming from the wall and tell Claire I think I've got it; I think I can stand; she can let go.

"Are you sure?" she asks, holding on.

"Pretty sure."

I wrench the pipe downward with all the force I have. The pipe breaks off at the joint with a metallic squeal and the cold water gushes out in a ropey snarl. Left arm up, slipping through Claire's fingers, then I've got her by the wrist and I swing my body toward her, rotating my hips to maximize the blow, and slam the jagged edge of the broken pipe into her neck.

I wasn't sure I could break a steel pipe with my bare hands, but I was pretty sure.

I have been enhanced.

67

CLAIRE STAGGERS AWAY, blood pouring from the two-inch puncture wound in her neck. The fact that I didn't drop her doesn't surprise me; I'd assumed she would be enhanced, too, but I'd hoped to get lucky and sever her carotid artery. She fumbles in the pocket of her lab coat for the kill switch. I anticipated that. I toss the broken pipe away, grab the bolted-in shower rod, break it from its brackets and smash one end into the side of her head.

The impact barely rocks her. In a millisecond, faster than my eyes can follow the motion, she has the end of the rod in her grip. I let go in half a millisecond, so when she yanks there's nothing holding the other end, and she stumbles back into the wall, hitting with enough force to crack the tiles. I barrel toward her. She swings the rod toward my head, but I anticipated that, too—counted on it, when I rehearsed this in the thousand silent hours beneath the constant glow.

I grab the other end of the rod as it arcs toward me, first with my right hand, then with the left, hands shoulder-width apart, and power the rod into her neck, spreading my legs for the balance and leverage necessary to crush her windpipe.

Our faces are inches apart. I'm close enough to smell the cyanide breath trickling out of her parted lips.

Her hands are on either side of mine, pushing back while I push forward. The floor is slick; I'm barefoot, she isn't; I'm going to lose the advantage before she blacks out. I have to drop her—fast.

I slide my foot to the inside of her ankle and kick out. Perfect: She falls to the floor and I follow her down.

She lands on her back. I land on her stomach. I clamp my knees tightly against her sides and shove the rod down hard into her neck.

Then the door behind us flies open and Jumbo Recruit lumbers in, gun drawn, shouting incoherently. Three minutes in and the light in Claire's eyes is fading, but it's not all the way out, and I know I have to take a risk. I don't like risk, never did; I just learned to accept it. Some things you can choose and some you can't, like Sullivan's Crucifix Soldier, like Teacup, like going back for Zombie and Nugget because not going back meant there's no value to anything anymore, not life, not time, not promises.

And I have a promise to keep.

Jumbo's gun: The 12th System locks in on it and thousands of microscopic droids go to work augmenting the muscles, tendons, and nerves in my hands, eyes, and brain to neutralize the threat. In a microsecond, objective identified, information processed, method determined.

Jumbo doesn't have a prayer.

The attack happens faster than his unenhanced brain can process it. I doubt he even sees the curtain rod whizzing toward his hand. The gun flies across the room. He goes one way—for the gun—while I go the other—for the toilet.

The tank lid is solid ceramic. And heavy. I could kill him; I don't. But I smack him hard enough in the back of head to put him out for a long time.

Jumbo falls down. Claire rises up. I sling the lid toward her head. Her arm rises to block the projectile. My enriched hearing picks up the sound of a bone snapping from the collision. The silver device in her hand clatters to the floor. She dives for it as I step forward. I slam one foot on her outstretched hand and with the other kick the device to the other side of the room.

Done.

And she knows it. She looks past the barrel of the gun leveled at her face—beyond the tiny hole filled with immense nothingness—into my eyes, and hers are kind again and her voice is soft again, the bitch.

"Marika . . ."

No. Marika was slow, weak, sentimental, dimwitted. Marika was a little girl clinging to rainbow fingers, helplessly watching the time wind down, teetering on the razor's edge of the bottomless abyss, exposed behind her fortress walls by promises she could never keep. But I will keep her final promise to Claire, the beast who stripped her naked and baptized her in the cold water that still roars in the broken shower. I will keep Marika's promise. Marika is dead, and I will keep her promise.

"My name is Ringer."

I pull the trigger.

68

JUMBO SHOULD HAVE a knife on him. Standard issue for all recruits. I kneel beside his unconscious body, slip the knife from its sheath, and carefully cut out the pellet embedded near the spinal cord at the base of his skull. I slip it between my cheek and gums.

Now mine. No pain when I cut it out, and only a small amount of blood trickles from the incision. Bots to deaden sensation. Bots to repair damage. That's why Claire didn't die when I rammed a broken pipe into her neck and why, after the initial gush, the bleeding quickly stopped.

Also why, after six weeks flat on my back with very little food and a burst of intense physical activity, I'm not even out of breath.

I insert the tiny pellet from my neck into Jumbo's. *Track me now, Commander Asshole.*

Fresh jumpsuit from the stack under the sink. Shoes: Claire's feet are too small; Jumbo's much too large. I'll work on shoes later. The big kid's leather jacket might come in handy, though. The jacket hangs on me like a blanket, but I like the extra room in the sleeves.

There's something I'm forgetting. I glance around the small room. The kill switch, that's it. The screen got cracked in the melee, but the device still works. A number glows above the flashing green button. My number. I swipe my thumb over the display and the screen fills with numbers, hundreds of sequences representing every recruit on the base. I swipe again to return to my number, tap on it, and a map pops up showing my implant's precise location. I zoom out and the screen fills with tiny, glowing green dots: the location of every implanted soldier in the entire base. Jackpot.

And checkmate. With a swipe of my thumb and a tap of my finger, I can highlight all the numbers. The button on the bottom of the device will light up. A final tap and every recruit neutralized, gone. I can practically stroll out.

I can—if I'm willing to step over several hundred corpses of innocent human beings, kids who are no less victims than I am, whose sole crime is the sin of hope. If the wage of sin is death, then virtue is a vice now: A defenseless, starving child lost in a wheat field is given shelter. A wounded soldier cries out for help behind a row of beer coolers. A little girl shot by mistake is delivered to her enemies in order to save her.

And I don't know which is more inhuman: the alien beings that created this new world or the human being who considers, if only for an instant, pressing the green button.

Three large clumps of stationary dots hover on the right side of the screen: the sleeping. A dozen isolated individuals on the periphery: sentries. Two in the middle: mine in Jumbo's neck, his in my mouth. Another three or four very close, on the same floor: the sick and injured. One floor down, the ICU, where only one green sphere glows. So: barracks, observation posts, hospital. A couple of the sentry dots are manning the magazine building. I won't have to guess which two. I'll know in a few minutes.

Come on, Razor, let's go. I've got one last promise to keep.

Watching the gusher pour from the broken pipe.

69

"DO YOU PRAY?" Razor asked me after an exhausting night of chaseball, while he packed up the game board and pieces.

I shook my head. "Do you?"

"Damn right I do." Nodding his head emphatically. "No atheists in foxholes."

"My father was one."

"A foxhole?"

"An atheist."

"I know that, Ringer."

"How did you know my father was an atheist?"

"I didn't."

"Then why did you ask if he was a foxhole?"

"I didn't. It was a freaking—" He smiled. "Oh, I get it. I know what you're doing. The disturbing thing to me is *why.* Like you're not trying to be funny but trying to prove how superior you are. Or think you are. You're not either. Funny *or* superior. Why don't you pray?"

"I don't like putting God on the spot."

He picked up the queen and examined her face. "You ever checked her out? She is one scary-looking she-bitch."

"I think she looks regal."

"She looks like my third-grade teacher, a lot of *man* and very little *wo.*"

"What?"

"You know: heavy on the *male,* light on the *fe.*"

"She's just fierce. A warrior queen."

"My third-grade teacher?" He studied my face. Waiting. Waiting. "Sorry, tried that joke once. Epic fail." He placed the piece in the box. "My grandma belonged to a prayer circle. You know what a prayer circle is?"

"Yes."

"Really? I thought you were an atheist."

"My father was an atheist. And why couldn't an atheist know what a prayer circle is? Religious people know about evolution."

"I know what it is. I've got it," he said thoughtfully, dark, intense eyes still on my face. "You were, like, five or six and some relative remarked in a very positive way what a *serious* little girl you were, and from then on, you thought seriousness was attractive."

"What happened in the prayer circle?" Attempting to get him back on track.

"Ha! So you *don't* know what it is!" He set the box down and scooched farther onto the bed. His butt now touching my thigh. I eased my leg away. Subtly, I hoped. "I'll tell you what happened. My grandma's dog got sick. One of those purse dogs that bites everybody and lives about twenty-five years, biting people. So her petition had to do with God saving that mean little dog so it could bite *more* people. And half the old ladies in her group agreed and half didn't, I'm not sure why, I mean a God who doesn't like dogs wouldn't be God, but anyway, there was this big debate about wasted prayer, which became an argument about if there could be such a thing as wasted prayer, which turned into a fight about the Holocaust. So in five minutes it went from a nippy old purse dog to the Holocaust."

"So what happened? Did they pray for the dog?"

"No, they prayed for the souls of the Holocaust. Then the

next day the dog died." And now he was nodding thoughtfully. "Grandma prayed for him. Prayed every night. Told all us grandkids to pray, too. So I prayed for a dog that terrorized and hated me and gave me this." He swung his leg onto the bed and pulled up his pants to expose his calf. "See the scar?"

I shook my head. "No."

"Well, it's there." He pushed down the pants leg but kept his foot on the bed. "So after it died, I said to Grandma, 'I prayed really hard and Flubby still died. Does God hate me?'"

"What did she say?"

"Some BS about God wanting Flubby in heaven, which was impossible for my six-year-old brain to process. There are nippy old purse dogs in heaven? Isn't heaven supposed to be a *nice* place? It bothered me for a long time. Like, every night, while I said my prayers, I couldn't help but wonder if I even *wanted* to go to heaven and spend eternity with Flubby. So I decided he must be in hell. Otherwise, theology falls apart."

He wrapped his long arms around his upraised knee, where he rested his chin and stared into space. He was back in a time when a little boy's questions about prayer and God and heaven still mattered.

"I broke a cup once," he went on. "Playing around in Mom's china cabinet, part of her wedding set, this dainty little cup from a tea set. Didn't totally break it. Dropped it on the floor and it cracked."

"The floor?"

"No, not the floor. The cu—" His eyes widened in shock. "Did you just make the same . . . ?"

I shook my head. He pointed his finger at me. "Naw, I caught you! A moment of lighthearted levity from Ringer the warrior queen!"

"I joke all the time."

"Right. But they're so subtle that only *smart* people get them."

"The cup," I prodded him.

"So I've cracked Mom's precious china. I put it back in the cabinet, turning its cracked side toward the back so maybe she won't notice, even though I know it's only a matter of time before she does and I'm dead meat. Know where I turn for help?"

I didn't have to think hard. I knew where the story was going. "God."

"God. I prayed for God to keep Mom away from that cup. Like, for the rest of her life. Or at least until I moved away to college. Then I prayed that he could heal the cup. He's God, right? He can heal people—what's a tiny freaking made-in-China cup? That was the optimal solution and that's what he's all about, optimal solutions."

"She found the cup."

"You bet your ass she found the cup."

"I'm surprised you still pray. After Flubby and the cup."

He shook his head. "Not the point."

"There's a point?"

"If you'd let me finish the story—yes, there is a point. Here it is: *After* she found the cup and *before* I knew she'd found it, she replaced it. She ordered a new cup and threw away the old one. One Saturday morning—I guess I'd been praying for about a month—I went to the cabinet to prove the prayer circle wrong about wasted prayer, and I saw it."

"The new cup," I said. Razor nodded. "But you didn't know your mom replaced it."

He threw his hands into the air. "It's a fucking miracle! What's cracked has been uncracked! The broken made whole! God exists! I nearly crapped my pants."

"The cup was healed," I said slowly.

His dark eyes dug deep into mine. His hand fell to my knee. A squeeze. Then a tap.

Yes.

70

IN THE BATHROOM, the gush becomes a stream, the stream becomes a trickle, the trickle becomes an anemic dribble. The water slows and my heart quickens. My paranoia was getting the better of me. A decade passed while I waited for the water to be cut off: the go signal from Razor.

The hall outside is deserted. I already know that thanks to Claire's tracking device. I also know exactly where I'm going.

Stairs. One flight down. One last promise. I pause long enough on the landing to slip Jumbo's sidearm into the jacket pocket.

Then I slam through the door and hit the hall running. Straight ahead is the nurses' station. I sprint straight toward it. The nurse pops out of her chair.

"Take cover!" I shout. "It's going to blow!"

I swerve past the counter and race toward the swinging doors that lead to the ward.

"Hey!" she shouts. "You can't go back there!"

Any day now, Razor.

She hits the lockdown button on her desk. It doesn't matter. I hurtle into the doors at full speed and smash both off their hinges.

"*Freeze!*" she screams.

The entire length of the hallway remains; I won't make it. I've been enhanced, but I can't outrun a bullet. I skitter to a halt.

Razor, I'm serious. Now would be a very good time.

"Hands on your head! *Now.*" Struggling to catch her breath. "Good job. Now walk toward me, *backward.* Slow. Very slow, or I swear to God I'll shoot you."

I obey, shuffling toward the sound of her voice. She orders me to stop. I stop. I'm still, but the mechanisms inside me aren't. Her position is fixed: I don't have to see her to know exactly where she's standing. The hub's dispatched the managers of my muscular and nervous systems to execute the directive when called upon. I won't have to think when the time comes. The hub will take over.

But I won't owe my life entirely to the 12th System: It was my idea to grab Jumbo's jacket.

And that reminds me:

"Shoes," I murmur.

"What did you say?" Her voice is quivering.

"I need shoes. What size are you?"

"Huh?"

At the speed of light the hub's signal fires. My body doesn't move quite that fast, but double the speed that is probably necessary.

Right hand jams into Jumbo's baggy sleeve, where I slipped the ten-inch knife, pivot to the left, then throw.

And down she goes.

I pull the knife from her neck, slide the bloody blade back into the left sleeve of the jacket, and check out her shoes. A pair of those white, thick-soled nurse's shoes. A half size too big, but they'll work.

At the end of the hallway, I step into the last room on the right. It's dark, but my eyes have been enhanced: I can see her clearly in the bed, fast asleep. Or doped. I'll have to determine which.

"Teacup? It's me. Ringer."

The thick, dark lashes flutter. I'm so jacked up by this point, I swear I can hear the tiny hairs thrumming the air.

She whispers something without opening her eyes. Too soft for the unenhanced to hear, but the auditory bots transmit the information to the hub, which relays it to the inferior colliculus, the hearing center of my brain.

"You're dead."

"Not anymore. And neither are you."

71

THE WINDOW BESIDE the bed jiggles in its frame. The floor quivers. Bright orange light floods the room, winks out, then an earsplitting roar and a fine mist of plaster floating down from the ceiling. The sequence repeats. Then again. Then again.

Razor's hit the magazine building.

"Teacup, we have to go." I slide one hand behind her head and lift gently.

"Go where?"

"As far as we can."

Bracing the back of her head with one hand, I hit her in the forehead with the heel of the other. The precise amount of force, no more, no less. Her body goes limp. I heave her out of the bed. Another blast as the ordnance in the magazine continues to detonate. I kick out the window. Bitter cold air crashes into the room. I sit on the sill facing the bed, cradling Teacup against my chest. My intent alerts the hub: I'm two stories above the ground. Reinforcements race to the bones and tendons in my feet, ankles, shins, knees, and pelvis.

We deploy.

I flip as we drop, like a cat falling off a countertop. We land safely, like a cat, except Teacup's head bounces up on impact and smacks me hard under the chin. In front of us the hospital. Behind us the blazing ammunition storehouse. And to our right, exactly where Razor said it would be, the black Dodge M882.

I throw open the door, shove Teacup into the passenger seat, jump behind the wheel, and take off across the parking lot, cutting hard to the left to make the turn north toward the airfield. A siren screams. Floodlights blare. In the rearview mirrors, emergency vehicles race toward the burning magazine. The fire brigade will have a hard time of it since *someone* has shut down the pumping station.

Another hard left, and now straight ahead are the hulking bodies of the Black Hawks, glistening like the bodies of black beetles in the harsh light of the floods. I grip the wheel hard and take a deep breath. This is the trickiest part. If Razor couldn't kidnap a pilot, we're all screwed.

A hundred yards away, I see someone jump from one of the choppers' holds. He's wearing a heavy parka and toting an assault rifle. His face is partially obscured by the hood, but I'd know that smile anywhere.

I hop from the M882.

And Razor says, "Hi."

"Where's the pilot?" I ask.

He jerks his head toward the cockpit. "I got mine. Where's yours?"

I pull Teacup from the truck and jump inside the chopper. A guy wearing nothing but a drab green T-shirt and a matching pair of boxer shorts sits behind the controls. Razor slides into the co-pilot seat beside him.

"Fire her up, Lieutenant Bob." Razor grins at the pilot. "Oh. Manners. Ringer, Lieutenant Bob. Lieutenant Bob, Ringer."

"There's no way this is going to work," Lieutenant Bob says. "They'll come after us hard."

"Yeah? What's this?" Razor holds up a mass of tangled electrical wire.

The pilot shakes his head. So cold, his lips are turning blue. "I don't know."

"Neither do I, but I'm guessing they're very important for the proper operation of a helicopter."

"You don't understand . . ."

Razor leans toward him and all his playfulness is gone. His deep-set eyes burn as if backlit and the coiled force I sensed from the beginning springs free with such ferocity, I actually flinch.

"Listen to me, you alien sonofabitch, you fire this mother-effing stick buddy up ASAP or I'm—"

The pilot shoves his hands into his lap and stares straight ahead. After getting one into the chopper undetected, my biggest concern was getting a pilot to cooperate. I lean forward, grab Bob by the wrist, and bend his pinky finger backward.

"I'll break it," I promise him.

"Go ahead!"

I break it. His teeth clamp down on his bottom lip. His legs jerk. His eyes swim with tears. That shouldn't happen. I press my fingers against the back of his neck, then turn to Razor.

"He's implanted. He isn't one of them."

"Yeah, well, who the hell are *you*?" the pilot squeals.

I pull the tracking device from my pocket. There's the hospital and the magazine surrounded by a swarm of green dots. And there are three dots glowing on the airstrip.

"You cut yours out," I say to Razor.

He's nodding. "And left it under my pillow. That was the plan. Or was that the plan? Shit, Ringer, wasn't that the plan?" A little panicky.

I drop the knife into my hand. "Hold him."

Razor understands immediately. He grabs Lieutenant Bob and puts him in a headlock. Bob doesn't put up much resistance. I worry now that he might go into shock. If he does, it's over.

There isn't much light and Razor can't hold him perfectly still, so I tell Bob to chill or I might sever his spinal cord, adding paralysis to the problem of a broken finger. I pull out the pellet, toss it onto the tarmac, yank Bob's head back, and whisper in his ear, "I'm not the enemy and I haven't gone Dorothy. I'm just like you—"

"Only better," Razor finishes. He glances through the window and says, "Uh, Ringer . . ."

I see them: The glow of headlights expanding like a pair of stars going supernova. "They're coming, and when they get here, they will kill us," I tell Bob. "You too. They won't believe you and they will kill you."

Bob stares into my face, tears of pain streaming down his.

"You have to trust me," I say.

"Or she'll break another finger," Razor adds.

A deep, shuddering breath, shaking uncontrollably, cradling his wounded hand, blood trickling down his neck and soaking into the collar of his T-shirt. "It's hopeless," he whispers. "They'll just shoot us down."

On impulse, I reach forward and press my hand against his cheek. He doesn't recoil. He becomes very still. I don't understand why I touched him or what's happening now that I am, but I feel something opening inside me, like a bud spreading its delicate petals toward the sun. I'm freezing cold. My neck is on fire. And the little finger on my right hand throbs to the beat of my heart. The pain brings tears to my eyes. *His* pain.

"Ringer!" Razor barks. "What the hell are you *doing*?"

I pour my warmth into the man I touch. I douse the fire. I caress the pain. I soothe his fear. His breath evens out. His body relaxes.

"Bob, we really have to go," I tell him.

And two minutes later, we do.

72

AS WE ASCEND, the truck screeches to a stop and a tall man steps out, and his face is a study in deep shadows thrown by the floods, but I see his eyes with eyes enhanced, bright and hard like the crows' in the woods, polished blue while the crows' were black, and it must be a trick of light or shadow, the small, tight smile he seems to wear.

"Keep us low," I order Bob.

"Where are we going?"

"South."

The chopper banks; the ground rushes toward us. I see the magazine burning and the spinning lights of the fire trucks and recruits swarming around like ants. We pass over a river, black water sparking in the spillover light from the floods. Behind us now, the camp is an oasis of light in a desert of winter dark. We plunge into that dark, skimming six feet above the treetops.

I slide into the seat next to Teacup, lean her into my chest, and pull her hair to one side. I hope this is the last time I have to do this. When I'm done, I crush the implant with the heel of the knife.

Razor's voice squawks in my headset: "How's she doing?"

"Okay, I think."

"How're *you* doing?"

"Good."

"Glitches?"

"Minor. You?"

"Smooth as a newborn baby's ass."

I ease Teacup back into the seat, stand up, and open compartments until I find the chutes. Razor rattles on as I check the assemblies.

"Anything you want to say to me? Like, I don't know, *Thank you, Razor, for saving my ass from a lifetime of alien servitude after I punched you in the throat and generally acted like a douchebag*? Something along those lines? You know, it wasn't exactly like taking a walk in baseball, secret codes embedded in bogus games and slipping laxative in pudding and rigging explosives and stealing trucks and kidnapping pilots with fingers for you to break. Maybe *Hey, Razor, I couldn't have done it without you. You rock*. Something like that. Doesn't have to be word-for-word, just something to capture the general spirit."

"Why did you?" I ask. "What made you decide to trust me?"

"What you said that day about the kids—turning kids into bombs. I did some asking around. Next thing I know, I'm in the Wonderland chair and then they take me to the commander and he's all down on my ass about something *you* said, and he orders me to stop talking to you because he can't order me to stop *listening,* and the more I think about it, the stinkier it gets. They train us to terminate Teds and then load down toddlers with alien ordnance? Who're the good guys here? And then I'm like, who am *I* here? It got really angsty, a real existential crisis. What tipped it for me, though, was the math."

"Math?"

"Yeah, math. Aren't all you Asians really good at math?"

"Don't be racist. And I'm three-quarters Asian."

"'Three-quarters.' See? *Math*. It comes down to simple addition. As in it doesn't add up. Okay, so maybe we get lucky and seize the Wonderland program from them. Even super-superior aliens can screw up, nobody's perfect. But we don't just snatch Wonderland. We have their bombs, we have their track-and-kill implants, their super-sophisticated nanobot system—shit, we even have the technology capable of *detecting them.* Wha duh fuh? We've got more of their weapons than they do! But the real kicker came that day they jacked you up, when Vosch said they lied to us about the organism attached to human brains. Unbelievable!"

"Because if that's a lie . . ."

"Then everything's a lie."

Below us the land is covered in a blanket of white. The horizon is indiscernible in the dark, lost. *Everything is a lie.* I thought of my dead father telling me that I belonged to them now. Instinctively, I gather Teacup's little hand into mine: *truth*.

I hear Bob say in the headset, "I'm confused."

"Relax, Bob," Razor says. "Hey, *Bob*. Wasn't that the major's name at Camp Haven? What's it with officers and the name Bob?"

An alarm sounds. I return Teacup's hand to her lap and shuffle forward. "What is it?"

"Company," Bob says. "Six o'clock."

"Choppers?"

"Negative. F-15s. Three of them."

"How much time before they're in range?"

He shakes his head. Despite the cold, his shirt is soaked in sweat. His face shines with it. "Five to seven."

"Bring us up," I tell him. "Maximum altitude."

I grab a couple parachute rigs and drop one into Razor's lap.

"We're bailing?" he asks.

"We can't engage and we can't outrun. You're with Teacup. Tandem jump."

"I'm with Teacup? Who are you with?"

Bob glances at the other rig in my hand. "I'm not bailing," he says. And then, just in case I didn't hear or don't understand: "I'm. Not. Bailing."

No plan is perfect. I'd planned for a Silencer Bob, which meant my plan entailed killing him before we bailed from the chopper. Now it's complicated. I didn't kill Jumbo for the same reason I don't want to kill Bob. Kill enough Jumbos, murder enough Bobs, and you've plunged to the same depths as the ones who shove a bomb down a toddler's throat.

I shrug to hide my uncertainty. Toss the rig into his lap. "Then I guess you get incinerated."

We're at five thousand feet. Dark sky, dark ground, no horizon, all dark. The bottom of the lightless sea. Razor is looking at the radar screen, but he says to me, "Where's your chute, Ringer?"

I ignore the question. "Can you give me a sixty-second ETA on their range?" I ask Bob. He nods. Razor asks the question again. "It's math," I tell him. "Which I'm three-quarters really good at. If there are four of us and they mark two chutes, that leaves at least one of us on board. One, maybe two of them will stay with the chopper, at least until they can take it down. It'll buy time."

"What makes you think they'll stay with the chopper?"

I shrug. "It's what I'd do."

"Still doesn't answer my question about your chute."

"They're hailing us," Bob announces. "Ordering us to set it down."

"Tell them to suck it," Razor says. He stuffs a piece of bubble gum into his mouth. Taps his ear. "Popping's bad." Jams the gum wrapper into his pocket. Notices I'm watching and smiles. "Never noticed all the crap in the world until there was nobody left to pick it up," he explains. "The Earth is my charge."

Then Bob calls out, "Sixty seconds!"

I tug on Razor's parka. *Now.*

He looks up at me and says slowly and distinctly, "Where's your freaking chute?"

I haul him out of the seat one-handed. He chirps in surprise, stumbling toward the back. I follow him, squat in front of Teacup to remove her harness.

"Forty seconds!"

"How are we going to find you?" Razor yells, standing right next to me.

"Head for the fire."

"What fire?"

"Thirty seconds!"

I haul open the hatch door. The blast of air that punches into the hold blows Razor's hood off his head. I scoop up Teacup and press her into his chest.

"Don't let her die."

He nods.

"*Promise.*"

Nods again: "I promise."

"Thank you, Razor," I say. "For everything."

He leans forward and kisses me hard on the mouth.

"Don't ever do that again," I tell him.

"Why? Because you liked it or because you didn't?"

"Both."

"Fifteen seconds!"

Razor maneuvers Teacup over his shoulder, grabs the safety cable, and shuffles back until his heels touch the jump pad. Silhouetted in the opening, the boy and the child over the boy's shoulder, and five thousand feet beneath them, the limitless dark. *The Earth is my charge.*

Razor releases the cable. He doesn't seem to fall. He is sucked out into the ravenous void.

73

I HEAD BACK to the cockpit, where I find the pilot's door unlatched, the seat empty, and no Bob.

I wondered why the countdown stopped; now I know: He changed his mind about the whole bailing issue.

We must be in range, which means they don't intend to shoot us down. They've marked the location of Razor's drop, and they'll stay with the chopper until I bail or it runs out of fuel and I'm forced to bail. By this point, Vosch has figured out why Jumbo's implant is on this aircraft while its owner is in the infirmary being treated for a very bad headache.

With the tip of my tongue, I push the pellet from my mouth and lick it onto my palm.

Do you want to live?

Yes, and you want that, too, I tell Vosch. *I don't know why and, hopefully, I never will.*

I flick the pellet from my hand.

The hub's response is instantaneous. My intent alerted the central processor, which calculated the overwhelming probability of terminal failure and shut down all but the essential functions of my muscular system. The 12th System has the same order I gave Razor: *Don't let her die.* Like a parasite's, the system's life depends on the continuation of mine.

The instant my intent changes—*Okay, fine. I'll parachute out*—the hub will release me. Then and only then. I can't lie to it or bargain with it. Can't persuade it. Can't force it. Unless I change my mind, it can't let me go. Unless it lets me go, I can't change my mind.

Heart on fire. Body of stone.

There's nothing that the hub can do about my snowballing panic. It can respond to emotions; it can't control them. Endorphins release. Neurons and mastocytes dump serotonin into my bloodstream. Other than these physiological adjustments, it's as paralyzed as I am.

There must be an answer. There must be an answer. There must be an answer. What is the answer? And I see Vosch's polished, birdlike bright eyes boring into mine. *What is the answer? Not rage, not hope, not faith, not love, not detachment, not holding on, not letting go, not fighting, not running, not hiding, not giving up, not giving in, not not not, knot, knot, knot, naught naught naught.*

Naught.

What is the answer? he asked.

And I answered, *Nothing.*

74

I STILL CAN'T MOVE—not even my eyes—but I've got a pretty good angle on the instruments, including the altimeter and fuel gauge. We're five thousand feet up and the fuel won't last forever. Inducing paralysis might stop me from jumping, but it won't keep me from falling. The probability of terminal failure in that scenario is absolute.

It has no other option: The hub releases me, and the sensation is like being hurled the length of a football field. I'm *shoved* back into my body, hard.

Okay, Ringer 2.0. Let's see how good you are.

I grab the handle of the pilot's door and kill the engines.

An alarm sounds. I kill that, too. There is the wind now and only the wind.

For a few seconds, momentum keeps the chopper level, then freefall.

I'm thrown to the ceiling; my head smacks against the windshield. White stars explode in my vision. The chopper begins to spin as it drops, and I lose my grip on the door. I'm tossed around like a die in a Yahtzee cup, grasping at empty space, searching for a handhold. The chopper flips, nose up, and I'm flung twelve feet into the rear of the aircraft, then slung back as it flips again, smashing chest-first into the back of the pilot's seat. A hot knife rips across my side: I've broken a rib. The loose nylon strap of the pilot's harness smacks me in the face and I snatch it before I'm thrown again. Another flip, and the centrifugal force whips me back into the cockpit, where I smash into the door. It flies open and I jam my white-soled nurse's shoe against the seat for leverage and heave myself halfway out. Release the strap, lock my fingers around the handle, and push hard.

Roll, pitch, flip, somersault, flashes of gray and black and sparkling white. I'm hanging on to the handle as the chopper rolls pilot side up and the door slams closed on my wrist, snapping the bone and tearing my fingers from the handle. My body bounces and twists along the length of the Black Hawk until it whacks into the rear wheel, rocketing straight up, and when the tail rotates skyward, I'm shot toward the horizon like a rock from a slingshot.

I have no sensation of falling. I'm suspended on the updraft of warmer air pressing against the colder, a hawk sailing in the night sky on outstretched wings, behind and below me the tumbling helicopter prisoner to the gravity that I deny. I don't hear the explosion when it crashes. Just the wind and the blood roaring in my ears, and there is no pain from the beating inside the chopper. I am deliriously, exhilaratingly empty. I am nothing. The wind is more substantial than my bones.

The Earth rushes toward me. I am not afraid. I've kept my promises. I've redeemed the time.

I stretch out my arms. I spread my fingers wide. I lift my face toward the line where the sky meets the Earth.

My home. My charge.

75

I AM FALLING at terminal velocity toward a featureless landscape of white, a vast nothingness that gobbles up everything in its path, exploding toward the horizon in all directions.

It's a lake. A very big lake.

A frozen-over very big lake.

Going in feet-first is my only option. If the ice is more than a foot thick, I'm done. No amount of alien enhancement will protect me. The bones in my legs will shatter. My spleen will rupture. My lungs will collapse.

I have faith in you, Marika. You did not come through fire and blood only to fall now.

Actually, Commander, I did.

The white world beneath me shines like pearls, a blank canvas, an alabaster abyss. A screaming wall of wind pushes against my legs as I draw my knees to my chest to execute the rotation. I have to go in at ninety degrees. Straighten too soon and the wind will knock me off-kilter. Too late and I'll hit with my ass or my chest.

I close my eyes; I don't need them. The hub's performed perfectly so far; time for me to give it all my trust.

My mind empties: blank canvas, alabaster abyss. I am the vessel, the hub the pilot.

What is the answer?

And I said, *Nothing. Nothing is the answer.*

Both legs kick out hard. My body swivels upright. My arms come up, fold themselves over my chest. My head falls back, my face to the sky. My mouth opens. Deep breath, exhale. Deep breath, exhale. Deep breath, *hold*.

Vertical now, released by the wind, I fall faster. I hit the ice straight on, feet-first, at a hundred miles an hour.

I don't feel the impact.

Or the cold water closing over me.

Or the pressure of that water as I plummet into inky darkness.

I feel nothing. My nerves have been shut down or the pain receptors in my brain turned off.

Hundreds of feet above me, a tiny point of light, a pinprick, faint as the farthest star: the entry point. Also the exit point. I kick toward the star. My body is numb. My mind is empty. I've completely surrendered to the 12th System. It isn't part of me anymore. The 12th System *is* me. We are one.

I am human. And I am not. Rising toward the star that shines in the ice-encrusted vault, a protogod ascending from the primordial deep, fully human, wholly alien, and I understand now; I know the answer to the impossible riddle of Evan Walker.

I shoot into the heart of the star and hurl myself over the edge onto the icecap. A couple of broken ribs, a fractured wrist, a deep gash in my forehead from the pilot's harness, totally numb, completely out of breath, empty, whole, aware.

Alive.

76

I REACH THE SMOLDERING wreckage of the chopper by dawn. The crash site wasn't hard to find: The Black Hawk went down in the middle of an open field covered in a fresh fall of snow. You could see the fire's glow for miles.

I approach slowly from the south. To my right, the sun breaks the horizon and light shoots across the winterscape, setting ablaze a crystalline inferno, as if a billion diamonds had fallen from the sky.

My water-soaked clothes are frozen, crackling like kindling when I move, and sensation has been returned to me. The 12th System perpetuates my existence to perpetuate its own. It's calling for rest, food, help with the healing process; that's the purpose of giving me back my pain.

No. No rest until I find them.

The sky is empty. There is no wind. Smoke curls from the mangled remains of the chopper, black and gray, like the smoke that rose over Camp Haven carrying the incinerated remains of the slaughtered.

Where are you, Razor?

The sun climbs and the glare coming off the snow becomes blinding. The visual array adjusts my eyes: A dark filter with no discernable difference from sunglasses drops over my vision, and then I see a blot in the perfection of white about a mile to the west. I lie flat on my stomach, using a breaststroke motion to dig myself a small trench. At it draws closer, the dark imperfection takes on a human shape. Tall and thin, wearing a heavy parka and carrying a rifle, moving slowly against the ankle-gripping snow. Thirty minutes crawl by. When he's a hundred yards away, I rise. He drops as if shot. I call his name, not loudly, though; sound carries farther in winter air.

His voice floats back to me, high pitched with anxiety. "Holy shit!"

He slogs for a few steps, then takes off running, lifting his knees high and pumping his arms like a determined cardio fiend on a treadmill. He stops an arm's length from me, warm breath exploding from his open mouth.

"You're alive," he whispers. I see it in his eyes: *Impossible.*

"Where's Teacup?"

He jerks his head behind him. "She's okay. Well, I think her leg might be broken . . ."

I step around him and start walking the way he came. He trudges after me, fussing for me to slow down.

"I was about to give up on you," he puffs. "No chute! What, you can fly now? What happened to your head?"

"I hit it."

"Oh. Well, you look like an Apache. You know, war paint."

"That's the other quarter: Apache."

"Seriously?"

"What do you mean, you think she broke her leg?"

"Well, what I mean is I think her leg might be broken. With the help of your x-ray vision, maybe you can definitively diagnose—"

"This is strange." I'm studying the sky as we walk. "Where's the pursuit? They would have marked the location."

"I've seen *nothing*. Like they just gave up."

I shake my head. "They don't give up. How much farther, Razor?"

"Another mile? Don't worry, I got her tucked away nice and safe."

"Why'd you leave her?"

He looks at me sharply, dumbstruck for a second. But only for a second. Razor doesn't stay speechless for long. "To look for you. You told me to meet you by the fire. Sort of generic directions. You could have said, 'Meet me at the crash site where I put this chopper down. *That* fire.'"

We walk for a few minutes in silence. Razor is out of breath. I'm not. The arrays will sustain me until I reach her, but I have a feeling that when I crash, I'll crash hard.

"So what now?" he asks.

"Rest up a few days—or as long as we can."

"Then?"

"South."

"South. That's the plan? *South*. A little elaborate, isn't it?"

"We have to get back to Ohio."

He stops as if he'd run into an invisible wall. I trudge on for a few steps, then turn. Razor is shaking his head at me.

"Ringer, do you have any idea where you are?"

I nod. "About twenty miles north of one of the Great Lakes. I'm guessing Erie."

"What are you— How are we— You do realize Ohio is over a hundred miles from here," he sputters.

"Where we're going, more like two hundred. As the crow flies."

"'As the . . .' Well, too fucking bad, we aren't crows! What's in Ohio?"

"My friends."

I continue walking, following the imprint of his boots in the snow.

"Ringer, I don't want to burst your bubble, but—"

"You don't want to burst my bubble butt?"

"That sounded suspiciously like a joke."

"I know they're probably dead. And I know I'll probably die long before I reach them, even if they're not. But I made a promise, Razor. I didn't think it was a promise at the time. I told myself it wasn't. Told *him* it wasn't. But there're the things we tell ourselves about the truth, and there're the things the truth tells about us."

"What you just said makes no sense. You know that, right? Must be the head injury. You usually make a lot."

"Head injuries?"

"Now, that *definitely* was a joke!" He frowns. "Made a promise to who?"

"A naïve, thick-headed, stereotypical jock who thinks he's God's gift to the world when he isn't thinking the world is God's gift to him."

"Oh. Okay." He doesn't say anything for a few shuffling steps, then: "So how long has Mr. Naïve Thick-headed Stereotypical Jock been your boyfriend?"

I stop. I turn. I grab his face with both hands and kiss him hard on the mouth. His eyes are wide and filled with something that closely resembles fear.

"What was that for?"

I kiss him again. Our bodies pressed close. His cold face cradled in my colder hands. I can smell the bubble gum on his breath. *The Earth is my charge.* We are two pillars rising from an undulating sea of dazzling white. Limitless. Without borders, without boundaries.

He brought me from the tomb. He raised me from the dead. He risked his life so I might have mine. Easier to turn aside. Easier to let me go. Easier to believe the beautiful lie than the hideous truth. After my father died, I built a fortress safe and strong to last a thousand years. A mighty stronghold that crumbles with a kiss.

"Now we're even," I whisper.

"Not exactly," he says hoarsely. "I only kissed you once."

77

AS WE APPROACH, the complex seems to rise from the snow like a leviathan from the deep. Silos, conveyors, bins, mixers, storage and office buildings, an enormous warehouse twice the size of an airplane hangar, all surrounded by a rusty chain-link fence. It seems creepily symbolic, fitting somehow, for this to end at a concrete plant. Concrete is the omnipresent human signature, our principal artistic medium on the world's blank canvas: Wherever we went, the Earth slowly disappeared beneath it.

Razor pulls aside a section of the rotting fence for me to duck through. Color high in his cheeks, nose bright red from the cold, soft, soulful eyes darting about. Maybe he feels as exposed as I do in the open, dwarfed by the towering silos and massive equipment, beneath the bright, cloudless sky.

Maybe, though I doubt it.

"Give me your rifle," I tell him.

"Huh?" He's clutching the weapon against his chest, trigger finger nervously tapping.

"I'm a better shot."

"Ringer, I've checked it all out. There's nobody here. It's perfectly—"

"*Safe,*" I finish for him. "Right." I hold out my hand.

"Come on, she's right over there in the warehouse . . ."

I don't move. He rolls his eyes, tips his head back to consider the empty sky, looks back at me.

"If they were here, you know we'd already be dead."

"The rifle."

"*Fine.*" He shoves it at me. I pull the rifle from his hands and smash the stock against the side of his head. He drops to his knees, eyes on my face, but there's nothing in those eyes, nothing at all.

"*Fall,*" I tell him. He pitches forward and lies still.

I don't think she's in the warehouse. There's a reason he wanted me to go in there, but I don't believe that reason had anything to do with Teacup. I doubt she's within a hundred miles of this place. I have no choice, though. A slight advantage with the rifle and Razor neutralized, and that's all.

He opened up to me when I kissed him. I don't know how the enhancement opens an empathetic pathway into another human being. Maybe it turns the carrier into a kind of human lie detector, gathering and collating data from a myriad of sensory inputs and funneling it through the hub for interpretation and analysis. However it works, I felt the blank spot inside Razor, a nullity, a hidden room, and I knew something was terribly wrong.

Lies within lies within lies. Feints and counterfeints. Like a desert mirage, no matter how hard you ran toward it, it stayed forever in the distance. Finding the truth was like chasing the horizon.

As I enter the shadow of the building, something loosens inside. My knees begin to shake. My chest aches like I've been hit with a battering ram. I can't catch my breath. The 12th System can sustain and strengthen me, supercharge my reflexes, enhance my senses tenfold, heal me, and protect me against every physical hazard, but there's nothing my forty thousand uninvited guests can do about a broken heart.

Can't, can't. Can't go soft now. What happens when we go soft? What happens?

I can't go inside. I must go inside.

I lean against the cold metal wall of the warehouse, beside the open door, where darkness dwells, profound as the grave.

78

ROTTEN MILK.

The stench of the plague is so intense when I step inside that I gag. The olfactory array immediately suppresses my sense of smell. My stomach settles. My eyes clear. The warehouse is twice the size of a football field and sectioned into three ascending tiers. The bottom section, in which I'm standing, had been converted into a field hospital. Hundreds of cots, wads of bedding, and tipped-over carts of medical supplies. Blood everywhere. Glistening in the light streaming through the holes in the partially collapsed ceiling three stories over my head. Frozen sheets of blood on the floor. Blood smeared on the walls. Blood-soaked sheets and pillows. Blood, blood, blood everywhere, but no bodies.

I climb the first set of stairs to the second tier. Supply level: bags of flour and other dry goods, ripped open, contents strewn by rats and other scavengers, stacks of canned goods, jugs of water, barrels of kerosene. Stockpiled in anticipation of winter, but the Red Tsunami caught them first and drowned them in their own blood.

I climb the second set of stairs to the third tier. A column of sunlight cuts through the dusty air like a spotlight. I've reached the end. The final level. The platform is littered with corpses, stacked six high in some places, the ones on the bottom wrapped carefully in sheets, the ones closer to the top hastily tossed there, a discordant jumble of arms and legs, a twisted mass of bone and desiccated skin and skeletal fingers grasping uselessly at the empty air.

The middle of the floor has been cleared. A wooden table sits in the center of the column of light. And on the table, a wooden box and, beside the wooden box, a chessboard, set up in an endgame that I instantly recognize.

And then his voice, coming from everywhere and nowhere, like the whisper of distant thunder, impossible to place.

"We never finished our game."

I reach forward and topple the white king. I hear a sigh like a high wind in the trees.

"Why are you here, Marika?"

"It was a test," I whisper. The white king on his back, blank stare, the eyes an alabaster abyss looking back at me. "You needed to test the 12th System without me knowing it was a test. I had to believe it was real. It was the only way I'd cooperate."

"And did you pass?"

"Yes. I passed."

I turn my back to the light. He's standing at the top of the stairs, alone, face in shadow, though I swear I can see his bright blue, birdlike eyes glittering in the charnel dark.

"Not quite yet," he says.

I aim the rifle at the space between those glittering eyes and pull the trigger. The clicks echo from the empty chamber: *Click, click, click, click, click, click.*

"You've come so far, Marika. Don't disappoint me now," Vosch says. "You must have known it wouldn't be loaded."

I drop the rifle and shuffle backward until I knock against the table. I press my hands on the top to steady myself.

"Ask the question," he orders me.

"What did you mean, 'Not quite yet'?"

"You know the answer to that."

I pick up the table and hurl it at him. He slaps it away with one arm, and by that time I've reached him, launching myself from six feet away, hitting him square in the chest with my shoulder and wrapping my arms around him in a bear hug. We fly off the third level and smash onto the second. The boards beneath us give a thunderous *crack*. The impact loosens my grip. He wraps the long fingers of one hand around my neck and slings me twenty feet into a tower of canned goods. I'm on my feet in less than a second, but he still beats me, moving so fast, his rising traces an afterimage in my vision.

"The poor recruit in the washroom," he says. "The nurse outside the ICU, the pilot, Razor—even Claire, poor Claire, who was at a distinct disadvantage from the beginning. Not enough, not enough. To truly pass, you must overcome what cannot be overcome."

He spreads his arms wide. An invitation. "You wanted the opportunity, Marika. Well. *Here it is.*"

79

THERE'S LITTLE DIFFERENCE between what happens next and our chess game. He knows how I think. He knows my strengths, my weaknesses. Knows every move before I make it. He pays particular attention to my injuries: my wrist, my ribs, my face. Blood streams from the reopened wound on my forehead, steaming in the subzero air, running into my mouth, my eyes; the world turns crimson behind a bloody curtain. After I fall a third time, he says, "Enough. Stay down, Marika."

I get up. He puts me down a fourth time.

"You'll overload the system," he cautions me. I'm on my hands and knees, watching dumbly as blood spatters from my face to the floor, a rain of blood. "It could crash. If that happens, your injuries might kill you."

I'm screaming. Pouring from the very bottom of my soul: the death howls of seven billion slaughtered human beings. The sound ricochets around the cavernous space.

Then I'm up again for the last time. Even enhanced, my eyes can't follow his fists. Like quantum particles, they're neither here nor there, impossible to place, impossible to predict. He flings my limp body from the platform to the concrete floor below, through which I seem to fall forever, into darkness thicker than that which engulfed the universe before the beginning of time. I roll onto my stomach and push myself up. His boot slams into my neck and stamps down.

"What is the answer, Marika?"

He doesn't have to explain. Finally, I understand the question. Finally, I get the riddle: He isn't asking about *our* answer to the problem of them. He never was. He's asking about *their* answer to the problem of us.

So I say, "Nothing. Nothing is the answer. They're not here. They never were."

"Who? Who's not here?"

My mouth is full of blood. I swallow. "The risk . . ."

"Yes. Very good. The risk is the key."

"They're not here. There are no entities downloaded into human bodies. No alien consciousness inside anyone. Because of the risk. The risk. The risk is unacceptable. It's a . . . a program, a delusional construct. Inserted into their minds before they were born, switched on when they reached puberty—a lie, it's a lie. They're human. Enhanced like me, but human . . . human like me."

"And me? If you are human, what am I?"

"I don't know . . ."

The boot presses down, crushing my cheek against the concrete.

"*What am I?*"

"I don't know. The controller. The director. I don't know. The one chosen to . . . I don't know, I don't know."

"Am I human?"

"I don't know!" And I didn't. We'd come to the place I could not go. The place from which I could not return. Above: the boot. Below: the abyss. "But if you are human . . ."

"Yes. Finish it. If I am human . . . what?"

I am drowning in blood. Not mine. The blood of the billions who died before me, an infinite sea of blood that envelops me and bears me down to the lightless bottom.

"If you are human, there is no hope."

80

HE LIFTS ME from the floor. He carries me to one of the cots and gently lays down my body. "You are bent, but not broken. The steel must be melted before the sword can be forged. You are the sword, Marika. I am the blacksmith and you are the sword."

He cups my face. His eyes shine with the fervor of a religious zealot, the look of a street-corner crazy preacher, except this crazy holds the fate of the world in his hands.

He runs his thumb over my bloody cheek. "Rest now, Marika. You're safe here. Perfectly safe. I'm leaving him to take care of you."

Razor. I can't take that. I shake my head. "Please. No. Please."

"And in a week or two, you'll be ready."

He waits for the question. He's very pleased with himself. Or with me. Or what he has achieved in me. I don't ask, though.

And then he's gone.

Later, I hear the chopper come to take him away. After that, Razor appears, looking as if someone shoved an apple under the skin that covered his cheek. He doesn't say anything. I don't say anything. He washes my face with warm, soapy water. He bandages my wounds. He binds my fractured ribs. He splints my broken wrist. He doesn't bother to offer me water, though he must know I'm thirsty. He jabs an IV into my arm and hooks up a saline drip. Then he leaves me and sits in a folding chair by the open door, cocooned in the heavy parka, rifle across his lap. When the sun sets, he lights a kerosene lamp and places it on the floor beside him. Light flows up and bathes his face, but his eyes are hidden from me.

"Where's Teacup?" My voice echoes in the vast space.

He doesn't answer.

"I have a theory," I tell him. "It's about rats. Do you want to hear it?"

Silence.

"To kill one rat is easy. All you need is a piece of old cheese and a spring-loaded trap. But to kill a thousand rats, a million rats, a billion—or seven billion—that's a little bit harder. For that you need bait. Poison. You don't have to poison all seven billion of them, just a certain percentage that will carry the poison back to the colony."

He doesn't move. I have no idea if he's listening or even awake.

"We're the rats. The program downloaded into human fetuses—that's the bait. What's the difference between a human who carries an alien consciousness and a human who *believes* that he does? There is no difference except one. Risk. Risk is the difference. Not our risk. Theirs. Why would they risk themselves like that? The answer is *they didn't*. They aren't here, Razor. They never were. It's just us. It's always been just us."

He bends forward very slowly and deliberately and extinguishes the light.

I sigh. "But like all theories, there are holes. You can't reconcile it with the big rock question. Why bother with any of it when all they had to do was throw a very big rock?"

Very quietly now, so quietly I wouldn't hear him without the enhancement array: "Shut up."

"Why did you do it, Alex?" If Alex is really his name. His entire history could be a lie designed by Vosch to manipulate me. The odds are it is.

"I'm a soldier."

"You were just following orders."

"I'm a soldier."

"It's not yours to reason why."

"I. Am. A. SOLDIER!"

I close my eyes. "Chaseball. Was that Vosch's, too? Sorry. Stupid question."

Silence.

"It's Walker," I say, my eyes snapping open. "It has to be. It's the only thing that makes sense. It's Evan, isn't it, Razor? He wants Evan and I'm the only path to him."

Silence.

The implosion of Camp Haven and the disabled drones raining from the sky: Why did they need drones? The question always bothered me. How hard could it be to find pockets of survivors when there were so few survivors left and you had plenty of human technology in your possession to find them? Survivors clustered. They crowded together like bees in a hive. The drones weren't being used to keep track of *us*. They were being used to keep track of *them,* the humans like Evan Walker, solitary and dangerously enhanced, scattered over every continent, armed with knowledge that could bring the whole edifice crashing down if the program downloaded into them malfunctioned—as it clearly did in his case.

Evan is off the grid. Vosch doesn't know where he is or if he's alive or dead. But if Evan is alive, Vosch needs someone on the inside, someone Evan would trust.

I am the blacksmith.

You are the sword.

81

FOR A WEEK, he is my sole companion. Guard, nursemaid, watchman. When I'm hungry, he brings me food. When I hurt, he eases my pain. When I'm dirty, he bathes me. He is constant. He is faithful. He is there when I wake and there when I fall asleep. I never catch him sleeping: He is constant, but my sleep never is; I wake several times a night, and he's always watching from his spot by the door. He is silent and sullen and strangely nervous, this guy who effortlessly conned me into believing him and *in* him. As if I might try to escape, when he knows I can but won't, when he knows I am imprisoned by a promise more binding than a thousand chains.

On the afternoon of the sixth day, Razor ties a rag over his nose and mouth, clumps up the stairs to the third level, and comes back carting a body. He carries it outside. Then back up the stairs, his tread as heavy empty-handed as it is burdened with a corpse, and another body descends to the bottom. I lose count at one hundred twenty-three. He empties the warehouse of the dead, piling them in the yard, and at dusk, he sets the pile on fire. The bodies have mummified and the fire catches quickly and burns very hot and bright. The pyre can be seen for miles, if there are any eyes to see it. Its light glows in the doorway, laps across the floor, turns the concrete into a golden, undulating seabed. Razor lounges in the doorway watching the fire, a lean shadow haloed like a lunar eclipse. He shrugs out of his jacket, removes his shirt, rolls up the sleeve of his undershirt to expose his shoulder. The blade of his knife glimmers in the yellow glow as he etches something into his skin with the tip.

The night wears on; the fire dwindles; the wind shifts and my heart aches with nostalgia—summer camps and catching lightning bugs and August skies aflame with stars. The way the desert smells and the long, wistful sigh of wind rushing down from the mountains as the sun dips beneath the horizon.

Razor lights the kerosene lamp and walks over to me. He smells like the smoke and, faintly, like the dead.

"Why did you do that?" I ask.

Above the rag, his eyes swim with tears. I don't know if he's teary from the smoke or something else. "Orders," he says.

He pulls the IV from my arm and wraps the tubing over the hook on the stand.

"I don't believe you," I say.

"Well, I'm shocked."

It's the most he's spoken since Vosch left. I'm surprised that I'm relieved to hear his voice again. He's examining the wound on my forehead, face very close because the light is dim.

"Teacup," I whisper.

"What do you think?" he says crossly.

"She's alive. She's the only leverage he has."

"Okay, then. She's alive."

He spreads antibacterial ointment over the cut. An unenhanced human being would have needed several stitches, but in a few days no one will be able to tell that I was injured.

"I could call his bluff," I say. "How can he kill her now?"

Razor shrugs. "Because he doesn't give a shit about one little kid when the fate of the whole world is at stake? Just a guess."

"After all that's happened, after everything you heard and everything you saw, you still believe him."

He looks down at me with something that closely resembles pity. "I *have* to believe him, Ringer. I let go of that and I'm done. I'm *them.*" He nods toward the yard where the blackened bones smolder.

He sits on the cot next to mine and pulls down the makeshift mask. The lantern between his feet and the light that flows over his face and the shadows that pool in his deep-set eyes.

"Too late for that," I tell him.

"Right. We're all dead already. So there is no leverage, right? Kill me, Ringer. Kill me right now and run. *Run.*"

I'd be off the cot before he could blink again. A single punch to his chest and the augmented blow would shove a shattered rib into his heart. And then I could walk out, walk away, walk into the wilderness where I can hide for years, decades, until I am old and beyond the capability of the 12th System to sustain me. I might outlive everyone. I might wake one day the last person on Earth.

And then. And then.

He must be freezing, sitting there with nothing but a T-shirt on. I can see a line of dried blood across his biceps.

"What did you do to your arm?" I ask.

He pulls up his sleeve. The letters are crudely drawn, big and blocky and shaky, the way a little kid makes them when he's first learning:

VQP

"Latin," he whispers. "*Vincit qui patitur.* It means—"

"I know what it means," I whisper back.

He shakes his head. "I really don't think that you do." He doesn't sound angry. He sounds sad.

Alex turns his head toward the doorway, beyond which the dead are borne toward the indifferent sky. *Alex.*

"Is Alex really your name?" I ask.

He looks at me again and I see the playfully ironic smile. Like hearing his voice again, I'm surprised at myself for missing it. "I didn't lie about any of that. Only the important stuff."

"Did your grandmother have a dog named Flubby?"

He laughs softly. "Yes."

"That's good."

"Why is that good?"

"I wanted that part to be true."

"Because you love mean little nippy purse dogs?"

"Because I like that once upon a time there were mean little nippy purse dogs named Flubby. That's good. That's worth remembering."

He's off the cot before I can blink again, and he's kissing me, and I plunge inside him where nothing is hidden. He's open to me now, the one who sustained me and the one who betrayed me, the one who brought me back to life and the one who delivered me back to death. Rage is not the answer, no, and not hate. Layer by layer, that which separates us falls away, until I reach the center, the nameless region, the defenseless stronghold, an ageless, bottomless ache, the lonely singularity of his soul, unspoiled by time or experience, beyond thought, infinite.

And I am there with him—I am *already* there. Within the singularity, I am already there.

"That can't be true," I whisper. Within the center of everything, where nothing is, I found him holding me.

"I don't believe all of your bullshit," he murmurs. "But you're right about this: Some things, down to the smallest of things, are worth the sum of all things."

Outside, the bitter harvest burns. Inside, he slips the sheets down, and these are the hands that held me, the hands that bathed and fed and lifted me when I could not lift myself. He brought me to death; he brings me to life. That's why he removed the dead from the upper tier. He banished them, consigned them to the fire, not to desecrate them but to sanctify us.

The shadow that wrestles with light. The cold that contends with fire. *It's a war,* he told me once, and we are the conquerors of the undiscovered country, an island of life centered in a boundless sea of blood.

The piercing cold. The searing heat. His lips sliding over my neck and my fingers feeling his shattered cheek, the wound I gave him, and the wounds on his arm—*VQP*—that he gave himself, then my hands sliding down his back. *Don't leave me. Please don't leave me.* The smell of bubble gum and the smell of smoke and the smell of his blood, and the way his body slides over mine and the way his soul slices into mine: *Razor.* The beat of our hearts and the rhythm of our breath and the spinning stars we could not see, marking the time, measuring the shrinking intervals until the end of us, him and me and everything else.

The world is a clock and the clock winds down, and their coming had nothing to do with that. The world has always been a clock. Even the stars will wink out one by one and there will be no light or heat, and this is the war, the endless, futile war against the lightless, heatless void rushing toward us.

He entwines his fingers behind my back and pulls me tightly against him. No space between us anymore. No spot where he ends and I begin. The emptiness filled. The void defied.

82

HE LINGERS BESIDE ME until our breath evens and our hearts slow, running his fingers through my hair, staring at my face intently as if he cannot leave until he's memorized every aspect. He touches my lips, my cheeks, my eyelids. Runs the tip of his finger along the length of my nose, around the curve of my ear. His face more in shadow, mine more in light.

"Run," he whispers.

I shake my head. "I can't."

He rises from the cot, but I have the sensation of falling as he remains still. He pulls on his clothes quickly. I can't read his expression. Razor has closed himself off to me. I am bound inside the emptiness again. I can't bear it. It will crush me, the absence I lived with for so long that I hardly noticed. Unnoticed until this moment: He showed me how enormous the emptiness was by filling it.

"They won't catch you," he presses. "How could they ever catch *you*?"

"He knows I won't run as long as he has her."

"Oh Christ. What is she to you, anyway? Is she worth your life? How can one person be worth your whole life?" It's a question he already knows the answer to. "Fine. Do what you want. Like I care. Like it matters."

"That's the lesson they taught us, Razor. What matters and what doesn't. The one truth at the center of all the lies."

He picks up his rifle and slings it over his shoulder. He kisses me on the forehead. A blessing. A benediction. Then he picks up the lamp and walks unsteadily to the doorway, the watchman, the caretaker, the one who does not rest or grow weary or falter. He leans against the open door, facing the night, and the sky above him burns with the cold light of ten thousand pyres marking the time ticking down.

"Run," I hear him say. I don't think he's speaking to me. "Run."

83

ON THE EIGHTH DAY, the chopper returns for us. I let Razor help with my clothes, but besides a couple of sore ribs and a pair of weak legs, the twelve arrays collectively known as Ringer are fully operational. My face has completely healed; not even a scar remains. On the ride back to the base, Razor sits across from me, studying the floor, looking up at me only once. *Run,* he mouths. *Run.*

White land, dark river, the helicopter banks hard, swooping around the control tower at the airfield, close enough for me to see a tall, solitary figure behind the tinted windows. We set down in the same spot from which we took off, another circle complete, and Razor puts his hand on my elbow to guide me into the tower. On the ride to the top, his hand wraps briefly around mine.

"I know what matters," he says.

Vosch stands at the other end of the room with his back toward us, but I can see his face reflected dimly in the glass. Beside him stands a burly recruit gripping a rifle to his chest with the desperation of someone hanging over a ten-mile-deep gorge by a shoestring. Sitting next to the recruit, wearing the standard-issue white jumpsuit, is the reason I'm here, my victim, my cross, my charge.

Teacup starts to get up when she sees me. The big recruit puts his hand on her shoulder and pushes her back down. I shake my head and mouth to her, *No.*

The room is quiet. Razor is on my right side, standing slightly behind me. I can't see him, but he's close enough that I can hear him breathing.

"So." Vosch draws out the word, a prelude. "Have you solved the riddle of the rocks?"

"Yes."

I see him smile tightly in the dark glass. "And?"

"Throwing a very big rock would defeat the purpose."

"And what is the purpose?"

"For some to live."

"That begs the question. You're better than that."

"You could have killed all of us. But you didn't. You're burning the village in order to save it."

"A savior. Is that what I am?" He turns to face me. "Refine your answer. Must it be all or nothing? If the goal is to save the village from the villagers, a smaller rock would have achieved the same result. Why a series of attacks? Why the ruses and deceit? Why engineer-enhanced, delusional puppets like Evan Walker? A rock is so much more simple and direct."

"I'm not sure," I confess. "But I think it has something to do with luck."

He stares at me for a long moment. Then he nods. He seems pleased. "What happens now, Marika?"

"You're taking me to his last known location," I answer. "You're dropping me in to track him down. He is an anomaly, a flaw in the system that can't be tolerated."

"Really? And how could one poor human pawn pose any danger whatsoever?"

"He fell in love, and love is the only weakness."

"Why?"

Beside me, Razor's breath. Before me, Teacup's uplifted face.

"Because love is irrational," I tell Vosch. "It doesn't follow rules. Not even its own rules. Love is the one thing in the universe that's unpredictable."

"I would have to respectfully disagree with you on that point," Vosch says. He looks at Teacup. "Love's trajectory is entirely predictable."

He steps close, looming over me, a colossus cut from flesh and bone with eyes clear as a mountain lake boring all the way down to the bottom of my soul.

"Why would I need you to track him or anyone down?"

"You lost the drones that monitor him and all the others like him. He's off the grid. He doesn't know the truth, but he knows enough to cause serious damage if he isn't stopped."

Vosch raises his hand. I flinch, but his hand comes down on my shoulder, which he squeezes hard, his face glowing with satisfaction. "Very good, Marika. Very, very good."

And beside me, Razor whispers, "Run."

His sidearm explodes beside my ear. Vosch backpedals toward the window, but he isn't hit. The big recruit goes down to his knees, ramming the recoil pad of his rifle against his shoulder, but he isn't hit, either.

Razor's target was the smallest thing that is the sum of all things, his bullet the sword that severs the chain that bound me.

The impact hurls Teacup backward. Her head smacks into the counter behind her; her stick-thin arms fly into the air. I whip to my right, toward Razor, in time to see his chest blown apart by the kneeling recruit's round.

He pitches forward and my arms come up instinctively, but he falls too fast. I can't catch him.

And his soft, soulful eyes lift up to mine, at the end of a trajectory that even Vosch failed to predict.

"You're free," Alex whispers. "*Run.*"

The recruit swings the rifle toward me. Vosch steps between us with an enraged, guttural cry.

The hub lights up the muscular array as I sprint straight for the windows overlooking the landing field, leaping from six feet away and rotating my right shoulder toward the glass.

And then I'm in the open air, falling, falling, falling.

You're free.

Falling.

VIII
DUBUQUE

84

COVERED IN ASH and dust, five gray ghosts occupying the woods at dawn.

Megan and Sam finally drifting off to sleep, though more of a passing out than a drifting off. She was clutching Bear to her chest. *Wherever there is someone in need,* Bear said to me, *I will go.*

Ben watching the sun rise with his rifle across his lap, silent, wrapped tight with anger and grief, but mostly grief. Dumbo, the practical one, digging in his rucksack for something to eat. And me, wrapped tight, too, with anger and grief, but mostly anger. Hello, good-bye. Hello, good-bye. How many times do I have to relive this cycle? What happened wasn't hard to figure out; it was just impossible to understand. Evan found the baggie that Sam dropped and blew (literally) both Grace and himself to lime-green oblivion. Which had been Evan's plan from the beginning, the self-sacrificing, idealistic, alien-human hybrid asshole.

Dumbo came over and asked if I wanted him to take a look at my nose. I asked him how he could miss it. He laughed. "Take care of Ben," I told him.

"He won't let me," he said.

"Well," I said, "the real wound your medical mojo can't touch, Dumbo."

He heard it first (the big ears maybe?), head coming up, looking over my shoulder into the trees: the snap and crackle of the frozen ground breaking and dead leaves crunching. I stood up and swung my rifle toward the sound. In the deep shadows, a lighter shadow moved. A survivor of the crash who followed us here? Another Evan or Grace, a Silencer finding us in his territory? No. Couldn't be. No Silencer would be caught dead tramping through the woods with all the stealth of a bull in a china shop—or they would be caught dead doing it.

The shadow raised its arms high in the air and I knew—knew before I heard my name—that he'd found me again, keeper of the promise he couldn't make, the one I had marked with my blood and who had marked me with his tears, a Silencer all right, *my* Silencer, stumbling toward me in the impossibly pure light of a late winter's sunrise promising spring.

I handed my rifle to Dumbo. I left him. The golden light and the dark trees glistening with ice and the way the air smells on cold mornings. The things we leave behind and the things that never leave us. The world ended once. It will end again. The world ends, then the world comes back. The world always comes back.

I stopped a few steps from him. He stopped, too, and we regarded each other across an expanse wider than the universe, within a space thinner than a razor's edge.

"My nose is broken," I said. Damn that Dumbo. Made me self-conscious.

"My ankle's broken," he said.

"Then I'll come to you."

ACKNOWLEDGMENTS

Going in, I didn't fully appreciate the toll this project might take. One of my flaws as a writer (one of many, God knows) is that I tend to dive too deeply into the inner lives of my characters. I ignore the sage advice to remain above the fray, to be as indifferent as the gods to the suffering within my creation. When you're writing a long story spanning three volumes about the end of the world as we know it, you're probably better off not taking it too seriously. Otherwise, you're in for some dark nights of the soul, as well as fatigue, malaise, untoward mood swings, hypochondria, crying jags, and puerile hissy fits. You tell yourself (and the people around you) that acting like a four-year-old who cries because he didn't get what he wanted for Christmas is a perfectly normal way to behave, but deep down you know you're being disingenuous. Deep down you know that, when the clock has wound down and the time is up, there will be more than acknowledgments owed; there will be apologies, too.

To the good people at Putnam, particularly Don Weisberg, Jennifer Besser, and Ari Lewin: Forgive me for getting lost in the thickets, for taking myself and my books too seriously, for blaming others for my own shortcomings, for getting bogged down in the muddy trenches of the impossible dilemmas of my own making. You have been generous and patient and incredibly supportive.

To my agent, Brian DeFiore: Ten years ago, you had no idea what you were getting into. To be fair, neither did I, but thanks for hanging in there. It's nice to know that there's someone I can call anytime and yell at for no reason at all.

To my son, Jake: Thank you for always answering my texts and not freaking out when I was. Thanks for reading my moods and forgiving them even when you didn't understand them. Thanks for inspiring me and pushing me and always defending me against mean people. And thanks for not minding too much your father's annoying habit of peppering his speech with obscure quotes from books you haven't read and movies you haven't seen.

Finally, to Sandy, my wife of nearly twenty years, who recognized in her husband a dream unfulfilled and who understood better than he did how to make that dream real: My darling, you taught me courage in the face of overwhelming odds and incalculable loss. You showed me faith in the face of despair, courage in the hours of lightless confusion, patience in the shadow of looming panic over lost time and wasted effort. Forgive me for the hours of silence you endured, the inarticulate anger and hopelessness, the inexplicable swings from euphoria ("I'm a genius!") to angst ("I suck!"). The only fool I've ever seen you suffer gladly is me. Ruined holidays, forgotten obligations, unheard questions. Nothing is more painful than the loneliness of being with someone who is never completely there. I've incurred a debt that is hopeless for me to repay, though I promise to try. Because, in the end, without love all our effort is wasted, all we do is in vain.

Vincit qui patitur.

RICK YANCEY is the author of *The 5th Wave*, the highly acclaimed first book in the series, as well as several adult novels. *The 5th Wave* was the winner of the Red House Children's Book Award, a YALSA 2014 Best Fiction for Young Adults and a VOYA 2013 Perfect Ten. His first young-adult novel, *The Extraordinary Adventures of Alfred Kropp*, was a finalist for the Carnegie Medal. In 2010, his novel, *The Monstrumologist*, received Michael L. Printz Honor, and the sequel, *The Curse of the Wendigo*, was a finalist for the *Los Angeles Times* Book Prize. He also wrote the memoir *Confessions of a Tax Collector*. When he isn't writing or travelling the country talking about writing, Rick is hanging out with his family.

You can visit Rick Yancey at:

www.rickyancey.com

www.The5theWaveIsComing.com

RICK YANCEY Q&A

BE PREPARED.

RICK YANCEY **Q&A**

You're a prolific writer, with a memoir and several adult novels under your belt in addition to your various, more recent YA series. Did you set out to make a move into writing for teens, or did it happen organically?

Prolific? Naw. R. L. Stine and Stephen King are prolific. Next to those guys, I'm a slouch. I think of my series for teens (Alfred Kropp, The Monstrumologist, The 5th Wave) as three very long books broken into convenient reading segments, so that cuts down on my total count.

My foray into young adult lit was by no means planned. I wrote the first *Alfred Kropp* book as an adult novel, which everyone loved but no one would publish – until I changed my protagonist from a thirty-something P.I. into a fifteen-year-old kid. After that, it was off to the races and I am so GLAD. There's nothing like writing for that age group, so I consider what happened the happiest of accidents.

I always have ideas (usually half-baked) floating around in my head while I'm working on a series – but I'm the kind of writer (and person) who has to focus on one thing at a time or suffer creative schizophrenia. It's been a while since I've written a novel aimed at the adult market, but I never sit down and say to myself, 'Okay, now I'm going to write something for us old folks.' I get gripped by an idea and I go where the idea takes me.

BE PREPARED.

RICK YANCEY **Q&A**

When we first meet Cassie, she's about to be on the move and making the difficult choice of which books to keep in her travelling library. In the event of an alien apocalypse, which two titles would you want with you at all times?

I would take an old volume of poetry I still have from my college intro to American poetry course. In dark times, nothing beats verse. Second choice is harder. Maybe *How to Survive an Alien Apocalypse for Dummies*?

Did you feel any trepidation about embarking on another multi-book project after The Monstrumologist?

I always feel trepidation at the beginning of every project. I worry about so many things. Time to get it right, the skill to do it justice, the will to finish. I also worry about more mundane things, like what if my computer crashes and I've forgotten to back up the manuscript?

BE PREPARED.

RICK YANCEY **Q&A**

What sparked the idea for *The 5th Wave*? Was there a particular character/moment/setting from which the book emerged?

I've loved science and speculative fiction since I was a kid, so I guess it was inevitable I was going to try my hand at it. *The 5th Wave* evolved out of many separate strands. There was a discussion years ago between my wife and I about the most terrifying thing each of us could imagine.

For her, it was an alien abduction, for two reasons: first, it was a frigging alien abduction. Second, she knew afterwards NO ONE WOULD BELIEVE HER. It was the isolation that terrified her. The idea of being ALONE in the face of such a mind-blowing encounter led to an image of a survivor, alone, vulnerable, at the end of hope and maybe of life. Thus Cassie was born, trapped beneath an abandoned car.

***The 5th Wave* is a unique mash-up of survivalist drama (à la *The Walking Dead*) and alien-invasion story. Do you have favourite books/movies/shows from these genres, or one in particular that inspired you to write your own?**

I read *The Stand* years ago and remember liking it very much. I'm a huge movie fan, too. *The Matrix* blew me away. *The Alien* franchise is a favourite (well, I don't count *Prometheus*). I can't think of a particular book or movie that goaded me into *The 5th Wave*, though.

BE PREPARED.

RICK YANCEY **Q&A**

Having researched and written *The 5th Wave*, what advice would you offer the rest of us in the event of an alien invasion?

I'm like Cassie in the opening of the book: the aliens we imagine have been, on the whole, ridiculous, from what they might look like to why they might come here. Stephen Hawking and other scientists have pointed out – correctly, I think – that (a) yes, they probably are out there and (b) we better hope they never find us. If they do find us, my advice is Evan's from the book: 'Find something worth dying for.'

Any hints about what we can expect from the rest of the The 5th Wave series?

Some very bad stuff is going to happen as the Others roll out their answer to Cassie's defiance. Then . . . more bad stuff, some good stuff, and an affirmation . . . maybe not triumph, but an affirmation.